ALL OF US
ARE BROKEN

Also by Fiona Cummins

Rattle
The Collector
The Neighbour
When I Was Ten
Into the Dark

ALL OF US ARE BROKEN

FIONA CUMMINS

MACMILLAN

First published 2023 by Macmillan
an imprint of Pan Macmillan
The Smithson, 6 Briset Street, London ECIM 5NR
EU representative: Macmillan Publishers Ireland Ltd, 1st Floor,
The Liffey Trust Centre, 117–126 Sheriff Street Upper,
Dublin 1, DOI YC43
Associated companies throughout the world
www.panmacmillan.com

ISBN 978-1-5290-4020-3 HB
ISBN 978-1-5290-4021-0 TPB

1 3 5 7 9 8 6 4 2

A CIP catalogue record for this book is available from the British Library.

Typeset in Scala by Palimpsest Book Production Ltd, Falkirk, Stirlingshire
Printed and bound by CPI Group (UK) Ltd, Croydon, CRO 4YY

Visit **www.panmacmillan.com** to read more about all our books
and to buy them. You will also find features, author interviews and
news of any author events, and you can sign up for e-newsletters
so that you're always first to hear about our new releases.

For Sophie Lambert and Trisha Jackson,
the women who changed my world

And for the victims of shootings
who never make it home

'This road was so dimly lighted.
There were no highway signs to guide,
But they made up their minds
If the roads were all blind
They wouldn't give up till they died.'
— Bonnie Parker,
'The Story of Bonnie and Clyde'

PROLOGUE

The Lodge on the Loch: 8.59 p.m.

During the last few months of her life, Christine Hardwicke had thought a great deal about death. The injustice of knowing one light would be switched off while millions of others burned bright and strong. How it must feel to exhale, knowing each breath might be your last. Did an afterlife exist? Or were those countless moments of love and grief and joy that represent humanity lost to the ether when electrical activity ceased? Yes, she'd thought about death. But never her own.

Until now.

The gun was warm. She'd always thought gunmetal would feel cool to the touch but the heat of the muzzle against her temple made her flinch, like a burn against her wrist when she grazed it on the oven. From behind her, she could smell his sweat, taste it on her tongue.

Three bodies were slumped across the polished parquet of the ballroom. When the children were little, Christine had told them the foxes, badgers and occasional deer lying prone at the side of the road were sleeping, but there was no wrapping of unpalatable truths in the silk of a lie this time.

Blood darkened the wood, collecting in random pools,

1

their surfaces glinting under the subdued glow of the chandelier. The way the light hit these fjords of plasma and cells reminded her of their honeymoon in Norway, winding their way through the watery veins of the glacier-fed inlets and into the sharp, clean air of the mountains. Charlie had loved the landscape, the austere beauty of it. He'd loved her too with a hunger, an almost insatiable need, she did not expect to find again. This was an inappropriate thought, as fleeting as a butterfly landing on the fallen in a battlefield, but she recognized her brain was trying to protect her from shock. The arm of a young man – the hotel's concierge – twitched.

Her daughter Galen, glassy-eyed and trembling, was standing by a set of heavy drapes drawn across double-height windows that gazed upon the lodge's twenty-five acres of woodland. A woman with a mouth that needed editing and a crucifix at her throat was pointing a pistol at the teenager's stomach, words pouring from her.

'Tell him to shut his fucking mouth or I'll do it for him.'

Christine dug her fingernails into her palms as Galen bent over her younger brother, wiping the tears and snot that streamed from him with the pads of her thumbs.

'Hush now, Tom. Pretend it's a game.' She flicked a glance at the woman, and then a brief, wordless plea at her mother. Galen squeezed the boy's shoulder and put her hand across his mouth. 'Stop crying. It's making her cross.'

He tugged at her fingers and threw his head from side to side in denial, as if this might erase the events of the last hour, his cries rising in volume and intensity. An eight-year-old boy – young for his age – who had witnessed more than any child should. Christine started towards him but the pressure of the gun against her skin – the unrestrained

2

violence of it – was enough to deaden even the most powerful maternal instinct. *Come on, captain. Hold it together.*

A wash of blue and red spilled across the flocking on the wall. The repetitive wail of sirens filled the space between the bodies on the floor, the man and woman with the guns and the Hardwicke family.

The air was sticky with expectation and fear. Christine's heart was running in her chest, harder and faster with every electronic pulse of sound that drifted from the sweeping drive outside. Through a gap in the drapes she could see cars – nine or ten of them, at least. *The police are here. Thank God.*

The man – she hadn't caught his name although the woman had whispered it at the beginning, when the Hardwickes had stumbled into this nightmare – stepped from behind her, gun still trained on her head. Despite the autumn chill that had begun to descend, semi-circles of perspiration darkened his blue chambray shirt.

His female accomplice jerked her weapon at Galen, gesturing at her to move. With her free hand, the woman dragged Tom by his wrist, tearing a cry from him. Her lips, a slash of colour in the inverted pentagon of her face, thinned into a line.

'They'll try to negotiate.' The man's gaze slid to the window, his voice wet and warm, as if his mouth was filled with too much saliva. His tongue poked at a sore that had opened up, a pinprick of blood forming at the edge of the scab before he licked it away. 'Missy, did you hear me?'

Missy turned to him, her body angled so that Christine could see her expression of – not excitement, although it was close – *triumph.*

'I heard you.'

Missy's eyes were twin stars, bright and hard, and a radiance seemed to emanate from them. She glanced towards the drapes. Those blue and red lights pulsed again, a neon heartbeat. She turned back towards the man. He was talking in short bursts, the machine-gun fire of his words bouncing around the high ceilings and alcoves. Panicked. Agitated. Out of control.

'Calm down.' Missy's voice was amplified in the still of the room but he carried on talking, the vowels and consonants like bullets, ricocheting between the walls, directionless and dangerous. She raised it a notch. 'Fox.' At the sound of his name, the man stopped mid-sentence. The pressure of the gun against Christine's temple eased. Missy's expression hardened to match her tone. 'We always knew how this would end.'

Fox staggered forward, a wild light in his eyes. 'Of course we did. But it feels—' He gestured towards the bodies on the floor. 'Not enough.' His eyes travelled to the children. 'Remember what we said? We need something more.' Flicked back towards Missy. 'So they never forget us.'

Missy smiled at Fox, lips shaped like a bent pin, transforming her face into something sly and hard. Christine and the children watched this interplay, fear swelling their lungs. Something passed between the couple, a shorthand the Hardwicke family did not understand, but all three of them recognized its malignancy. The air sparked with tension.

Tom began to cry again, quiet sobs he tried to muffle with his fist. Galen pressed her own hand against his mouth but it was not enough to evade the spotlight of Missy's attention, a feverish, searching thing.

Thirteen hours ago, the Hardwickes had left their home

in Essex, brimming with excitement at their trip to the Scottish Highlands. Now Christine didn't know if they would make it through the next ten minutes. But she wouldn't look away. She owed her children that.

Missy signalled to Fox, and in one synchronized movement, they'd each flanked a child, their guns bruising the tender hollows of Tom and Galen's cheeks with a dark symmetry.

'Do you *want* to live?' Missy was gazing at Christine, head cocked to one side. Her lashes were thick and long, and when she blinked, it reminded Christine of her childhood doll, that same dead-eyed vacuity. The smattering of acne on Galen's face was obscured by the gun. Her daughter's eyes met hers. She read fear in them. And determination.

'Yes.' Christine was abrupt. Urgent. She buttoned down the panic that was rising in her and tried again, softer this time. 'Yes. Of course I do. We all do.' She could not risk antagonizing this woman, who radiated a fearless fatalism.

Yes. Missy imitated her and Fox laughed. He tried it. *Yes.* With his free hand, he mimed firing a gun at Christine. 'Boom.' His eyes darted back to the window again and he ran his fingers around his collar. A sheen of perspiration gilded his forehead. In contrast, Missy looked cool and fresh in her long-sleeved shift dress.

'At least your mother doesn't have to wash the sweat out of your shirts anymore.' Missy laughed as she said this, and Fox laughed too, although he looked confused, as if he couldn't work out whether she was being witty or cruel. 'I wonder if they'll give it back to her, full of bloodstains and bullet holes.' She eyed the drapes. 'Do you think the police marksmen have arrived?'

Christine stilled, drawing in a sharp breath and only releasing it when her lungs ached in protest. With a stab of clarity, she understood that both Missy and Fox had resigned themselves to death. But if it was infamy they craved, how far would they go in its pursuit?

'Do you want to live?' Missy again. Quizzical. Mocking.

'Yes. Please. *Yes.*'

'Then choose a child to die.'

That far.

Christine's world tilted and blurred. 'What do you mean?' The words were dust in her mouth. As soon as Missy had articulated her demand, Christine had understood what she was asking, but she needed to buy time. For herself and her children. *Think, Chrissy, think.*

'One child lives. One dies. You decide.' Missy giggled at the expression on Christine's face and fluffed up her own dark hair.

A physical pain consumed Christine. She imagined a hand squeezing her heart until the blood flow was cut off and the organ that had kept her alive for forty-two years withered and necrotized. This was followed by a floating sensation – a disconnect between her head and her body – and a pin-sharp awareness of every sound and smell. She glimpsed Tom's face, the rounded cheeks that reminded her of the baby he was, and the mess of curls, so like his father. Galen, her girl, her brave and beautiful girl, was sticking out her chin but a single tear tracked down her cheek.

'Oh, I forgot to say,' said Missy, still smiling. 'If you can't choose between them, we'll kill all three of you instead.'

The ballroom was freezing. Christine's breath became air that drifted upwards to meet the scent of pine from the forest outside. The police lights cast a glow that seemed otherworldly. Fox cocked his gun and pointed it at Christine. Missy followed suit, directing hers at Tom.

Galen's cry of anguish filled her mother's head and heart.

Time slowed until Christine felt sure the clock on the wall must have stopped, stuck at 8.59 p.m. forever. Her ears filled with a roaring sound. She glanced towards Galen. The girl's mouth was distorted, pleading with her, an unforgettable expression on that face she'd kissed a thousand times: a squally newborn who grew into a sunny girl, and now, a desperate teenager. Tom wouldn't look at her, his palms flattened across his eyes, the laces of one of his trainers untied, body wracked with sobs. Her boy. Her baby.

God, she loved them both.

From the inside pocket of the concierge's suit jacket, a mobile phone began to ring.

From outside, a disembodied voice identifying herself as Chief Inspector Shona McGill implored them through a tannoy to answer it.

The sounds echoed around the ballroom, silencing them all. Fox gave a shiver of excitement and bent forward, grinning at Missy. 'It's started.'

Missy readjusted her grip on the gun she was holding, slid her free hand into the bag she wore across her body and removed the lid of her lipstick before reapplying a coat. She inspected the bottom of the gold tube, where the shade was printed on a perfect scarlet disc. *Bang-Bang.*

Her finger tightened on the trigger and she smiled with her blood-red mouth, eyes half closed in a sort of ecstasy at the prospect of another kill.

'Three.'

Christine's gaze flicked between each of her children: Tom, his eyes screwed up and a thin mewl escaping from him; Galen, defiant but trembling.

'Two.'

An impossible choice. Unthinkable. But the alternative was worse. Lose one or lose both.

'Wait.'

Christine Hardwicke's voice thinned and cracked. Then she lifted her hand and pointed to the child she had chosen to die.

PART ONE

ENGLAND

1

Thirteen hours earlier

The Old Barn, Hawkstone, Essex: 7.12 a.m.

The morning sky was streaked with darkness, as if the night wasn't ready to let go. Christine Hardwicke loaded the last of the suitcases into the boot and breathed in the frozen air, particles of ice prickling her lungs.

The windscreen was thickened by the first frost of the season and it threw her back to the past when Charlie would warm the car for her before she left for work. No chance of that these days. Her divorced friends insisted they were glad to be rid of their husbands but she wasn't one of them. She missed him, especially today.

Her hands tingled in the cold. The rest of the houses in their hamlet were in shadow – it was too early on a Monday for most sensible folk – and she stamped her feet, intending to return inside for foil-wrapped sandwiches and flasks of hot chocolate before waking the children. A vixen slunk through the hedge and stood on their driveway, surprised into stillness. She had a scar on her left flank, puckering the skin. For a moment, Christine stared into her bright, watchful eyes – a brief connection between human and vulpine – and then she was gone, fleeing into the woods beyond. She must remember to tell Galen. Her daughter was obsessed with the natural world, especially wild animals.

Two weeks until Bonfire Night. She ought to think about sending invitations and stringing lights across the gabled windows and setting up the model-miniature of the burning Houses of Parliament that had belonged to her grandmother. The sight of those flames flickering in the darkness of the sitting room had entranced her as a child, and that sense of wonder had followed her into adulthood. But her heart wasn't in it. Tom would ask, though, and it wasn't fair to deprive him. There would be fireworks and parkin and a guy stuffed with newspaper. In a fit of organization, she'd bought fifty frozen sausages last week and six packets of sparklers. But it was difficult this year. More difficult than it had ever been.

Christine had told Galen's school, St Agnes's, the truth and they had authorized her absence. The headteacher had even sent a thoughtful handwritten note, which had arrived yesterday. She would pretend Tom had a sickness bug. His primary school was much stricter about this sort of thing – Mrs Birch, the head, had ambitions regarding pupil attend-ance records – and that would buy her two days' grace, at least.

She shut the boot carefully – *don't wake the neighbours* – and walked up the garden path. In the glow cast by the outside light, the frost gleamed. Charlie's favourite weather, cold and crisp. Even now, she expected to see him framed in the doorway, arms outstretched, ready to warm her up. But there was only an empty hall and the shadowed stairs beyond.

Stars, bright but distant, were still visible in the clear sky. Daylight would disappear them soon, painting over the constellations with the brushstrokes of a new day, and it saddened her. Memory was like that. Over time, it blurred, and new memories papered over the old ones. But they were always there, even if they were hidden.

Don't get maudlin, Chrissy.

The house was still with sleep. Tom was breathing deeply, his favourite knitted blanket tucked beneath his arm, and the heat rose from his cheeks. She worried about him. He'd been quiet of late, but whenever she'd probed him about how he was feeling, he'd dismissed her with a single word: 'Fine.' She leaned over and kissed him. 'Rise and shine, captain.'

He stirred, eyes closed but a lemon-wedge smile curving his mouth. 'Is it today yet?'

'Yes, it's today.' She dropped another kiss, this time on his forehead, and switched on the light. 'Get dressed into something warm. It's freezing outside.'

In Galen's bedroom, the curtains were open and the radiator was off, but her daughter had kicked off her covers, seemingly oblivious to the frigid air. Christine stood by the teenager's bed, watching her sleep. Her pyjama bottoms were too short for her, exposing her calf and the delicate nub of her ankle bone. Her arms and legs had lengthened, almost overnight. In video footage Christine had filmed at Charlie's last birthday, she'd seemed so young, excitedly handing her father his present and taking her turn at blowing out the candles. But now she was knocking on the door of womanhood.

She touched Galen's arm, a fleeting contact, knowing how

much her daughter hated to be woken up, favouring a gentle introduction to the new day. The corner of one of her posters – a photograph of a dolphin leaping from the water – had come unstuck from the wall and she smoothed it back into place, feeling the lump of Blu-Tack beneath her thumb.

'Honey. We need to be on the road in half an hour.'

Galen stirred, reaching for her duvet and burrowing into its softness. The girl opened her eyes and shut them again. On the bedside table, a framed photograph of her father had been placed face down. A surge of tenderness warmed Christine and she bent over to whisper in her ear. 'Nice try, sunshine. But it's time to get up.'

She slipped from the bedroom, knowing her girl would drag herself from bed when she was ready and not a moment before. It frustrated Christine, but Galen had never been late for school, so she'd learned to trust her. If she needed help, she'd ask for it. Even when the clock was turning over minutes at pace and the bagel she'd toasted had gone cold, Christine resisted the pull to sour the morning by shouting upstairs to hurry her along.

Tom was getting dressed. She could hear him singing, the clear high notes of a carol. *Too early, Tom. It's not even November yet.* But still, she paused on the landing, savouring the sweetness, the occasional stumble. The tune was familiar, conjuring the ghosts of Christmases past, drinking mulled wine and peeling vegetables with Charlie, their voices raised in joyful abandon. She could almost smell the orange slices they'd bake in the oven and string together in garlands, those repeating discs of sunshine a nod to the return of light after the winter solstice.

But she wouldn't bake oranges this year and the stairway

was dark and cold. She could hear the tick of the grandfather clock and her feet were chilled by the floorboards, covered only by a threadbare rug.

She longed to call him.

Her fingers touched the screen of her phone. She mustn't keep doing this. It wasn't healthy, not now. Ten months had passed. She should be moving on. At least, that's what Carmen said.

The clock chimed once, a rolling and melodious marking of the half-hour. Carmen's husband had left her for a woman at work, nine years younger and three stone lighter. It was the mornings that tormented her, her best friend explained, imagining the two of them in the cloaked intimacy of dawn. Every day for a month, Carmen had called him at this time, on some pretext or other, knowing that guilt would compel him to pick up. 'Why should he get to lie in bed with *her* while I keep the home fires burning? He's got three children. He should be thinking about them instead of shagging Miss Younger and Thinner.'

Christine didn't disagree. But she recognized the nuances of marriage in a way her younger self had not. The lines in the sand of her thirties – fidelity, honesty, loyalty, solvency – had been kicked over, blurred by the realities of life in all its messy glories. She didn't point out to Carmen that her acerbic criticisms, shopping addiction and refusal to spend time with her in-laws had probably contributed to her husband's dissatisfaction in the same way his alcoholism and quick temper had contributed to hers. Marriage was an imperfect state.

But in all the years they had been together – two decades and four months – she had considered herself lucky. Unlike

Carmen, who'd started to complain about her own husband within a year of their wedding, Christine had never wanted anyone but Charlie – and had never doubted his love, not once – which made his absence all the more painful.

She succumbed to temptation and dialled his number, wishing he'd pick up.

It rang once before going to voicemail. *Hey, it's Charlie Hardwicke. I can't come to the phone right now, but please leave a message after the tone.*

She imagined him lying in the dark somewhere, eyes closed, lost to the night. At least Carmen's husband answered his phone. Charlie never answered his. She'd caught Galen talking to him a few weeks ago, her voice a murmur through the bedroom door. Christine had lingered on the landing, torn between wanting to hear what her daughter was saying and the guilt of eavesdropping, of prying when it was none of her business.

In the end, she had compromised, standing as close to the door as she'd dared, fixing her gaze on the framed painting opposite instead of through the crack, as she'd wanted to.

'I miss you, Daddy. I wish you were here.' A pause.

Christine had stifled the sound that rose in her by driving the bulb of her thumb into her mouth and biting down. She could hear Galen crossing her carpet and fiddling with the bottles of nail varnish on her dressing table, followed by the tell-tale clink of her knocking them over.

'I came top in a science test again this week. Mrs McGovern says if I carry on at this rate, I'll be winning a Nobel Prize before too long. But I told her I'd rather be an explorer or rescuing animals.' A laugh. 'Or both.'

Another silence. Galen's laugh turned into a half-sob. Christine had held her breath, a pain in her chest, pressing down on an instinct to go to her, knowing that wouldn't be what she'd want.

'Mum cries a lot, but mostly when Tom is asleep and she thinks I'm chatting to my friends. She's not eating much either. I'm worried, Dad. About what happens to her when, you know—'

Tom's bedroom door had opened then and he'd wandered out, holding his blanket. 'What are you doing?' He'd blinked at her, waiting for her reply. 'Nothing much.' She had smiled, a quick quarter-turn that brooked no further questions and guided him back to bed. Not for the first time, she'd thanked her lucky stars he was easily distracted.

But that was last month, and she couldn't believe how quickly the weeks were sliding past. As a child, she'd been impatient, wishing her life away, longing for the next school holiday or birthday, but now she wanted time to slow down because, as it turned out, there was never enough of it.

She could hear voices, Tom chatting to his sister and Galen giggling at something he'd said. They would be down in a few minutes, and then they would hit the road. If Charlie was here, he'd be up there with them, joking around and making them laugh.

Christine lifted her mobile to her ear and pressed redial. *Hey, it's Charlie Hardwicke. I can't come to the phone right now, but please leave a message after the tone.*

Her heart clenched, tears spilling over. 'I miss you, Charlie. Please come home.'

2

The classroom was quiet and then it was not. The voices of thirty-three four- and five-year-olds filled the space, a flock of chattering birds, squawking over each other, jostling and chirping, hanging coats on their pegs and dropping their gloves, some laughing, one playing the fool. All of them vivid with youth.

Miss Smith, whose mouth tasted of stale white wine and regrets, could not decide which was causing her the most discomfort: the pounding in her head, the steadily rising volume in Reception or her ill-fitting bra. Even at 8.41 a.m., her patience was wearing thin.

Gerard said she looked like a slut in her flimsy scarlet knickers and the matching triangles of lace that covered her chest. 'Not suitable for work,' he'd said, but what he'd meant was not suitable for a staffroom filled with married men and their mid-life crises. A bit rich coming from a man who was still a virgin at twenty-seven. As if she gave a toss what he thought anyway. She *liked* knowing her underwear was sexy, at odds with her unofficial work uniform of fitted skirts and demure jumpers. She was hardly going to show it off to her colleagues, was she?

The deputy head, a florid, no-nonsense older man called Jonathan Blakeney, had been waiting by her desk when she'd arrived that morning, too late for the staff meeting and barely in time for registration. As she'd half run into the form room, hair still damp from the shower, his eyebrows had lifted but he did not comment. Instead, while she shrugged off her coat and searched for a pen to take the register, he'd reminded the pupils to sit and, for the love of God, to keep the noise down. The volume continued to rise.

Miss Smith knew this was her cue to assert her authority but all she could think about was the softness of her pillows and a few extra hours of sleep. Gerard had taken her out for dinner to celebrate their engagement and she'd kept drinking until he'd had to carry her home. She hadn't told him the reason she'd sought solace in the bottle was to blunt the edges of her disappointment. The diamond was embarrassingly small. She shouldn't have said yes but she'd felt sorry for him, asking in front of those teenagers, messing about on the beach and catcalling him. He was solid and dependable, even if he didn't believe in sex before marriage. And his flat was nice. She didn't want to move back home again. Who else would want her anyway?

When he'd punched the air and called his mother, it had felt too late to retract her acceptance. She would need to do something about that.

She ran her tongue around the inside of her mouth. It tasted sour. She'd overslept and missed breakfast. Mr Blakeney's eyes were upon her – she felt his censure too – but she tried to ignore him.

Instead she began to clap, a slow and repetitive sound designed to break through the Monday morning chaos. One by one, the class fell silent except for Dylan Adams, who was scribbling on Aakashi's phonics workbook, much to the young girl's chagrin.

'Stop that.' Too weak. Miss Smith bit her lip, waiting to see if he'd do as she'd asked. She wished Mr Blakeney would fuck off. Didn't he have an assembly to prepare?

Dylan tossed his pencil onto the desk but he didn't seem chastised. Even at his tender age, there was defiance in his expression, an attitude Miss Smith recognized because she saw it every day when she looked in the mirror.

She pointed to a chart on the wall, a fat yellow sunshine with an upturned smile and a dark storm cloud a few centimetres below. 'Do you want to start this week on the cloud?'

Dylan shrugged. 'I don't care.'

'I don't think that's true.'

'Is.'

'Well, okay then.'

Every pupil in Reception was presented with a laminated magnetic rectangle printed with their name when they joined the school. Miss Smith found the one with DYLAN on it and placed it on the cloud. His was the only name there. His face fell but only briefly, and then he laughed and hit Aakashi on the arm.

'Dylan.' Her reprimand was sharp. 'You will sit here where I can see you.'

The boy sulked his way to the empty chair at the table in front of her desk. The classroom door opened. Helena Wilson, a teaching assistant with a second home in France and grown-up daughters, walked in with Zayn Costello, who was wearing too-big trousers borrowed from Lost Property.

'Sorry.' She mouthed the words. 'Bathroom emergency.'

'Miss Smith,' said Mr Blakeney, now Helena was back to supervise. 'A word outside, if I may.'

She followed him into the corridor. His mouth was fixed in a sour-milk smile. He had been her mentor since she had joined the school and although she didn't know him well, she knew enough to read his displeasure. He wiped his palms on his trousers and sucked in air through his teeth. 'You missed the staff meeting this morning. It's the third time you've been late this term.'

'I overslept. And then my car wouldn't start.'

'You do realize you're on probation?'

A headache thrummed between her eyes. She rubbed the bridge of her nose to excise the pain but it made no differ-ence. She didn't care – gave precisely zero fucks – but she couldn't say that out loud. She hated teaching, had realized her mistake as soon as she had started, and only the need for money had prevented her from quitting. 'I'm sorry. It won't happen again.'

'You're right. It won't.' His eyes slid to her chest and lingered there. 'I suppose I ought to let you get back to class. The register won't take itself.' She started to leave but then he reached for her wrist, to stall her. 'I can put in a good word for you, if you like.' That sour-milk smile glistened as he wet his lips with his tongue. 'With the head, I mean. We could talk about it over dinner tonight.'

The feel of his hand against her skin repulsed her. He was thirty years older than her, at least. The glint of gold confirmed his marital status. She did what she always did when men like this – and there were so many of them – approached her.

She leaned into him, her breath warm against his ear. He stilled, not quite believing his luck. Her voice dripped with honey. 'I would rather impale myself on a rusty nail than spend a moment longer with you than I have to.'

3

The Coastguard's Lookout, Midtown-on-Sea: 7.59 a.m.

The kittiwakes were scavenging offal and discards from the fishing boats, their screams piercing the cold air. A man in oilskins was hefting baskets of herring onto the jetty while the engine of a nearby tug thrummed in the stillness, its rudder spiralling cracks across the surface of the sea.

The detective Saul Anguish had been awake all night, and now the first rays of dawn were breaking over the marshland, he rubbed the tiredness from his eyes and stood in the upstairs bedroom of the coastguard's lookout, watching the birds fight over the scraps.

It was sixteen hours since he'd heard from Blue. Sixteen hours since she'd messaged or called or updated her social media feeds. She'd spent the previous day preparing to appear as an expert witness in court – her real name was Dr Clover March and she was a talented forensic linguist – and then she had planned to have dinner with her sister. Followed by an arrangement to spend the secret dark hours with him. But she hadn't showed up.

Saul had lain awake, watching his phone but pretending not to. It was a loose arrangement, after all. They were not boyfriend and girlfriend, but now-and-again lovers when their schedules allowed. They were still unwrapping the layers of each other. Still uncertain and hesitant and feeling their way.

But he couldn't deny he felt protective over her, especially since that afternoon last year when he'd found her, dazed and wandering, with her shirt undone, sexually assaulted by a police officer during one of her narcoleptic episodes. Detective Constable Douglas Lynch, who had an extreme phobia of birds, had paid dearly for his actions. By way of retribution, Saul and Blue, under cover of night, had filled his house with dozens of lovebirds, budgerigars, finches and canaries, their bond strengthened by this shared transgression. But their friendship ran far deeper than that.

Both were naturally distrustful. Both hid secrets in the darkest reaches of their souls. But a fire burned between them and they did not – could not – fight it. They did not discuss what was happening. Instead they lost themselves in the liquid heat of their lust whenever they could. Saul would not admit he wanted more and Blue had not suggested it.

But that didn't stop him from wondering why she hadn't been in touch, or shield him from the sting of what felt like her rejection. He wanted to kiss her, to press himself against the furnace of her body. To hide them both behind the cloak of the night and burn with her. But he would not call her. Not because he didn't want to. But he tried not to pressure her. He respected her boundaries. She always called him.

Except last night.

For fuck's sake, Saul. Get a grip.

The kittiwakes rose in a tornado of cries and beating wings, their brief sojourn to shore over before returning to the sea where they wintered. Saul watched them wheel across the iron skies before dressing quickly and heading into the new day.

4

Midtown Primary School: 8.59 a.m.

The birds were squawking when she returned, like fledglings that had fallen from the nest, demanding attention from their mother. The completed register was on her desk. Helena, efficient as ever. Dylan was scribbling on his chair with a black felt-tip pen.

Miss Smith had read his file when he'd joined Midtown Primary. On the surface, he had everything going for him. A well-kept family home with a spacious garden, and parents with good jobs. Loving grandparents and extended family. A playroom full of toys and expensive gadgets.

But his mother and father were rarely home. He was shunted between his grandparents and babysitters and au pairs that changed with the seasons. She had visited the homes of all her new charges before they started school and his had been the only one with neither parent present.

She knew what it was to be a victim of parents who didn't care.

His grandfather, a soft-bodied man with liver spots on his temples and glasses that were too big, had talked her through Dylan's early years. 'He's a spirited boy, a bit over-enthusiastic at times.' When Dylan had thrown a car at the television and cracked the screen, she'd admonished him, even though it wasn't her place to do so, but his grandfather had offered up an indulgent smile. 'It's not the first time. Boys will be boys, eh?'

Boys will be boys.

How many times had their bad behaviour been excused because it was expected? Is that when it started, when they were four and their boundaries were so elastic they might as well not exist? Was this why Mr Blakeney, a key part of the senior leadership team, thought it appropriate to ask her – a newly qualified teacher – out for dinner? What about girls? Or women? Were they allowed to be bad too? Gerard didn't think so. In his eyes, women should be compliant and grateful, and why did she accept his proposal last night when she had no intention of marrying him?

Why was her life such a fuck-up?

Her head was full of noise, the abrasive kick of a katydid's wing on a summer night. *Katy-did. Katy-did. Katy-did.* She shook herself, trying to dislodge the buzzing that filled all the gaps in her mind and left no room for clarity or precision of thought. She tried to concentrate on the morning's lesson. *Phonics. Story-time. Number recognition.* But she couldn't silence the rasp and click of the insects. She needed water. Something to eat. A reprieve from her cotton-wool brain overstuffed with feral children, and the wet lips of Mr Blakeney, and Gerard's wedding proposal.

'Miss Smith—'

She spun around, a dazed expression on her face. The noise in the classroom was building again. From the corner of her eye, she could see three or four children out of their seats. Helena was holding a stack of brightly coloured cards

26

printed with phonemes, her voice tight, a frown crumpling her forehead. 'Shall we press on with the lesson?' A step closer, quieter now. 'The children are getting restless.'

'Sit down, children,' she said. But her voice was little more than a whisper.

One of the boys was standing by the sink. He turned on the tap and flicked water at his friend, who laughed and flicked him back. The spray landed on one of the girls – Aakashi again – sitting at a nearby table, and she screamed and started to cry. Dylan ran over, cupped his palms beneath the running tap and flung it towards her. Another girl – Aakashi's best friend – jumped up from her chair and pushed him, determined but lacking in power.

Miss Smith opened her mouth to chastise them – to call her class to order – but no sound emerged.

The following sequence of events, no longer than five or six seconds, seemed to unfold in slow motion.

Dylan placed his palms on the girl's chest and shoved her back. He was one of the oldest in the year and a sturdy boy, used to wrestling and rough play. Her name was Katie Andrews and she was slight, smaller than average, with limbs like freshly grown branches, thin and vulnerable.

Katie stumbled backwards, arms pin-wheeling, trying to maintain her balance. But she tripped over Aakashi's foot and couldn't right herself, her four-year-old body clumsy and lacking the more refined co-ordination of an older child.

The back of her head struck the enamel sink with a crack that sounded like the firing of a gun and there she lay, still as the clay sculptures they had made the previous week.

Silence settled across Reception, the quietening of birds that sense an approaching storm.

The teaching assistant was the first to react, commanding the children back to their seats. Her voice broke the spell and the children began to cry out, Dylan loudest of all.

'Katie did it first. Katie did it first.'

Miss Smith stared at him until his face became a featureless blur. She knew he was speaking but his words were lost to the buzzing in her head. *Katy-did. Katy-did. Katy-did.* In some distant part of her mind, she knew she ought to do *something*, but she couldn't muster the energy to care about these whiny babies who wouldn't do as they were told.

She was aware of Helena marshalling the most sensible children – 'Go to the office quickly and get Mrs Jefferies and Mr Underwood' – and tending to Katie, who had not yet opened her eyes, but still she did not move.

The girl's lips were pale. A picture of innocence. Dylan wasn't innocent though, was he? He was cruel, a pint-sized bully. But perhaps that wasn't all his fault. The adults in his life should bear some responsibility for the boy's behaviour, his hunger for attention, his need to be noticed and listened to. Innocence could be stolen without hesitation or permission, a creeping and insidious act. She knew all about that.

The children eddied around her, despatched in pairs to fetch the school's welfare officer and its headteacher. A handful of those who remained behind began to cry, disturbed by the sight of their classmate lying prone on the linoleum. Their panic was contagious. Soon, almost all of Reception was crying, their wails inflating the space like too much air in a tyre. Helena called to her twice, sharp and impatient, her words bladed with intent.

Still she stood there, the noise crashing over her in polyphonic waves.

'Miss Smith.' *Katy-did*. The sound of crying that would not stop.

If Katie was seriously hurt, there would be an internal investigation. Miss Smith had only been at Midtown Primary since September, still on her probationary year. They would let her go. Helena, with her frown and her experience, and Mr Blakeney, smarting from rejection, would make sure of that.

She thought about her papa's face, the curled lip of his disapproval, which still hurt, in spite of their distance, the rarity of her visits. She didn't know why she bothered to see him when he wasn't a proper father anyway. Force of habit, she supposed, some residual sense of duty. Gerard would be smug. 'I knew you wouldn't last five minutes.' Dash wouldn't care though. He'd laugh and offer to buy her a drink. He'd called her boring the last time she'd messaged him because she had a full-time job and a boyfriend. Sorry, *fiancé*. She didn't think he'd laugh about that.

The noise hurt her head and it was growing louder. Helena was talking urgently on her phone, requesting an ambulance, holding Katie's hand. She shouted at Miss Smith. Something about CPR and rescue breaths. Mobiles were supposed to be kept in their lockers in the staffroom as a safeguarding measure. She hadn't pegged Helena as a rule-breaker, but people surprised her all the time.

The door opened and Mr Underwood ran in, followed by two pupils. His eyes surveyed the scene and he clapped – hard and loud – until the only sound in the room was muffled sniffling and Helena's voice, giving out the school's address. When Mrs Jefferies arrived twenty-three seconds later and began to administer chest compressions, the children were already standing in a line to be taken to the hall.

The headteacher crouched next to the women huddled around Katie. Helena, who had been relaying instructions to Mrs Jefferies from the emergency operator, put her hand over the mouthpiece and leaned into him, her gaze sliding towards Miss Smith. Miss Smith couldn't hear their exchange but their body language – closed off, rigid – indicated their anger. More than anger. Fury. She was in trouble. Serious fucking trouble.

A part of her – the part that had always been wonky – wanted to laugh.

When all the children had been led away by another teacher, Mr Underwood stood up and moved towards her, an unreadable expression on his face. She wondered if his wife knew he'd bought Helena a silver necklace for her birthday, and that she wore it every day.

But she would never find out what he intended to say because the noise in the classroom swelled until it was impossible to distinguish between the sounds inside and outside her head.

Mrs Jefferies counting under her breath. The wail of sirens. The thump of the paramedics' boots crossing the halls of Midtown Primary School. Voices, low and urgent, using words she did not fully understand like ventricular tachycardia and epinephrine and shockable rhythm.

In the confusion of the ambulance's arrival, the rush of activity and the undercurrent of panic, she made a decision. With cool fingers, she removed the security lanyard from around her neck and laid it on her desk.

Miss Smith had always dreamed of being famous, and although she didn't know it yet, that laminated photograph of her face, her name, would be in every newspaper across Britain and beyond by Tuesday morning.

No one tried to stop her from leaving the school. No one noticed. As she walked out of the classroom and away from the life she had known for twenty-three years, the katydids sang to her.

There would be no coming back from this, no second chances. A chain of events had been set in motion that could not be undone, even if she had wanted it to. But she had no regrets. For so many years, she'd been desperate to belong, to be some*one* or part of some*thing*, but it had always seemed to elude her. Today she would realize a truth that had been concealed inside her all along – she'd just been coming at it from the wrong direction. She would discover a way to embrace the infamy she craved, the validation she had longed for in a way that felt like she'd come home.

And she knew exactly where she was going to start. By the end of the day – in exactly twelve hours' time – Melissa Mary Smith, together with her accomplice Dashiell Lloyd, would have killed or been pivotal in the deaths of ten men, five women and a child.

5

Midtown-on-Sea Police Station: 9.04 a.m.

Midtown-on-Sea police station was full of cats. They slunk through Saul's legs and under the waiting-room chairs and behind the bin. A tabby sat on the windowsill, licking her paws.

The young police constable trying to round them up looked harassed. One of the cats dragged its claws down his arm and he swore under his breath. Another disappeared through the front doors before he could catch it.

'What's happened?' The detective in Saul was curious. He bent to stroke the thick fur of a tortoiseshell. *Felis silvestris catus*. The domestic cat. Two hundred and thirty bones in her skeleton. Powerful jaws. Needle-sharp teeth. A digitigrade, her heels never touching the ground.

'A woman just came in here and dumped them.' The desk sergeant didn't look up from his paperwork. 'Said they belonged to her neighbour, she was sick of them making a mess in her garden and as we were doing nothing about it, we could deal with them instead.' He grinned, and with a flash of humour, raised his voice to the young PC, who held a squirming calico kitten in his arms. 'Isn't that right, Alex?'

Something about the muscular, sinuous movements of

the felines reminded Saul of a collector he once knew. The man – a shadow from his past – had collected medical curiosities and had told him about a kitten born with two faces, a Janus cat.

He blinked away the memory. Mr Silver didn't deserve to be remembered.

Upstairs, the Major Crime Unit was quiet, but Saul had arrived early. Detective Inspector Angus O'Neill respected commitment to the job and Saul desired his admiration, if not his friendship. A couple of officers coming to the end of a night shift were gathered around a desk but the phones were silent for once. Two major homicide investigations had been tied up over the last few weeks and three ongoing murder inquiries were cut and dried with suspects in custody or dead. Midtown was calm today. Or calmer than usual.

Saul drank his coffee. Wandered back downstairs. PC Alex Talbot was still rounding up cats.

'Do you need a hand?'

'It's DC Anguish, isn't it? Are you sure? I mean, I know you're with the Murder Club.' He said it with a kind of enthusiastic awe. Talbot was a couple of years younger than Saul, a fresh-faced new recruit who'd joined Midtown police six months after he had and who often found himself assigned to the jobs no one else wanted.

Saul shrugged. He had a soft spot for the underdog. 'I've got a few minutes.'

An ambulance sped past the station, its blue lights flashing but no sirens. As he often did, Saul wondered who was inside and whether they would live or die. At twenty-five, he'd stared into darkness more times than was healthy for a man of his tender years. Most of his contemporaries believed in justice and redemption and hope, but he under-stood the truth in a way the others did not. Those who walked the path of shadows rarely found their way again, but ventured deeper into depravity.

After all, he should know.

They carried the cats in two plastic boxes to a vet's on the high street. The pavements were icy and Talbot lost his footing, almost upending his. Blue still hadn't messaged.

While they waited to see if the animals were microchipped, they drank terrible coffee from a vending machine and chatted about being part of the Murder Club. 'What's it like? Seeing dead bodies all the time?'

Saul considered the question. There was no relish in Talbot's tone, no hunger. But the young officer was curious and he didn't begrudge him that. 'It depends.' He wasn't being awkward but truthful. And the truth was deserving of respect.

When it became clear DC Anguish wasn't planning to elaborate further, Talbot said, 'On what?'

'Whether they're children. How they died.' A pause. 'If they deserved it.'

Talbot's eyes widened. 'I'm not sure about that. No one *deserves* to die.'

Saul didn't reply.

'Is it creepy, though? Seeing someone who's been mur-dered?'

The detective put down his polystyrene cup. 'You never forget your first body. And there will be one, I promise. You can't be a police officer without forming an intimate acquaint-ance with death.'

Talbot laughed, from nerves or embarrassment, it wasn't clear. 'Is death an intimate acquaintance of yours, then?'

Saul didn't reply to that either.

The veterinary receptionist was full of smiles when she returned. 'Fortunately, all five of them are microchipped with the same address. Do you want me to contact the owner?'

'No, I'll pop round there now and have a word.' Talbot grimaced. 'There's probably some kind of neighbourly dispute. Can we leave the cats here in the meantime?'

'Of course.' A flirtatious grin from the young woman. 'And do I get your number in return?' Talbot blushed. Saul hid a grin. 'I'll leave you to it,' he said. 'See you back at the station.'

The call came through seventeen minutes later. Saul had been tasked with getting coffee for the rest of the team when his mobile rang. Mouthing an apology to the barista, he snatched it up, hopeful it was Blue.

'Hello?'

No one spoke. All he could hear was the sound of sobbing, broken and hurt-filled, the kind of emotional pain that comes from deep within. At first, he thought it was a prank by one of his MCU colleagues, but the timbre was too ragged, too serious.

'Who is this?' The voice that replied was garbled and incoherent. Saul recognized it but he couldn't place it. He didn't know the number either. And then the shape of some words he couldn't understand. 'I'm sorry.' Calm and patient. 'I didn't catch that.'

The voice repeated itself. He listened, close and careful. Deciphered it. *It's Alex Talbot.* An address. *Come now. Please.*

DC Saul Anguish had heard that kind of desperation before. Without hesitation, he abandoned the coffees and protocol. He would call it in when he got there.

The house was on the outskirts of Midtown. It was neat and tidy, the outside painted in cream and blue with a grey slate roof that matched the sky, and ceramic pots filled with plants.

A car was parked on the driveway, polished and gleaming, and the front door was ajar, but there was no sign of anyone. A piece of paper was held in place by the heavy brass knocker. Six words written in thick black ink: *Do Not Enter. Call The Police.* Saul pushed against the door and went in.

He found himself standing at the end of a hallway. Paintings – wild seascapes, mostly – lined the walls. A red and white lifebuoy was hanging on a hook. On a bureau was a large ship constructed from matchsticks and a model of a lighthouse with jaunty stripes. A faint smell of cats. Not a thing out of place.

But Saul's eyes weren't drawn to the nautical adornments. Instead they followed the white floorboards and the bloodied paw prints that tracked across them.

A mewl caught his attention. The cat who'd escaped through the police station doors was cleaning her paw with delicate movements. Her eyes – amber fire – watched him.

Something dark and unholy unfurled itself in Saul.

The hall smelled of paint – the boards were bright and freshly done – and the blood looked incongruous, like fallen blossoms against snow. He followed the trail which led to a door off the hallway, careful not to smudge the tracks.

The man was slumped at the kitchen table with the left side of his face missing. A mess of blood and bone. Under his chin was a circle rimmed with abraded skin. The tidiness of a bullet hole always surprised him.

Saul knew a bit about gunshot wounds. He knew that bullets

streak through the brain faster than the speed at which con- nective tissues and fibrous membranes split apart. But he also knew that in the aftermath of a bullet's trajectory, the resultant shock waves tear through the soft parts of a body and splinter its bones, creating a catastrophe ten times its size.

The blood was everywhere. It had spread under the oven and washing machine, sticky underfoot. He knew that if it was left too long, it would become jelly-like and, yes, the police and ambulance would come, but when they had left, as they always did, the blood would still remain for the family to clear up, and while it was possible to disinfect the tiles, to wipe clean the floor, it was harder to do that to the memory and the soul.

On a windowsill that overlooked the sink was a pot plant and a framed photograph of a smiling family. A father. A mother. A daughter. A son.

Except the glass was strafed with bodily matter and the father was dead.

Saul Anguish, with an eye for the darker detail, processed all this information in less than twenty seconds. Then his gaze fell on PC Alex Talbot.

He was huddled in the corner of the kitchen, in a space between the washing machine and the wall. The mundane in a place of horror. He was holding one of the kittens, stroking it over and over again, and tears were streaking down his face. His phone was on the floor and the blood, so much of it, was inching closer to him, like a rising tide.

Saul crouched next to him.

'Alex, listen to me. I know it's hard but have you called this in yet?'

PC Talbot did not answer. Could not.

Saul picked up the phone from the floor and, with gentle hands, pressed the young officer's thumb to the screen. It sprang into life. The last call he had made was to Saul's mobile fifteen minutes earlier.

Saul closed his eyes and inhaled, a breath – a moment – to steady himself. By the time he released it, he'd made his decision.

With Talbot's phone, he began to take photographs: of the spreading pool of blood on the floor; the man at the table; the walls; the bullet wound. Instinctively, he looked for the gun but could not find it. Talbot must have bagged it. The scene spoke of a man who had reached the end of his tether, a father in such pain he had chosen the one-way road to self-obliteration.

Talbot's hands were cold. Classic sign of shock. Saul wondered if the young officer's questions about death had been answered and whether he recognized the irony of their earlier exchange.

'Come on,' he said, crouching behind Talbot and sliding his hands under the stricken man's armpits, dragging him upwards. Not impatient but firm, no room for dispute.

'I can't.' Talbot's voice was a scratched record. 'I can't.'

'You can. And you will. You can't go to pieces. They'll sideline you, even though they'll say they won't.' Saul had seen the derision, the culture of toxic masculinity in some sectors of the police force. The public efforts of the Police Federation – well-being courses and a structured support plan for those with mental health issues – and the private stigma, the whispers behind hands, teasing laced with cruelty but dressed up as banter. 'No one will know or care exactly what time you got here, but you have to call it in now.'

The kitten, a black and white tom, pranced to the edge of the crimson pool. He lapped at it with his tongue and droplets collected on his muzzle. Saul watched the cat but did not stop him. He felt no repulsion but the kindling of a scientific interest.

Whether it was Saul's arrival or the sight of the kitten feasting on his owner's blood, something galvanized Talbot. He wiped the back of his hand against his nose. Mumbled an apology.

Saul held out the phone. 'I've taken some pictures but you need to secure the scene. Just in case. Call for back-up, okay?'

'Okay.'

'Now.'

Talbot repeated the instruction. 'Now.'

The detective was halfway to the kitchen door when he turned back. The police constable had the phone to his ear and a haunted look in his eyes. Death had stripped away the bravado of early adulthood and left behind a boy, exposed and frightened. But while the ever-present shadows of his own past had hardened Saul instead of dismantling him, he felt a flicker of kinship. 'Don't feel shame. This is a brutal job. It gets easier.'

Outside, the air was sweet with bonfire smoke from the allotments down the road. By the time Saul had reached the petrol station about half a mile away, he could hear the sounds of approaching sirens. He could have waited with him. Perhaps he should have done. But they would rip Talbot to shreds if they sensed a weakness. It was better this way, to make it look as if Talbot had handled it by himself. Poor lad. This life was not for everyone, but Saul knew he belonged in it. For now, anyway.

He slid his hand into his pocket and pulled out one of the evidence bags he carried everywhere with him. Something glinted in the greyness, a gold filling embedded in a cracked and bloodstained tooth. Saul couldn't explain what drove him to pocket these mementoes, only that he must. He was a collector, he knew that now. Blue understood. Of course she did. But he had no idea where she was.

It was only when Saul arrived back at the station with a tray of coffees and a bag of muffins to apologize for his tardiness that it occurred to him he'd forgotten to ask Talbot about the gun.

6

The traffic was heavier than Christine had expected. A string of red tail-lights stretched ahead as far as she could see, bisecting the gloom. They reminded her of her mother's jewellery box, and the brightly coloured glass beads Galen used to beg from her for dressing-up games.

Her mother would spend hours sharing stories about this antique brooch and that diamond ring, placing necklace after necklace around Galen's throat. The little girl would drape herself in a faded silk chemise, a turban and a handbag, tottering around their sprawling home in too-big high heels. Those happy days, full of Sunday lunches and card games and laughter, seemed a long time ago. Her mother and father were dead now, and they'd seen Charlie's parents once in the past decade, a few months previously. Contact had been sporadic over the years. A few birthday cards. The odd phone call. He'd been devastated when they'd moved to Northumberland without telling him, and their relationship, already fractious, had ruptured. Her stomach performed a lazy back-flip. Their estrangement would end later today. Christine and the children were expected for a late lunch.

Galen was looking out of the window, her face reflected

in the glass. She'd hardly spoken this morning, her hands folded between her thighs, lost in thought. Christine had forgotten how to reach her, couldn't find the words to comfort her or make her laugh. It hadn't always been like that. They'd been thick as thieves when Galen was younger, baking and painting together, building plasticine models or hosting fairy picnics in the garden. Trips to the farm and horse-riding lessons.

But when Charlie left them, Galen had been at school. She blamed her mother for that, even though none of them had seen it coming on that bitter Wednesday afternoon when the world had been consumed by a pandemic – that tidal wave of Omicron – and the rumblings of an impending war, when their tragedy had felt small compared to the horrors unfolding, but was everything to them.

'Do you want a sandwich?' She kept her voice light, her eyes on the road.

'Can I have some crisps instead?' Tom had been buried in his game, silent in the back seat apart from muted beeps and exclamations of triumph, but the prospect of food had caught his attention.

'No, it's too early.' Galen rooted around in the bag and found some fruit loaf to soften her bossiness. 'Have this instead.'

'What about you?' Christine pretended not to notice that Galen had answered her brother's question but ignored her own. 'Aren't you hungry, sweetheart?'

'Nope.'

'You need to eat.' Christine tried not to nag but it was difficult sometimes, that desire to wrap her eldest in cotton wool. 'There's some bananas or those oat bars you like.'

Galen didn't reply.

The motorway was choked with cars and lorries. Their early start had not been early enough. Christine suppressed the sigh that threatened to spill from her. Tom was a sunny child, easy to get along with and popular with his peers. Everyone wanted to be his best friend, to invite him to a sleepover or for tea after school.

Galen was different. Prickly. Impossible to read. In the last few months, her friends had stopped coming over. Christine had asked tentative questions, trying to strike that hard-to-reach note between not prying but wanting to understand. But Galen had insisted it was her choice to be alone. And then she had stopped talking about it. About anything. Blood from a stone. But with her father gone, it was easy to understand why. Her mother forgave her everything. Of course she did.

'How long until we're at the dolphins?' said Tom, his mouth full of the sweet bread, plump with cinnamon and raisins. He brushed at the pile of crumbs that had fallen onto the knitted blanket on his lap, which he took everywhere with him.

'It's about eleven hours' drive,' said Christine. 'But we'll stop before then. We're staying in a hotel tonight.' She prepared herself. 'And your grandparents have invited us for lunch.'

'What? No way.' Galen met her mother's gaze in the rear-view mirror. 'You didn't say yes, did you?'

'I did, actually. It seemed like a nice idea.'

'I can't believe you did that. What would Dad say?'

What *would* Charlie say? She didn't know, to be honest. But Daphne and Frank were never going to tell him, so it wasn't something she needed to worry about. She'd thought carefully about accepting their invitation. Daphne had never liked her, or her mother and father. Over time, she had come to accept that. There would never be shared Christmases or anniversary celebrations or birthdays, full of bonhomie and joy.

When she and Charlie had first got together, she'd tried so hard to win them over. It was Christine who'd persuaded him to invite them out for regular dinners, and it was Christine who'd reminded him to phone home every week. But his mother was a brittle, selfish woman, seasoned with the bitterness of her own disappointments, and his father was too weak to challenge her.

As the years passed, the ties that bind family – blood and DNA and proximity and history – had withered to nothing except the scantest of threads.

But a few months ago, when Daphne had walked into their home for the first time in a decade, something had shifted. She'd caught sight of Tom with his neatly brushed hair and his pressed shirt, and tears had slid from the older woman's eyes.

His paternal grandmother had not met him before, their estrangement entrenched by the time he was born. But she watched him from afar, fascinated by the way he moved and talked. 'He looks just like Charlie did at that age.' She'd breathed it out loud with a sort of wonderment that made Christine uncomfortable, although she couldn't say why.

They'd stayed for one cup of tea and a triangle of salmon and cucumber sandwich. It was a start. Christine had wanted to unleash the full force of her fury: for the way they'd distanced themselves over the years; for their lack of support when things had been so difficult. But she'd resisted. Charlie had always believed in second chances and she'd wanted to support him.

And now, several months after he'd left, they'd extended this olive branch. She didn't know why, but she could guess. By being better grandparents to his son, they could correct all the mistakes they'd made with Charlie.

She wasn't sure how she felt about that, because what if they hurt Tom in the way they'd hurt their own child? But was it fair to deny her children a relationship with their only set of grandparents? In any case, she had her own reasons for wanting to see Daphne and Frank, but would they listen to what she had to tell them?

She didn't have the answers to any of these difficult questions and it wasn't something she could talk through with Charlie now. That ship had sailed. Her family had contracted – first her parents, and now her husband – and she was stranded on an island that would soon be uninhabited. She loved her children with a fierce passion, but they would leave her too.

She'd never expected to be alone at forty-two. Charlie had always talked about the party they would throw for their golden wedding but they hadn't even made it to fifteen years. The last few months had softened that hurt and anger. She didn't blame him anymore.

As the familiar heat rose behind her eyes, she blinked twice and composed herself. Galen was still waiting for an answer, so she forced herself to grin into the rear-view mirror.

'He would probably say, "Do what you think best, Chrissy."'

Her teenager rolled her eyes.

'I like Granny,' said Tom. 'She sent me all that money for my birthday.'

'At least she remembered yours.'

Tom's face fell and Galen nudged her brother to show she didn't hold it against him. He punched her on the arm in return, playful and laughing. Christine breathed a sigh of relief, as she always did, that her children appeared to like rather than loathe each other, recalling the stories of sibling rivalry she'd heard from her friends.

The traffic inched forward. The sun had risen now and the day had revealed itself as cold and bright. Despite the circumstances, Christine's heart lifted. She was on an adventure with her children. In a few hours, they would find themselves wending through the wide open spaces of the lochs and hills. Too late in the year to walk the carpet of heather that rolled across the wetlands in all its purpling glory, but in time to watch the changing colours of the landscape as she donned her autumn clothes. She would not think beyond these few days. Couldn't. For now, she would enjoy spending time with those she loved most of all.

Galen's phone made a vibrating sound. Christine's eyes flickered between the road and her daughter's face. As the teenager checked her messages, a cloud passed across the sun, dimming the light.

'Everything okay?'

Galen's face was in shadow. 'Fine.'

But as the sun reclaimed its place in the morning sky, sending a stream of fire through the windscreen, Christine caught the glint of tears in her daughter's eyes.

7

Melissa reapplied her lipstick until it was precision-perfect, checking in the wing mirror of a parked car that it had not bled into the feathery lines beginning to scar her skin. Papa believed that make-up was a profanity. But from the age of ten, her mother had impressed upon her that no woman should leave the house without it, even if it was first thing in the morning and she was on her way to buy a pint of milk.

'Like it or not, women are judged on the way we look,' said Aurelia Smith. 'Don't give those bastards a chance to find you wanting, my girl.' She had placed her hands on her waist and shaped her mouth into an over-exaggerated pout. 'Hips. Lips. Tits. Power. At all times.'

And Melissa had listened to that. Because she liked the taste of power.

Less than an hour ago, she'd walked out of her primary school, knowing she'd never teach again. She'd left a pupil dying on the classroom floor. There was no coming back from the gravity of that. As predicted, her papa, when she'd dropped by shortly afterwards, had reacted badly, but then so had she. Melissa asked herself if she cared – felt her way around the question – and found that she did not.

47

Those wonky edges again.

But it wasn't yet ten o'clock and the day was still unfolding. The school had called an ambulance. The police would surely follow. There would be interviews and statements, and Katie's parents to deal with, not forgetting the headteacher and school governors. Procedure. She didn't have the stomach for all that bureaucracy. To grovel and smooth over the sharp edges of her misjudgements.

She wasn't like other women.

Her friends – were they friends? – were so agreeable and yielding. Smiling, warm and confident, with lives as perfect as their teeth. She didn't know how to be like that. She used to want it. Longed for it. Tried to squeeze herself into the shape of belonging. But it was uncomfortable to become someone she wasn't. A cardboard cut-out. An imposter.

Most of the time, she suspected they tolerated her because of their shared history. They had known each other since school. But she'd always been on the periphery. No one wanted to meet her for coffee or lunch unless the others were there. Her life milestones were low-key affairs. She thought back to the messages they had exchanged earlier, the ones she had found time to send to her friends, even though she was running late for work. She – Melissa Mary Smith – wasn't enough.

ENGAGEMENT DRINKS

[7.56 a.m.] *Melissa:* Gerard proposed last night!!!! Drinks to celebrate?

[7.57 a.m.] *Natasha:* Congratulations! Sounds great. When?

[7.57 a.m.] *Melissa:* Friday?

[7.58 a.m.] *Natasha:* Perfect.

[8.07 a.m.] *Claire:* I can't make it then, unfortunately, but you guys go ahead. Congrats, Melissa!

[8.11 a.m.] *Lisette:* Sorry, Melissa. Neither can I. But have a fantastic night. Such exciting news. When's the wedding going to be?!

[8.17 a.m.] *Natasha:* Argh. Just checked my diary and I forgot I'm already going out on Friday. Another time?

[8.21 a.m.] *Melissa:* Sure. No problem. I'll let you know.

She wouldn't, though. She never did. It had been that way for most of her life. Which is why scrolling through the options available to her now was not an inspiring prospect.

Natasha and Claire were stay-at-home not-mothers with rich husbands and too much spare time. Their lives were the gym and shopping and lunches with other stay-at-home not-mothers. Lisette worked intense hours as a beauty therapist. Her shifts were long and her flat was small.

Melissa had always been the odd one out. At the edge of their friendship circle, treading a path around its circumference rather than through its centre. Sometimes the other three met up without her. For weekends away and dinner parties and country walks. She'd seen their photographs on social media.

They'd laughed at her when she'd confided in them her dreams of stardom, her hunger for fame. Melissa Mary Smith, her name up in lights.

'Famous for what though, Melissa?' Natasha had sipped her cocktail and nudged Claire. 'A legend in your own lunchtime, isn't that right?'

With a jolt that saddened but didn't surprise her, she realized these women were fair-weather friends, not a port in the storm offering shelter and solace.

If not her friends, what of her family? She gave a hollow laugh. Her mother and papa had separated years ago, interested enough to criticize her for her mistakes but not interested enough to help her unmake them. In the past, she had considered severing all contact but found herself pulled back like lassoed cattle.

Papa's house was a short walk from here. She hadn't seen him for a long while – tired of his scrutiny, his disappointment and disdain – and when she'd turned up unannounced this morning, he'd fired the same old questions at her. *Why are you wearing so much make-up? Why aren't you at work? You've been sacked, haven't you? Idiot girl.*

The insects buzzed inside her head.

Katy-did. Katy-did. Katy-did.

She shivered in the wind's scrutiny. Her hands were cold from when she'd washed them in the public toilets and the dryer had been vandalized. Checking all her coat buttons were fastened for the third time, Melissa pulled the belt around her, as tightly as she could, cinching her waist.

Gerard worked from home and she couldn't face his tepid sympathy. She didn't want to go to any of the local cafes in case she ran into someone she knew. Her mother would give her a cup of tea, at least. Allow her to gather her thoughts. But she would expect Melissa to strike out alone. She would not lend her money. Or make her a meal. Or invite her to stay at her modest bungalow with its silk wallpaper and fringed lampshades. Aurelia believed in letting her daughter stand on her own two feet, no matter how much she might need help and whatever the cost to their relationship.

Her handbag was still at school which meant her keys, mobile phone and money were also still at school. She had the clothes she was standing up in, her coat and a lipstick she had found in its pocket. And a secret.

Avoiding the main roads, she weaved her way through the quiet suburban streets until she found herself in one of the Victorian shelters by the cliffs on the seafront. Her lungs inflated with salted air. The wind cooled her cheeks. Above her, a flock of gulls crested the thermals. Something in her stirred. She watched them for a few minutes, their wings spread in symmetry, beaks dipped to the sun. Their freedom was intoxicating. No restraints. No boundaries. Choosing their own path, the sea and sky before them.

Across the road from the shelter was an old-fashioned telephone box, one of a handful remaining in the town that still worked. She looked away, her eyes catching on the horizon and the paper handkerchief boats anchored at low tide. She shouldn't. She mustn't. Where would it lead? Into an unlit alleyway she'd be wise not to travel down.

But once the thought had made itself at home in her head, she couldn't evict it. Gerard would hit the roof if he knew she was even considering it. He was solid and dependable, yes. But jealous too. He would punch the wall until the plaster gave way. Drive his fist through their glass door until his knuckles were shredded and the blood slid between them like stigmata. But he was probably on a conference call about compliance, or health and safety in the workplace, glasses pushed up his nose, his pink tongue nudging out of the corner of his mouth.

To stave off the chill, she buried her hands in her pockets, fingers snagging against the surprising hardness of a coin lost in old tissues, and the sticky residue of a sweet wrapper. Driven by an instinct she couldn't explain, Melissa drew out the five-pence piece and flipped it as high as she could, watching it spinning and falling as it made its descent.

Heads or tails, Melissa?

Heads.

The coin landed on the back of her outstretched hand, cold to the touch in that autumn morning. She placed her other palm over it, a prickle of premonition raising the hairs at the back of her neck. Heart revving, she lifted her hand and a portrait of Queen Elizabeth in profile gazed back at her.

Her mouth dried. Decision made. No going back.

Melissa swallowed, at a crossroads. Isn't this what she'd wanted? A decision made for her. Perhaps there would be other chances to salvage her future, but she couldn't conceive of the truth in that. She didn't have much of a future to salvage.

She didn't love Gerard. Despised her job. Her friends were fair-weather, no use in a storm. Her family was distant, wrapped up in their own lives and not interested in hers. Ever since she was small, she'd envied those with families who surrounded them with love. Now misfortune had found her, she had no one to turn to and nowhere to go.

That revelation was a knife in her heart.

But she was Melissa Mary Smith. She would drag herself upright, still bleeding if she had to, as she'd done for most of her life. Her choices might be limited. But there was still one avenue left to explore.

It had been almost two years since she'd seen him. Two years since he'd pressed his mouth, hard, against hers and told her that he would do anything for her, if only she would let him. She had closed off her feelings; closed off the things she had wanted in her dark and secret self. Because she had known then what would happen if they ever reunited. Like water on an oil fire, an explosive but disastrous combination.

But the thought of him – his hazel eyes and hair that flamed like a fox's pelt – liquefied her insides.

So Melissa crossed the road and did what any self-respecting woman in her circumstances would do. She reversed the charges and called Dashiell Lloyd, her ex-boyfriend, former convict and a very bad man indeed.

8

Midtown-on-Sea Police Station: 10.04 a.m.

A blue bird's egg was waiting on his desk.

As soon as he saw it, resting on a witness statement that still needed some work, Saul knew it was from her. Blackbird? Or starling? Perhaps a song thrush. The shell was unblemished. Too small to be from a supermarket carton. Too big to be a fake. But it was autumn and the season for nesting had passed. He glanced around the room but there was no tell-tale flash of hair, no sign at all that she'd been there. But she was safe. And that was enough for now.

'Did you hear about Talbot?' DC Williams couldn't hide his smirk as he parked himself on the edge of Saul's desk in the Major Crime Unit. 'Lost his shit when he saw a dead body. Cried like a fucking baby. He'll probably want to take the next six weeks off to deal with it.'

From the moment he'd been assigned to Eliot Williams, an experienced officer with a history of mentoring new recruits, Saul had disliked him. He was not a fan of the detective's particular brand of machismo. He wrapped the egg in a napkin left over from yesterday's lunch and slipped it into his drawer before his colleague could comment. Only then did he notice the underside of the shell had cracked and its yolk had spilled over his paperwork.

'So did I. Couldn't *stop* crying, to be honest.' It was a lie but Saul didn't care about that. He wanted to deflate Williams's overblown ego. 'Better make sure O'Neill doesn't hear you say that. You might find yourself on a disciplinary.'

DC Williams narrowed his eyes. 'Well, he didn't. So I don't have to worry about that, do I?' He fixed his gaze on Saul. He didn't say anything else, but DC Anguish recognized an attempt at intimidation when he saw one.

'Anyway, O'Neill wants a couple of extra pairs of eyes down at the scene to give it the once-over. Make sure it's a suicide and nothing more sinister.' He grinned at Saul, oblivious to his distaste. 'I volunteered us.'

He saw her before she saw him. She was crouched outside the house, inspecting the note that was still in situ on the front door. His breath caught at the back of his throat. Leather boots. Her houndstooth jacket. And that glorious shock of blue hair.

DC Williams walked past her and into the house without acknowledgement, not even a nod. She was too spiky for his tastes, too sarcastic, but Saul relished the sting of her tongue. She was a forensic linguist, after all. She understood the power of words.

He, on the other hand, didn't know what to say or how to say it. He knew how he *felt*. Relief that her eighteen hours of silence wasn't because she'd hurt herself during a narcoleptic episode. Confusion at her nonchalance when he'd give up almost anything to spend a few hours in her company. Acceptance – painful though it was – that her absence had become a physical thing, an ache that hollowed out his abdomen and hurt his heart.

But he didn't say any of that. Instead he did what he always did. Masked his vulnerabilities. He cleared his throat so he didn't startle her and offered up a quarter-grin. 'Hello, stranger.'

She turned, smiled up at him, although her eyes were tired. 'Hello yourself.'

He wanted to ask her where she'd been, but the words dried on his tongue. He waited to see if she would offer an explanation, a justification for her disappearing act, but she turned back to the note on the door, tracing the thick black strokes of writing with her finger, not touching it, but following its curls and flourishes.

'It's an extravagant style of handwriting, isn't it? Almost a work of penmanship.' Her voice quieted. 'It's a lot of effort for what's essentially a suicide note.'

Straight to business then. 'Have you been inside yet?'

'No.' She stood up. He could smell the scent of her hair: apples and lemons. A couple of buttons at the top of her shirt had come undone and he noticed a necklace of bruises around her collarbone. He wanted to ask her how she had got them. But he was tongue-tied. Awkward. Saul Anguish, a young detective who trod the narrow way between light and dark, who had walked towards death, his own and other men's, could not shape those words into a question. She felt distant, a long way from him. As she did not mention it, neither did he.

PC Talbot was still there. He was standing in the hall-way, methodically checking the contents of a bureau, full of old receipts and keys and bits of string. His face was chalky but he half nodded at Saul, although he wouldn't meet his eyes.

'Have you informed the next of kin yet?'

'We're still trying to confirm his identity.'

Neither of them was crass enough to acknowledge that photographic identification was going to be difficult because of the state of his face.

DC Williams emerged from the kitchen, two high spots of colour at the tops of his cheeks, the shadow of a smile playing across his lips.

'Bit of a bloody mess in there.' Saul and Talbot stared at him. Neither of them laughed. The older detective shook his head in mock despair. 'Come on, lads. Lighten up a bit.'

'I'm sure they would if your jokes were funny.' Blue smiled at DC Williams. He didn't smile back. The three of them – Saul, Talbot and Blue – stood shoulder to shoulder.

'None of you will last five minutes in the police if you can't see the funny side of the job.'

'We can all appreciate humour,' said Blue. 'But that wasn't it.'

DC Williams was prevented from answering by a call. 'It's the boss.'

Saul and Detective Inspector O'Neill, a leading light in the Major Crime Unit, had got off to a rough start when they'd met a few months ago, but their working relationship had been smoothed out by the younger officer's sharp eyes and sharper brain. Williams flapped his hand at them. 'Why are you lot still standing around? Get back to work.' He walked away but he was still audible. 'Yes, sir. It's all under control here. We're trying to get a picture of what's going on.'

Saul was used to Williams and his superiority complex by

now, but it grated to be ordered around by an officer so lazy he'd slept on a sofa for six months because he couldn't be bothered to build his new bed.

He rolled his eyes at Blue, but she was flicking through the pages of an address book that Talbot had discovered in the bureau, an intent expression on her face. The police constable pulled out some old birthday cards, held together by an elastic band. The pile trembled in his hands.

Saul didn't touch him. He hated to be touched by those he didn't know well. But he could see the physical toll this was taking on the young officer, and checking that Williams and Blue were out of earshot, he guided him down the hallway, murmuring so only Talbot could hear.

'Did you bag the gun?'

Talbot stilled, as if Saul had pressed pause on the moment. His eyes, bloodshot, flicked towards the front door, where the other officer was still talking on the phone to O'Neill. The shaking began again, more pronounced this time.

'I thought you'd done it.'

Saul pressed the heel of his hand against his forehead. 'What? Why did you think that? It was your shout, remember, not mine.'

The two men looked at each other.

In perfect synchronicity, they moved together down the hallway towards the kitchen. In the short time since Saul had been here, the air had sharpened with the smell of iron and abattoir.

The man – estimated as being in his early to mid-fifties – was in the same position, slumped across the kitchen table. The blood on the floor had begun to solidify into jelly-like clots. A mop would not clean the mess, rather a dustpan would be needed to scoop up the remains and a bucket to dispose of them. His hands hung by his sides. One slippered foot lolled on its side.

Without speaking, Saul and Talbot cast around the room, methodical and focused, for the weapon that had killed him. In these kinds of tragic circumstances, a gun might slide to the floor or end up in an unexpected place for all sorts of reasons like recoil velocity or involuntary muscle spasm. But after a few minutes' searching, neither man could deny the truth: it was nowhere to be found.

'What now?' Talbot's lack of experience was beginning to show like skin through worn fabric.

Saul had always believed that suicide was the untold story of gun violence. With careful attention, he'd studied the statistics during his training. How suicides jumped 100-fold in the month after buying a firearm. How the risk for women was four times greater than for men.

But that subconscious itch that had prompted him to pocket the broken tooth was back. If his instincts were sound, this house was now officially a crime scene.

'We'll have to tell O'Neill we can't find it. Ask for gunshot residue testing on his hands. Start trying to build a coherent picture of his life.'

Talbot scratched his head. 'If there's no gun, it means he can't have killed himself.' Saul almost heard the penny hit the slot. 'But if he didn't kill himself—'

'Who did?'

9

The M1: 11.30 a.m.

Galen pretended to be asleep. It was easier that way. Otherwise her mother would ask questions that did not stop. The concern oozed from her, cloying and palpable.

It was later now, mid-morning. The traffic had eased and they were making steady progress, the motorway flanked by fields. In the background, the radio played softly. A country song. Her father's favourite. She leaned her head against the car door and felt the vibrations ripple through her body.

Tom shifted next to her. He'd kicked off his trainers a few miles ago, and he rested his feet against her leg, a ball of warmth. She thought he might be looking at her, so she feigned the slow and steady breaths of slumber.

Behind her eyes were swirls of colour. Geometric patterns in the shape of a chessboard. Solar flashes. According to her book, this was a phenomenon known as phosphene. Her body's visual support system – the eyes and brain – did not shut off when denied light.

The not-quite-black background, what she had always thought of as the back of her eyelid, was called *eigengrau*, a German word that translated roughly as intrinsic grey. She loved that word, the hard shape of it. And its meaning. It resonated with how she felt.

A gecko had excellent night vision, 350 times more sensitive than humans'. Colour-detecting cells in the eyes of dogs were designed to pick up yellow and blue light.

But if Galen was a colour, *eigengrau* is what she'd be. Nondescript and forgettable.

Her mother would never understand what that might feel like. She was vibrant and funny and kind. Stylishly attired. The house was always full of her mother's friends, drinking and talking loudly. Making pots of chilli and rice, or bowls of spaghetti. When Galen was seven, her father, half drunk, had confided that her mother was the most beautiful woman in the world. If Christine Hardwicke was a colour, she would be vermilion.

Galen's body ached. She was more tired than she was prepared to admit. Her mother had fussed about the length of the journey but she'd promised her that she and Tom would cope. For months, Christine had cried so much that neither child wanted to add to her burden. By unspoken agreement, Tom now confided all his worries in her – *'Seb Parker keeps taking my football at playtime. Why am I so rubbish at spelling? I came last in the running race.'* – and she had kept her own inside, hidden away like the core of rotting fruit.

If her mother had known what was happening at school, she would lose her shit. But nothing would persuade Galen to tell her. She had resolved to carry this alone.

For the first few months of Year Eight, she'd enjoyed it. Different teachers, interesting subjects, the joy of friendship. An all-girls school could be claustrophobic at times, but

Galen had embraced it. She'd learned about ecosystems in the Amazon rainforest and how different kinds of animals reproduced. In Biology, they'd dissected a chicken wing, and although it had made her feel queasy, the mechanics of it had interested her. But then word spread about her dad. One of the girls at choir had overheard her mother talking about the Hardwickes, and soon the whole class knew, courtesy of WhatsApp.

At first, Galen had been flattered by the attention, answering questions patiently, but then it had become intrusive and upsetting, and she'd started to ignore it, muting notifications in the fervent hope that interest would wane.

That had caused difficulties of its own. She'd missed an invitation to Aliyah Ramsey's thirteenth birthday disco and was the only girl in her class not to attend – to not even reply – offending Aliyah and her family. She might have ridden out that social faux pas if she hadn't made a second mistake a couple of weeks later. In Drama, she and her friends had been put into a group for an assessed performance, and Galen had been tasked with sourcing their props. But Tom had been upset that morning, and Galen had forgotten to pick up the bag, and her mother had had an appointment in London and couldn't drop it off. All six of them had been marked down.

She had apologized several times, but the girls, even her best friend Isla, did not appreciate that emotional turmoil at home was causing Galen to become distracted and withdrawn. Like many teenagers, they were too self-absorbed to know how to behave. All they saw was a friend disengaging from them, and instead of showing her empathy, they disengaged in return.

Matters came to a head one spring day after her music lesson. Galen had grabbed her packed lunch and headed outside to find her friends, who were sitting on a picnic bench near the science labs. They'd stopped talking as soon as she got close, and their silence surprised her, although she had no idea of what was coming next.

'Miss Clark was *so* annoying today. She made me practise the same piece of music at least five times.' She swigged from her water bottle. 'I'm going to ask my mum if I can give it up.'

She'd smiled down at them and waited for Isla to make room, as she always did. But Isla picked at the skin around one of her nails and, although she made a show of moving up, there was still not enough space for Galen. Gabrielle, the most confident of the girls, balled up the foil from her sandwich and tossed it at the bin. It missed and landed by a clump of daffodils. Galen bent to pick it up, but lost her footing and tumbled onto the grass. She didn't like littering in case an animal tried to swallow it.

Nobody said a word. Nobody helped her up.

'Have you all revised for the maths test this afternoon?' She tried again, her voice light although her stomach was a bolus of anxiety. A part of her wished she'd worn her coat. Despite the spring sun, the wind held a bitter edge.

Gabrielle folded her hands in front of her and rested them on the picnic table. Most of the other girls looked away, as if they knew what she was going to say, although Abigail, Galen's least favourite of the group, could not hide the gleam of anticipation in her eyes.

'The thing is, Galen, none of us wants to be friends with you anymore. We don't like hanging around with you. You're not much fun, to be honest.'

Her words were like a slap, stinging and unexpected. Galen's mouth filled with cotton wool. She swallowed, trying to moisten her tongue. Her heart was a loaded gun, ready to explode.

'What about Lily's sleepover on Saturday? Am I still invited?' It was the only thing she could think of to say, even though it made her sound weak, exposing her to the risk of yet more cruelty from her classmates.

Gabrielle turned to Lily, a petite girl with red curls. 'Is she?'

Lily blushed and tugged at the sleeve of her blazer. She wouldn't look at Galen. Mumbled the dis-invitation. 'Probably not a good idea.'

Tears threatened to spill from her then. But Galen would not give them the satisfaction. She looked around the table. Abigail had slipped off somewhere and Gabrielle was smirking. She pulled herself upright, her eyes bright and defiant. 'What about you, Isla? Are you dumping me too?'

Isla raised her eyebrows, her voice cool and distant in a way that Galen hadn't experienced before, not even when they'd been at primary school together. 'Well, you're not exactly making things easy for us, are you?' She had the grace to look slightly shamefaced while she said that, but once the words were out there, it was impossible to take them back.

At that dismissal from her best friend, her knees weakened, but she prayed they wouldn't buckle. As she grabbed her water bottle from the table, her fingers accidentally brushed against Gabrielle, who recoiled and made a sound of disgust. Holding herself straight, Galen turned away from these girls she had trusted, and made her way back to the school.

All around her, pupils were laughing or practising dance routines or huddled in corners of the playground, their phones in their hands. Her face was hot with humiliation and hurt, and she wanted to hide herself in the toilets and let the tears come.

She hurried into the building. Half an hour of lunch remained, so she'd collect her rucksack, head to the toilets, and if she felt composed enough, she could read her book in the library until the bell went.

As she turned into the corridor that housed the Year Eight lockers, she noticed the door to hers was ajar, its padlock missing. In her haste to meet her friends for lunch after her music lesson, she'd been too lazy to lock it. Galen felt for the tiny key in her blazer pocket but its presence was a rebuke: too late to do anything about her carelessness now.

She found herself trembling, from the shock of being cast off by her friends and at the unexpected sight of her open locker. She was tired too, her eyelid twitching. A muscle spasmed in her thigh and she rubbed at it. Her mother said she'd been pushing herself too hard. A sixth-former who ran the lunchtime conservation club walked past and smiled at her, grounding her in reality again. Galen admonished herself for being stupid and pushed open the locker door.

She almost laughed in relief. Her flute case was still there, and so was her rucksack and the hump of her overstuffed PE bag. A couple of science textbooks and a copy of *A Midsummer Night's Dream*. But then she realized there was something else in the locker that hadn't been there before.

A trickle of – she couldn't think of the word but it felt like ice-water – worked its way down her spine. She stared at it, trying to process why someone would choose to inflict this kind of pain, a deliberate and spiteful act.

Her mother had always commended her inner strength but Galen couldn't hold back her tears. They slid down her face, salting her lips and running off her chin and down her neck. She should tell a teacher. Or her mentor in the year above. Or the head of pastoral care. But she wouldn't do any of those things.

Instead she would take it home and bury it. Commit it to the earth as the perpetrator wished to commit her.

She touched the object with her finger. Instead of polished mahogany, it was rough and ugly. A splinter pricked her skin, a drop of blood blooming at its tip. As she sucked it clean, she tasted pennies and grief.

Soil – dark and damp, smelling of the under-spaces – spilled out of the locker and onto the floor.

Amidst the dirt were five or six worms, their bodies pink and squirming, and a wooden box in the shape of a coffin with these words written in a tidy hand: *RIP Galen Hardwicke.*

10

The Cliffs, Midtown-on-Sea: 10.01 a.m.

When he was fourteen, Dashiell Lloyd blinded a boy with a fish hook he'd taken from his father's tackle box. It had just been sharpened, ready for a trip at the weekend, and Elvin, thrilled by the unexpected visitor to his workshop, had pointed out to his son the bend, barb and shank, his tools caressing the metal until it gleamed. Later, when his father was at the pub and his mother was tending to his younger siblings, Dash slipped into the night and went back for it, selecting it because of its ferocity and heft.

As he drove it into the flesh of the boy's left eye, Dash recited the anatomy of the hook. *Bend. Barb. Shank.* It helped him to block out the screams of pain. He'd jumped the boy on his way to school, lying in wait near the path by the brook that pupils used as a cut-through. The boy hadn't done anything much to deserve it. Made a fool of him at lunchtime the day before. It was reason enough. Dash wanted to see whether the boy's eye felt mushy or rubbery, and what kind of damage he could wreak with the hook's whetted tip.

Quite a lot, it turned out.

The boy's eye – a pulpy mess – could not be saved and the wound became infected, spreading to his brain. Eleven days after the attack – and on his fifteenth birthday – the boy died in hospital. Dash didn't feel remorse, not even at the effect his impulse to violence had on his own mother. She cried every day of his trial and wrote to him in prison until he turned eighteen, although he never replied.

Dash served six years and three months for manslaughter and grievous bodily harm with intent. He was twenty when he emerged from the institution he'd been locked up in, and that dangerous boy had become a dangerous man.

Melissa knew all about Dash's past because he'd told her about it on the night they had met, a year or so after he'd been released, the walls of the swimming baths sweating in the summer heat.

He had stared at her across the rippling water – he on one side of the pool and she on the other – and they had moved towards each other, a magnetic impulse drawing them together until they were close enough to touch. She did not care about his limp and he did not care about the scar below her clavicle, which she had received as a child.

He eyed her in her swimming costume and she, brazen as he was, eyed him back.

Neither bothered to swim that night. Instead they both changed back into their clothes and she drove with him to the beach, where they sat on the rocks until the sun dipped behind the line of the horizon.

He didn't kiss her, not then. Even though she had wanted him to.

'I've done some bad things.'

'It doesn't matter.'

'I'd like you to know.'

His face, serious in the shadows, had mesmerized her.

And the flaming crown of his hair. As she leaned against him, she felt the muscularity of his body, inherited from generations of farmers and labourers.

In the cool of the moonrise, his history dripped with blood. But Melissa didn't care. She liked the taste of it.

But together they were bad news. Their relationship – short but passionately intense – had faltered when Dash had threatened to stab her papa during a family row, and he'd retaliated by reporting him to the police. Dash had been forced to disappear for a while and Melissa had cried every day for a month, wishing he had carried out his threat. But then the seasons had rolled on, and she'd met Gerard through a friend, and by the time Dash had got back in touch, she'd convinced herself that he would drag her down, even though she missed him. Even though the splashes of colour had been leached from her life.

Her reminiscences were brought to an abrupt halt by the arrival of a black car, a classic Ford V-8. It pulled up alongside the bus shelter. Dash had always loved cars, especially vintage ones. She whistled, trailing her fingers across the elegant paintwork. He had clearly gone up in the world. The door swung open. She leaned in, and there he was, an elbow resting on the steering wheel and a crooked grin on his face.

She hadn't seen him in the flesh for almost two years. But he'd come as soon as she'd called. That knowledge thrilled her in a way that it oughtn't to.

'Hello, Missy.'

'Hello, Fox.'

And just like that, their mouths shaping their familiar nicknames, the time they had spent apart turned to dust. She slid into the passenger seat, next to him. He smelled of oil and musk. He glanced at the diamond ring on her finger.

'What's that?'

'An engagement ring.'

His face darkened. 'You going to marry him?'

'No.'

She pointed to a fine chain he wore around his neck. 'Who gave you that?'

'My girlfriend.'

'Are you going to marry her?'

'No.'

That was the first and last time they spoke about Gerard and Grace, their respective lovers. She removed her ring and tucked it in her pocket, where it slipped through a hole and into the lining of her coat. He threw his chain out of the window. Some might call it callous. But even before they had spent an hour in each other's company again, even before they had fully realized how fateful this reunion would prove to be, Missy and Fox, bound by something intangible, were moving on.

On the back seat of the car was a well-used guitar and a leather overnight bag. Music was playing, a bluegrass banjo song by Merle Haggard. Missy – because that's who she was when she was with Fox, not stuck-up Melissa with her staff meetings and sharpened pencils – sang along under her breath. The darkness inside her heart shifted to let in the light.

'Where to, my lady?' He winked as he said it, and that coil of fear she'd carried inside her since walking out of Midtown Primary loosened with the knowledge she could finally be herself.

'I don't know,' she said. Because she didn't.

'Leave it with me.' His smile was lopsided. She'd forgotten how much she liked it.

The morning was still shiny and new as Fox navigated the car through leafy streets and towards the ring road that would take them north and beyond. He didn't ask questions and neither did she. Both savoured the other's presence, and while they were not yet able to articulate the sense of belonging that engulfed them when they were together, each recognized that life without the other had been a withered and empty thing.

They had been driving for one hour and twenty-two minutes when a police car appeared in the rear-view mirror. The pair were making for an empty cabin that belonged to his brother, a rural hideaway in a village not far from the motorway, but surprisingly cut off. A place to think, Fox said, that was all. Until she knew which direction she wanted to take.

It was brighter now, the sun making him squint, and he swore, not loudly but distinctly. Missy found she liked that too. She thought about asking him to pull over and kiss her, but she remembered that Fox preferred not to be interrupted.

The lights on the police car began to flash. Missy did not worry. She had told no one where she was going or who she was with. Her mobile phone was still at school, along with her credit cards and keys. She'd had to walk away from everything. Not a person in the world, except Fox, knew where she was at this moment in time. The feeling was liberating, as if she'd been let off the leash.

Fox swore again, his eyes on the mirror.

'What is it?' she said.

'Police.'

She turned in her seat, looking over her shoulder. The police car was behind them now, flashing its lights. Mesmerizing. But there was threat in it too. 'I think they want you to stop.'

'I know.' He pressed his foot on the accelerator and she noticed he was shoeless, just a sock between his skin and the pedal. 'But I can't.'

With a twist of the steering wheel, the car switched lanes, narrowly avoiding a lorry, whose driver pressed his fist into the horn, filling the air with its antagonistic blare. Fox did not react, but moved into the outside lane, the traffic blurring as he chased the spaces between cars, cutting back and forth, always ahead of the sirens on their tail.

But still the police car shadowed them, weaving through the sea of metal and fumes, closer and closer now.

Without warning, Fox veered back across the middle lanes and up the slip road that turned off from the motorway. A sharp left at the roundabout took them down a lane that ran into Cambridgeshire countryside almost immediately. Missy gripped the sides of her seat, some dark place inside her enlivened by the thrill of the chase.

She looked behind her again, but there was no sign of the police car. 'They're gone.'

Fox drove, the corner of his mouth curved into that quarter-smile. He turned left, right and left again, without purpose or pattern, to shake off their pursuers. Past a heritage centre. A church. The neat shape of a school. Missy looked away.

Fox was searching for something, but she didn't know what. His brother's cabin was on the outskirts of a village some miles away. Neither she nor Fox had been to this place before.

'Why were the police chasing you?'

He winked again. 'Mistaken identity.' He didn't mention it was because he was driving a stolen car that had been flagged by the Automatic Number Plate Recognition system of a passing police patrol.

A few minutes later, they turned into a lane bracketed by tall hedges and ancient oaks. The chocolate box idyll of Madingley. It was quiet here. Almost deserted. They drove past two or three houses, their manicured lawns and wide plots whispering money as distinctly as the wind through the trees.

Towards the end of a lane was a thatched cottage with a gabled roof. Parked on its gravel driveway was a classic car not unlike the one they were driving, except this was cream in colour and close to mint condition.

'Look at that beauty.' Fox exhaled in pleasure. He pulled in next to the box hedge, its leaves pressed tight against Missy's window, claustrophobic and dark. He lit a cigarette for himself and one for Missy.

'What now?'

He passed it to her. 'Patience, my love.'

My love. Her heart beat a little faster. She took a drag, savouring it. She hadn't tasted cigarette smoke for months. Gerard had pressured her into giving up. But the tobacco was sweet and familiar. It threw her back in time to the smell of her grandfather's jacket and sitting on the beach that first time with Fox, fragrant curls rising in the summer air.

Through the car window, she watched two squirrels chase each other around a tree trunk. Her old life was over now. She felt this certainty deep in her marrow.

When Fox had finished his cigarette, he bent down and pulled on his trainers, tying the laces into symmetrical bows.

From that first night, he'd been honest. He didn't like to drive in shoes. He couldn't. As she'd stood on the side of the swimming bath, he'd limped towards her, his gait uneven. When he'd asked if she'd noticed, it didn't occur to her to pretend. He was missing his big toe and half of his second. 'Yes, you poor thing. What happened?'

'There was a fight. In prison. A nasty one. One of the screws stamped on my foot, badly damaged it.' He'd shrugged, as if to say it didn't matter, and pointed to his absent digits. 'I cut them off.'

This shocked and fascinated her, that he was able to inflict such pain upon himself.

'Why?'

'So I could spend some time in Medical.' That flash of a grin again, defiant, not embarrassed. 'They were beating the shit out of me on a regular basis. At least I got a reprieve, and then I was paroled a few months later.'

'Didn't it hurt?'

'It was worth it.' His fingers had grazed her face as he'd tucked a strand of her hair behind her ear.

She didn't ask what he'd been in prison for. And he didn't tell her. Not then. By the time he'd told her everything, she loved him.

And now, two years on, she loved him still.

Fox got out of the car. Missy went to follow him but he held up his hand. She smiled. She remembered this. He opened the boot, slipped something into his jacket. With a mock bow and flourish, he opened her door. 'My lady.'

She stepped out into the autumn air. The sun had burned off the early-morning frost and the rays warmed her face. But she didn't unbutton her coat. 'What now?' she said again.

'That is the question.' He held out his arm and she slid her hand into the crook of his elbow. There was something old-fashioned, almost courtly, about his gesture.

He led her to the pretty cottage with the gravel drive, surrounded by fields as far as the eye could see. The gates were open but there was no one around. A lark was singing its full-throated song.

'What are you doing?' She half laughed, but was not surprised. Fox had always been unpredictable.

'Helping us out of a predicament.'

He knocked on the door, three sharp raps of the knocker against wood. No answer. Then an older man in overalls appeared from a barn behind them, wiping his hands on an oil-stained cloth.

'If it's stuff for the church sale, Annie's not here. She'll be back tomorrow evening.'

'That's a pity – we're heading up north after this.' Fox wrinkled his nose. 'I don't suppose we could leave it with you.'

'I've told Annie I don't want every Tom, Dick and Harry dropping by at all hours.'

'My name's Dashiell, so does that mean I'm excused?' He gave a roguish grin.

The man sighed, as if he was used to being ambushed by his wife's causes. 'I suppose so. But it's just me here at the moment and I'm not going back into the house in this state. You can leave it in the barn, if you must.' He turned back towards the building and Fox followed him, Missy still tucked into his arm. She tugged on his jacket, a questioning expression on her face, and he placed a finger to his lips.

The barn was set back from the house, behind the garage

and away from the road. It smelled of engine grease and grass cuttings. The man and Fox were talking about cars. The acreage of the cottage. His job as part-time vicar of the parish church. Missy was distracted by a faded painting of a nude woman propped up on a shelf and wondered if it was the man's wife, or if it was hidden away because it wasn't.

As that thought meandered through her mind, the tension in the air shifted and Fox's voice lifted, striated with aggression. She turned to see what was going on, the tempo of her heart rising, and what she saw made everything stop.

Fox was standing opposite the man, a gun pointed at his chest. Missy breathed his name, but no sound emerged. She twisted her hands together, trying to think of a way to intervene. His voice was hard, no bend in it.

'Give me the keys.'

The older man – his face marked with sun damage, hair silvered at the temples – picked up a wrench. His wedding ring glinted in the morning light. 'If you think an ignorant little shit like you is going to come onto my property and threaten me, you are very much mistaken.'

The katydids began to sing in Missy's head again. Fox – bottom of the class at school and always so conscious of his family's lack of wealth – hated to be sneered at. If Fox's masculinity was called into question, this would not end well.

Fox said nothing in return but stared at him, the pistol steady. The man laughed and took a step towards him. 'As if you'd have the balls to fire a gun.'

His chest erupted in a volcano of bone and blood.

Missy blinked twice. She didn't scream or gasp, but her

ears were ringing. The oddest sensation overtook her, as if she and her body were two separate entities. It was too late to stop Fox. He'd discharged a gun, and now a body was crumpled on the ground, a piece of human litter discarded when he'd served his purpose. She crouched next to the man. A stain spread across the front of his overalls. If she didn't know better, she'd have thought he'd spilled engine oil on himself.

'Don't touch him.' Fox tucked the gun into his jacket.

Missy peered at the man's face. His eyes had rolled back, displaying the whites. He was clean-shaven but soft-looking, his jowls spreading under his chin. She nudged the toe of her shoe into his hip, to check for signs of life, but it was obvious, even to her, that he was dead.

She didn't feel repulsed. Or shocked. In truth, she felt nothing much at all.

'What shall we do?'

Fox retrieved a set of car keys from a hook and dangled them on his forefinger. 'We get out of here.' He scouted around the barn for anything else he could steal, grabbing some tools, a full petrol can, a worn map of the British Isles and a cash-box marked CHURCH. Then he leaned over and tugged the man's wedding ring from his still-warm finger, sliding it into his pocket.

Missy followed suit, pulling a long silk scarf from an open bag of jumble and wrapping it several times around her neck.

Outside, the air was undisturbed. The gun had made a noise like an explosion, at least that's how it had sounded to Missy. But this was the countryside. It was full of guns.

Fox put his spoils on the gravel driveway and closed the

barn door. 'He said his wife won't be back until tomorrow. That will buy us some extra time.'

The house, the lane, the hamlet – everything was quiet, as if the last five minutes had not happened. But the colours seemed brighter, and when Fox whistled a tune, it was too loud to her ears. The clarity was scalpel-sharp because in that moment she recognized her old life, as she had known it, was over.

Back at the car, Fox opened the boot. Missy's eyes were saucers. Three air rifles. A sawn-off shotgun. A revolver. Two semi-automatic pistols. Several clips of ammunition.

He shoved them into an unzipped holdall, and she caught a glimpse of more guns and bullets. A handful of knives. Some rope. Missy knew she should be shocked. Angry. Furious that Fox had dragged her into this bloodied mess. But when she examined her feelings, there was nothing but her love for him, and the sense they were on the cusp of something momentous. He asked her to retrieve his guitar and the bag from the back seat.

'What about your car?'

'It's not mine.'

'Whose is it?'

Fox laughed. 'No idea. But it seems they've reported it stolen.'

That explained why the police had pursued them, and the reason – along with the guns in the boot – why he hadn't stopped. He pressed his dry lips to her cheek. 'Come on. We need to go.' But the kiss was over so quickly it felt like she'd imagined it.

His movements were deft and efficient. He unlocked the boot of their newly acquired vehicle, and deposited the guns and the items he'd taken from the barn. With his customary flourish, he released the passenger door and held it open. She laughed, drunk on adrenaline, and slipped into the seat, waiting for him to join her. This car smelled of leather and old money.

He started the engine and turned to her, a look of tenderness on his face. Behind his fiery hair, the sun was bright. It haloed him like a burning saint, an avenging angel. He'd come back into her life when she'd needed him most. Her twin flame.

With care, Fox drove out of the gates, the gravel crunching beneath the wheels. He exclaimed in pleasure at the car and the smoothness of her engine. Within a few minutes, they'd left the village behind them and were back on the road, travelling north.

'Where shall we go?'

'I don't know.' She didn't. But she knew they couldn't go home. Her mother had shown her a book once, full of photographs. A place with mountains and lochs. 'I've always wanted to go to Scotland.'

'Then to Scotland we shall go.'

Missy leaned back against the headrest as the car swallowed up the miles. She closed her eyes, the tension of the last couple of hours teased from her shoulders by the act of motion. In that pause before sleep pulled her under, the truth hit her.

Fox was a fugitive, and so was she. There was no turning back now.

11

The tone of the investigation had changed. Even if the man they had now identified as fifty-seven-year-old Graham Baxter had put a bullet in his head while sitting at his kitchen table, it did not explain where the gun had gone. However skilled he was in life, a dead man could not dispose of the weapon used to kill him.

A forensic team had been despatched to the house and the painstaking task of reconstructing a death had begun. DC Saul Anguish touched the broken tooth in his pocket and watched the white-suited Scenes of Crime officers crawl over the kitchen. His instincts for murder had proved sound yet again. While the others were distracted, he would use his knife to cut some hair from Mr Baxter. Blue had warned him about stealing evidence that could later incriminate him, but she was a collector too, and he wondered what had piqued her interest from this crime scene.

Whenever he whispered her name in his mind, the vowels and consonants lit up everything inside him like dopamine. But his impulse was to hold back. Be watchful. Withdraw.

They hadn't had much chance for conversation. He wanted

to find her now, to dismantle this odd distance that had sprung up between them, to peel back the layers of this woman until he revealed the truth of her.

But she got to him first.

'Saul?' Her voice was low, as if she didn't want anyone else to hear. He turned from the kitchen door to the hallway. From blood-soaked floor to sea-mist eyes. She wouldn't look at him, which unsettled him. The shape of her body was awkward, as if she was in some kind of pain, and the bruises garlanding her neck disturbed him. Subdued. Reduced. Not like Blue at all.

To make it easier for her, he said, 'Thank you for the gift. Where did you find it?' He smiled to show he appreciated its quirkiness, the thoughtful acknowledgement of his love of the natural world.

Her expression closed down, those sea-mist eyes turning the colour of a storm. 'What gift?'

'The bird's egg you left on my desk in the MCU.'

She bit the skin around her nail, making it bleed. The strands of her hair danced a denial. 'That wasn't me.'

Saul's throat dried. That would teach him for making assumptions. This changed everything. If it wasn't her, who, then, had left it for him and why? The hunted look in Blue's eyes suggested she might have an answer to that.

'But you do know something about it?' In his suspicion, his voice hardened. He'd once known a man who left rabbit bones at the scene of his abductions, and the echo of that played through him. Mr Silver was dead now but the clanging notes of his legacy remained.

As far as he was aware, Blue had never lied to him. Her truths could be painful, but she was forthright, and he respected that about her. But he could sense – could see – her internal struggle.

She opened her mouth. Pressed her lips together.

He was cold, a touch angry perhaps. Saul found it difficult to trust – but he'd trusted her. Now it seemed as if that might have been misplaced. 'What is it?'

She reached out her hand to him. It was cool, nothing like the burn of the nights they'd spent together. He could sense that she was girding herself, preparing him. She breathed twice, a deep drawing in of air, and then her eyes rolled back.

Saul caught her as she pitched forward. Blue suffered from narcolepsy, a condition that caused sufferers to fall asleep without warning, often multiple times a day and during moments of heightened stress. How many narcoleptic episodes had she experienced today? Yesterday? Last night? It distressed him that he didn't know.

When he'd met her, still furious at her diagnosis, she'd stopped taking the pills that controlled her condition. She'd promised to restart her medication if he promised not to tell a soul about her secret. It was an imperfect solution. The pills did not prevent the episodes, just lessened their frequency. He'd covered for her a few times when she'd lost herself to sleep, but he was used to it. If the team saw her now, she would die of shame. Not because she was embarrassed about her illness, but because it rendered her vulnerable.

From his earlier search of Graham Baxter's house, he knew there was a spare bedroom through one of the doors off the hallway. Without thinking, he half carried, half dragged her, pushing his body backwards into a room containing only a double bed and chest of drawers.

With careful hands, he lifted her onto the mattress. She shifted and rolled over, her eyelids twitching in her sleep. A shadow moved in the corner and he stiffened, heart thumping. A cat, sinuous and watchful, jumped onto the bed and curled into the comma of Blue's stomach.

Her narcolepsy was an inexact science. But he knew that intense emotions – pain, hurt, stress, fear – could trigger an episode. She had been about to tell him something important, he was sure of it.

But what?

He left her to sleep, gambling on the fact the Scenes of Crime officers would have their work cut out in the kitchen and she'd remain undisturbed.

Outside, in the front garden, Talbot sat with a glass of water, his head between his knees. Saul crouched beside him, weighing a pebble in his palm. An azure damselfly, late for the season, was dying in the grass. Saul vowed to return for it. His insect collection was missing this unusual winged specimen. Finding the perfectly preserved body of one was rarer still. Or perhaps, when they'd cleared the air, he would gift it to Blue.

Two uniformed officers he didn't recognize were making their way down the path towards Talbot. 'Come on, sunshine,' one of them said. 'We've been sent to pick you up. Time to get moving.'

Talbot lifted his head, his eyes red-rimmed. 'Where are we going?'

'Welfare check. Some young teacher has disappeared after an incident at the primary school and the staff are concerned about her whereabouts.'

Talbot didn't move. Saul willed him to stand up. The second

of the officers – a younger man who, at close quarters, seemed vaguely familiar – smirked. 'She's a looker, mate. Might catch her at home in her underwear if we're lucky.'

A fire flared in Saul. He stood to his full height, sunlight shining on his white-blond hair. 'Don't say that.'

The police officer did a slow turn until he was staring at Saul. It was a movement designed to intimidate, if Saul let it. But Saul was not so easily cowed. He stared back, his jaw tensed. The officer didn't flinch at all. Instead he took a step forward and narrowed the space between them.

The first officer – older but not by much, with the kind of worn face that suggested a lifetime of disappointment – moved his body until he was shielding them from the house and the back and forth of the Scenes of Crime team. His younger colleague leaned in to Saul, breath sour and warm on his skin.

'I know all about you,' he said. 'You don't scare me.'

Saul, coiled as a predator sizing up its prey, did not move but was poised to strike if necessary. 'Is that so?'

The officer laughed. 'I'd watch your step, if I was you.'

'Is that a threat?' Saul's eyes glittered. He turned the stone over in his hand and imagined himself burying it in the officer's temple, not aware he was raising his arm, not aware of the blank feeling of pressure in his ears. Talbot pushed himself to his feet, placing a warning hand on Saul's wrist.

'I could ask you the same question.' The officer smiled, and there was cruelty in it. 'We know what you did. And if the enemy of my enemy is my friend, then it follows that the enemy of my friend is my enemy.'

For the first time, Saul faltered. With a past as dark as

his, he did not know what the officer was referring to, and that uncertainty unnerved him. But he would not let his weakness show.

Talbot, sensing the tension between them elongate and harden, tried to change the subject. 'Shall we get going then?'

The second officer swung his attention back to the police constable. 'You just want to see how hot she is, right?'

He fiddled with his phone and pulled up a photograph he'd been sent of the missing woman, thrusting it in front of Talbot, who flushed. Saul dug his nails into his palms, but not before he'd caught a glimpse of the image.

Brunette. A slash of lipstick. Dark brows that were finely shaped. An elegant nose.

He'd seen that face before. More than once.

Saul watched the men stride down the path to the waiting patrol car, full of self-importance and testosterone. Talbot threw an apologetic glance over his shoulder. It wasn't his fault. Saul acknowledged that. But he wasn't going to help them. Not now.

He slipped back inside the house, moving with a fluidity that meant no one noticed him, and pushed the spare bedroom door open, checking on Blue. The room was empty – a rumpled sheet the only sign she'd been there – but he heard her voice coming from the kitchen, precise and emphatic. She was standing in the far corner, the floor a chequerboard of blood and tiles.

'Look, we need to call DI O'Neill. It couldn't be any clearer.' She was holding an evidence bag in one gloved hand but Saul didn't need to move closer to know what was inside it. Through the transparent plastic, he saw Graham Baxter's final note. In her other hand, she was holding a handful of greetings cards, her thumb slipped between one of them, marking her place.

'Show me,' he said.

'Mr Baxter lived alone, right? I checked a sample of handwriting from the shopping list on the side. It matches the writing on his wall calendar and in his address book. I'd say it's safe to assume they're all his.'

He nodded. 'Go on.'

'But look at the shape of the L on the note from the door.'

Saul examined it. Each of the three letters was identical, a long loop marking the page.

'Mr Baxter doesn't write his Ls like that. His are squat and square, more masculine, see?'

DC Saul Anguish did see. Dr Clover March was telling him that the person who wrote the note was not the same person who wrote the shopping lists and calendar entries, and that seemed obvious, even to his layman's eye.

'But that's not all.' She showed him the front of the card, its gaudy design. *Happy Birthday, Dad.* Then opened it up. Written in a neat hand were birthday greetings from his daughter, Melissa. And the L of her name was a perfect match with the note on the door. She showed him Christmas cards. Father's Day. They were all the same.

The cogs in Saul's brain whirred and clicked.

'Fuck.'

'What is it?'

'A young female teacher has absconded from her primary school.'

'And?'

He edged around the kitchen, careful not to disturb the white-suited officer on the floor picking through bone fragments, until he reached the framed family photograph he'd noticed on the windowsill during his first visit. Father. Mother. Son. Daughter. He pointed to the young woman in the picture.

'That's her.'

12

Christine drove north. She drove until the urban landscape – the high-rises and retail parks, the grey monoliths of bricks and apathy – gave way to fields and the rolling beauty of the harvest. She drove until her foot felt numb on the brake and her eyes were gritty, and the children had lapsed into silence. She drove to forget. She drove until all she could concentrate on was the monotony of the road. It calmed her because she knew what lay ahead.

Charlie's parents lived in a picturesque town a few miles from the Scottish border. She had never visited this house and neither had her children. In the early years, she had spent time with Daphne and Frank, hoping to find a loving mother and father, not through blood but familial ties.

At first, Daphne had tried to befriend her with conversation starters about horoscopes and neighbourly feuds, neither of which interested Christine. But she had persevered because she loved Charlie and he loved her, and although their relationship was in its infancy, both recognized the inevitability of a future together. His mother could be difficult. He'd told her that. But he hadn't prepared her for Daphne's callousness, her indifference. Until one afternoon, a year after they'd started dating, she'd overheard his mother discussing her.

'She's so plain. You could do better, you know. You're such a good-looking young man, dynamic, and she's a bit . . .' – she'd paused, as if selecting the most demeaning word in her vocabulary – '. . . limp.' The clink of cutlery. 'Frank, you agree, don't you?'

Christine, on her way back from the toilet, had paused in the hallway. *Limp.* What an insulting descriptor. Six months earlier, during a work appraisal, a colleague had called her benign. She'd never forgotten the sting of it. But when she'd looked it up in the dictionary, she'd softened because it also meant friendly and amiable. But there was no such reprieve with limp: lacking in strength, vigour or firmness; drooping; spiritless.

She'd waited to see if Frank agreed with Daphne's verdict. Predictably, he had grunted something neutral but he hadn't chastised her. When Charlie cleared his throat, she'd held her breath.

'She's not limp, Mother. She's vivid and warm, and the kindest woman I've ever met.'

Her body had relaxed then, relief spinning through her. Charlie was the man she'd believed him to be, and that was all that mattered.

She knew she ought to return to the table to finish Sunday lunch and her glass of wine, but a part of her wanted to hear what poison Daphne would drip next into her son's unwilling ear.

'For a fling, perhaps, Charles, but not forever. You'll get bored. I know you will. You need something more than she can offer.'

Never had she felt so summarily dismissed. A wave of nausea overcame her. She wondered how Daphne would react if she vomited on her pale grey carpet.

'I'm afraid you'll have to get used to it because I'm going to ask her to be my wife.'

Even now, all these years later, that exchange remained imprinted on her memory, each word landing a blow until her relationship with Daphne was fractured beyond repair, a heap of broken pieces. She had gone back in to lunch and helped tidy the plates away and dry up, and on the journey home, she had told Charlie what she'd heard.

He had been mortified. Furious at his mother. That evening, he had telephoned her and it had erupted into a row which left him white-lipped and silent. He did not call Daphne again. And she did not call him. The days stretched into weeks and the weeks into months. Contact became a rarity. An occasional duty visit here and there. The odd birthday card or email. Christine and Charlie married. Had a daughter. A son. And the distance between them widened into a canyon.

That last week with Charlie, before he had left her, she'd pleaded with him to let her call his mother and attempt a reconciliation. He'd stared at the ceiling and hadn't answered. She had searched his face for a softening of hostilities, but he had remained expressionless, unmoved. Part of her thought she should ring them anyway, to lay that first brick in building bridges. But she'd wanted to respect his wishes. She couldn't pretend she didn't know how he felt because he'd answered in the same way every time she'd brought it up. 'She is not my mother anymore.'

Christine's fingers tightened on the steering wheel. All these years later, and that seed of anxiety was flowering inside her stomach again. But they had come for a specific reason. This was the right path to take. For her children.

For Tom, it would spark a new connection to his father. For Galen, it was complex and painful. But she would try. That's all she had left.

The house was more unkempt than she'd expected, the paintwork dull and the front garden overgrown. Leaves spilled over the lip of the gutter and a spread of moss was intruding on the roof.

Before she had finished pulling into their driveway, the front door opened and Daphne, clad in a soft jumper and skirt, stood watching, arms folded. Age had touched her hair and crumpled her skin. Her back was bent and her movements slower, but her face was a mask of discontent, set by years of bitterness.

Christine almost turned back then. But Tom had opened the car door and was already outside, his innocent face creasing into a smile. 'Hello, Granny. What's for lunch?'

Daphne smiled then, a warmth to her that Christine had forgotten. 'You're such a big boy now.' She took his blanket from him. 'You don't need that. Come and see your grandfather.' She draped an arm across Tom's shoulders and led him into the house without greeting Christine or Galen.

'This is going to be fun.' Galen's tone was dry as she took her mother's outstretched elbow and followed them inside.

Lunch was smoked salmon with capers and pickled shallots, and a side order of small talk. Daphne had forgotten that Galen was vegetarian and watched in disapproval as she ate triangles of buttered bread and nothing else. Tom poked at the fish and wrinkled his nose. In the end, she brought out a block of cheese, muttering about fussy eaters, and the children made sandwiches which they ate in embarrassed mouthfuls.

After a dessert of apple pie and ice cream, Daphne shot Frank a pointed look. 'Why don't we take the children into the garden and show them the tree?'

Tom's face lit up and he climbed down from the table, but Galen didn't move. 'I want to stay with Mum.'

Christine rested her hand on her daughter's and squeezed it. 'Is it okay if I come too?'

Daphne's mouth said yes but her face said no. Christine was beyond caring. It was clear to her this had been a mistake. While Tom had been fussed over and petted, Galen had been ignored. In a quiet moment, she had planned to explain everything to Daphne, but she had changed her mind. Her eyes filled with tears. Galen deserved better.

Their garden, a tidy square of lawn surrounded by shrubs, was ablaze with autumn glory. The five of them wandered towards an ancient oak with a rope-and-tyre swing.

'The previous owners put this in. We never got round to removing it.' Frank, in his gardening coat and boots, grinned at Tom and ruffled his hair. 'Have a go if you like.'

Galen stumbled over a divot in the grass and Christine steadied her, murmuring so the others didn't hear. 'You tired? It was an early start this morning.' Galen shook her head, brushing away her mother's concern.

At the far end of the garden was an ornamental pond, and water spilled like grief from the eyes of a stone frog. Daphne had moved ahead and was standing at the edge of a paved seating area, her face collapsed into an expression Christine knew well.

A silver birch stood by itself in a circle of rocks.

One by one, they joined her until they were standing in a circle too. The birds offered up their songs of sorrow. A wind with teeth attacked them, nipping at the exposed areas of their skin. In the sky above, the air thickened with the rolling notes of an approaching thunderstorm. But still they stood there, the sound and fury of nature swallowing them up.

Christine had loved him. And Charlie had known that, even through the most difficult parts of their marriage. Even through the pain and disbelief and injustice of it all. For Daphne, it was different. Christine read her hurt at the years of estrangement in the slope of her shoulders and the twist of her mouth and the lines that scored her face like scars. That loss was in every grey hair, every birthday and Christmas and Mother's Day spent without her only son. The taste of regret was in every room he hadn't slept in and each uneaten meal.

And now it was too late.

Christine, flanked by her children, reached for their hands. She squeezed them and they squeezed back. Their warmth comforted her. Frank stood a short distance from them, his head bowed. Daphne lifted a trembling hand to her mouth, the loneliest of all figures: a mother without her child.

A plaque was fixed to the base of the tree, the words engraved in a simple font that made Christine's heart drop like a stone in her chest, a reminder of all they had lost.

IN LOVING MEMORY OF CHARLES PETER HARDWICKE,
SON, NEPHEW, HUSBAND, FATHER.
GONE BUT NOT FORGOTTEN.
15 AUGUST 1981 – 22 DECEMBER 2021

13

Tickencote, Rutland: 12.54 p.m.

Fox and Missy had made their first mistake before they'd even left the grounds of the cottage. Or perhaps it wasn't a mistake at all, but a decision they'd taken with subconscious intent.

Either way, neither of them had covered their faces when they'd trespassed on the property of the part-time vicar, who was now lying dead in his Cambridgeshire barn. And neither of them had noticed the motion-sensor cameras that were dotted around the grounds, linked to his wife's mobile phone and triggered by movement.

For that reason, the vintage car which Fox had stolen was now the subject of an Automatic Number Plate Recognition alert, and screenshots of both their faces were on a Wanted circular that had been posted to the Police National Computer and would shortly be released to the media.

Unaware that their crimes had been uncovered so quickly, they had approximately seven minutes before this would start to become a problem.

For now, though, they were driving along a stretch of road that was quiet, looking for a place to break for lunch. Fox swerved down a lane and parked under a tree, its leaves drifting onto the windscreen, filling it with flames.

Missy watched him lay a napkin across his lap. He held out two paper bags. 'Chicken or tuna?'

She reached for the chicken and took a large bite, suddenly ravenous as she'd eaten nothing since dinner the previous night. 'They're going to catch up with us at some point.'

Fox shrugged. 'We knew that, didn't we?'

Did she? She wasn't sure she'd thought that far ahead. She seldom did. In some distant part of herself, she had known the police would want to talk to her about Katie, and all that had happened since. But it was an abstract knowledge, impossible to root in reality. She couldn't imagine the conversations, or pasting on the sincere and serious face she'd be expected to present. In truth, she was bored with life. Disillusioned. Different from everyone else. And for the first time in months, she felt truly alive.

'I guess.'

She studied him as she ate her sandwich. His long, lean fingers. The way his hair fell across his brow. In that moment, she understood she had never loved Gerard. It had only ever been Fox. She wanted to kiss him but it felt all wrong, like coffee and salt. He hadn't so much as looked at her with anything approaching lust. In the past, she would have taken the lead. But an odd shyness consumed her.

Fox was counting the cash in the church tin. 'Ninety-eight pounds and sixteen pence. We'll need more.'

Food. Petrol. A place to sleep. It all cost money. But how would they acquire it? Her mind touched on the answer, probing it like a tongue in the gap of an excavated tooth. *By violent means.*

She undid the top button of her coat.

Fox folded up his napkin and shook crumbs out of the

window. He closed his eyes. An occasional car drove past, but he was keeping to the back roads, which was a sensible move. His breathing deepened, his chest rose and fell.

Missy folded her hands in her lap. The katydids were quiet and the car was warm. She breathed in the silence and closed her eyes too.

When she opened them five minutes later, a police officer was looking through the window.

14

'Melissa Mary Smith. Twenty-three years old. Primary school teacher.' O'Neill had blown up a photograph of the young woman and stuck it on the wall. 'No previous convictions. At least, nothing on paper.'

He pointed to the photograph next to her. 'Dashiell Elvin Lloyd. Twenty-five. Six years in a young offenders' institution for manslaughter. Cookham Wood, I believe. Several convictions for GBH, theft and handling illegal weapons. Very bad news.'

In the last few minutes, Detective Inspector Angus O'Neill had pulled together a discreet and exclusive emergency briefing of Midtown's Major Crime Unit. The forensic team remained at Graham Baxter's home, but DC Saul Anguish, Dr Clover Marsh and DC Eliot Williams were among the four personnel who had been called in. PC Alex Talbot, back from interviewing staff at the school, had also been summoned by O'Neill, at Saul's behest.

Saul slid into his seat, the last to arrive, but O'Neill did not let him off the hook. 'You're late.' He was old-school, a stickler for punctuality. And his sharpness stung.

'As most of you know, a child who was in the care of Melissa Smith is currently in paediatric intensive care with a bleed on the brain. Prognosis is poor. Smith walked out of the classroom this morning after refusing to help the child.

'A man we believe to be a relative – pending formal identification – was found dead by gunshot wound at 9.45 a.m., but a note left on the door of his house was in Smith's handwriting.'

After this link between Baxter and Smith had been confirmed, O'Neill had instructed officers to post an alert on the Police National Computer, urging neighbouring forces to be on the lookout. As the team were about to discover, this quick thinking had paid off.

'A vicar – John Saint, would you believe – was killed by a bullet to the chest in a separate incident at his home less than two hours later. Both Lloyd and Smith were on the premises at the time, caught on security cameras and identified almost instantaneously through images on the PNC.'

O'Neill, who had been pacing the floor, stopped to rub his chest and tip an antacid onto the palm of his hand. 'This is a fast-moving investigation involving other police forces and jurisdictions. But as Smith is now a suspect in a murder inquiry here in Midtown, I want her and Lloyd in for questioning.'

Williams leaned back in his chair. 'Where are they now, boss?'

'We don't know. Their last known whereabouts was Madingley in Cambridgeshire but we think they're heading north. It's a fluid situation. The NPAS is on standby.' His gaze swept across his team and settled on DC Anguish. 'I want us to find them first.'

Saul's eyes bored into O'Neill's and they shared a wordless exchange. Their relationship was complex. Although Saul would not admit it, even to himself, he was beginning to regard O'Neill as a sort of father figure, the kind of steadying influence who'd been absent from his own life. A part of him understood O'Neill felt it too, that although they were wary of each other, they shared a burgeoning trust and respect. He knew that O'Neill wanted to nurture his talent. In return, he longed to impress him.

O'Neill played things by the book. Mostly. The police had changed since his younger days. He'd said as much to Saul a few weeks ago. How everyone was hog-tied by rules and regulations and corporate tick-boxes. 'There's no place for instinct, for old-fashioned policing.'

Saul had tested him then. 'It doesn't have to be that way, sir.' O'Neill had cocked his head, an unreadable expression crossing his features. 'Is that so?' He sensed in Saul something hungry and dark, which could be useful, even though his senior rank would never allow him to articulate that in an official capacity. But Saul knew it. And O'Neill knew it too.

With the National Police Air Service on standby, it was only a matter of time before Smith and Lloyd were apprehended. And it was highly likely they were still armed. There'd be a specialist firearms team. Armed Response Vehicles. Other officers from other police forces. But Saul would find them first, a wolf on the scent of blood.

'Be careful,' said O'Neill. 'Make sure you're wearing body armour. Arrest them if you can – but only if it's safe to do so. No heroics. Understood? This is a small team, working off the book, reporting directly to me. I need you to be discreet but I can't divulge why for operational reasons.'

O'Neill had looked away then, and Saul wanted to know what the detective inspector wasn't telling them. But Saul was not one for questions. Although his relationship with O'Neill was prickly at times, he respected him enough to trust his decisions.

'What about me, sir?' Talbot had that wide-eyed look of a rabbit in the headlights.

'You're going with them.'

'But I'm supposed to be on secondment to the traffic division tomorrow.'

'Change of plan. Unless you'd rather spend your days firing speed guns at spotty teenagers. You applied to join the Murder Club, didn't you? Here's your chance.'

DC Anguish hadn't told Talbot about the quiet word he'd had with O'Neill earlier but he was proud his DI had listened to him. Talbot would be an asset to the team – he just didn't know it yet.

The four of them were booked on an express train from London to Newcastle, which left in less than an hour and a quarter. It would be tight. But in the last few minutes, a petrol station attendant had called the tip-line after recognizing Smith and Lloyd from a Breaking News alert on a television bulletin. She'd overheard them talking about going to Scotland. Sticking a pin in the halfway point made sense. They could get off the train earlier if they needed to, but at least they'd be on their way. And rail travel was fast. O'Neill had jumped through a few hoops, but two unmarked cars would be waiting for them at the other end, on loan from another force.

'Do you want a ride to the lookout?' A smile – tentative but genuine – from Blue. 'To get your stuff.' She was making an effort. He acknowledged that. But he'd been hurt by her behaviour, even if he was too proud to show it. 'A ride?' Even he recognized how vacant he sounded. Then, 'Yes. Please.'

He glanced around the briefing room. Blue – icy, funny, complex, out of his league – was pulling on her houndstooth coat. Eliot Williams, an arrogant prick but razorblade-sharp, technically his superior, was sequestered in an alcove with O'Neill, symmetrical expressions of gravity.

And then there was PC Alex Talbot, who held a purity inside him that needed to be nurtured, an antidote to Saul's darkness that O'Neill's raggle-taggle team might benefit from.

His mouth tasted of metal, his body flooded with nor-epinephrine, a neurotransmitter released in heightened situations that altered his taste receptors. He was intoxicated with adrenaline. Drunk on cortisol. He itched to leave now, to hunt down Smith and Lloyd and mete out a brutal justice of his own. O'Neill might suspect him capable of deeds that others shied away from. The detective inspector had no idea how deep that seam of darkness ran.

'O'Neill wants to see you.' Williams jerked his head in the inspector's direction. Saul turned to Blue. 'Two minutes.'

'I'll be outside,' she said.

O'Neill waited until everyone had left before he spoke. He handed Saul a sealed envelope with a name written across the back. 'Keep this safe, and to yourself. Until I say other-wise, okay?'

Saul looked at him, a frown on his face, waiting for an

explanation. O'Neill shook his head. 'Not now. But I will tell you everything in due course, I promise.' And because Saul him, wanted to please him, he slid the letter into his pocket and he didn't breathe a word to anyone.

Blue's motorbike cut across the salt marshes, the wheels skidding on paths strewn with leaves, their veins touched with mould. His arms were anchored around her waist, a functional act, but even now, he could not ignore the memory of her skin. He burned to touch her again.

The coastguard's lookout – an old wireless transmission station that stood on a promontory overlooking the bay – had been Saul's home since arriving in Midtown-on-Sea the previous year. With no family left, his had been a rootless existence, but moving here was the closest he'd come to belonging.

Several gulls were circling above his garden when Blue pulled in. Two or three were on the lawn, fighting over the flesh of some unidentifiable animal. These were white-headed scavengers, known to kill and eat pigeons and rats, their beaks tipped with blood. He shooed them away, but did not have time to linger.

Blue always carried a change of clothes with her, and her neighbour would feed her cat Miss Meow, so she had no need to return to her flat, but the station was just under an hour away, and even though O'Neill had asked them to hold the train for his team, they would be cutting it fine. Talbot and Williams were already on their way to London.

The lookout was draughty and in need of attention. When the wind pushed in from the bay, the windows bowed at its display of strength, shaking in ill-fitting frames that might loosen their hold on the glass at any moment and send it spinning into the sea. Lived-in furniture. Threadbare carpets. No alarm, just a simple mortice lock in the ancient front door, a spare key hidden beneath the rusted anchor.

Because of this lax approach to security, Saul didn't see what had happened at first. He smelled it.

He slid in the key and it unlocked with a click, as usual. The sitting room was as he'd left it. But the air was filled with a peculiar scent, almost impossible to place. If he'd been asked, Saul would have said it was something unclean and foul, like meat that had turned or an on-farm slaughterhouse. It had the stink of animal about it. But an undercurrent of something darker too.

And it was warm. Stifling. As if the heating had broken and would not switch off.

His first thought was that the drains had overflowed or vermin – there had been an explosion of mice in Midtown – had crawled under the floorboards to die. But the scent waxed and waned. Until he reached the bottom of the stairs and had to cover his mouth.

Blue was sombre as she followed him inside, her nose wrinkled. 'Are you storing corpses in here?' It was a weak joke. He glanced at her; she was edging closer to the truth than she realized. While there were no bodies in Saul's house, he had killed more than once – but only when they'd deserved it.

'I don't know,' he said. 'But I think it's coming from upstairs.'

The smell intensified as he climbed the staircase but he was mystified by its cause. Everything was in its place. No signs of forced entry. When he'd left for work that morning, it had all been in order. Beads of sweat rolled off his forehead. He checked the thermostat on the landing. No wonder it was suffocating. It had been turned up to thirty-two degrees – and not by him.

His eyes narrowed. Blue was pale as clouds in her namesake sky. Saul pushed against his bedroom door. The smell was overpowering. Blue gagged and shook her head, retreating backwards onto the landing. Saul stood still and expressionless at the sight that met him.

Several dozen dead chicks were strewn across the room, a mass of pale fluff matted with blood and entrails. They were everywhere. All over his bed. Discarded on the rug in the centre of the floorboards. His wardrobe and chest of drawers had been pulled open, and they were tucked amongst his clean and folded clothes. They were piled on the windowsill, his bedside table. He'd made his bed that morning but his duvet had been thrown back and they were scattered across the sheet, the place he'd lain the night before, waiting for Blue.

He crouched, examining one of the birds more closely. A male chick, eyes shut, his beak no bigger than Saul's fingernail. He'd seen this before, at the pet shop he used to work at as a teenager. Day-old chicks taken from hatcheries, gassed and blast-frozen, and sold as feed for birds of prey and reptiles. He'd only been gone for a handful of hours, so it was apparent to him these had been deliberately defrosted and kept in a humid environment to make them reek before someone had dumped them here.

Oddly, he was not sickened by the sight of these creatures, limp and lifeless, although he felt a flicker of sorrow for he loved all that belonged to the natural world. But he was enraged by the violation of his private space. He felt exposed. His anger was not the bright red mist of impulsivity or the shimmering heat of incandescent rage, but cold and measured, like a surgeon's blade.

When he found out who was responsible for this, he would make them wish they had never heard the name Saul Anguish.

He turned off the heating and, clinical and disengaged, he collected up as many of the chicks as he could find and put them in a rubbish sack. The rest – the mess and the stink – would have to wait until he'd returned from the north. He considered alerting the landlord but dismissed the idea. He did not want to risk eviction.

He washed his hands, shoved the only clean clothes he could find into a bag, and shut the bedroom door behind him.

Blue was waiting for him downstairs, her face crumpled with distress. And something else, a blurring of knowledge and guilt. She did not ask questions and he did not volunteer a single syllable. Both were the type disinclined to waste words.

They did not speak again until they were outside, and Saul was tossing the birds across the grass for the animals, their bodies like tattered yellow ribbons.

'Saul—'

He turned to her, his face hard and uncompromising. 'I'll ask you again. Do you know anything about this?'

Her eyes filled with tears. He watched her wavering between the easy option and the truth. She chose the truth. 'Yes.'

He thought he heard his heart crack.

'But before you leap to conclusions, you have to let me explain.'

But Saul did not want her to explain. He did not want to hear excuses. He'd heard them all his life. From his mother and father. From social services. From the men who took pleasure in brutalizing children and women and deserved retribution. The part of him that was so drawn to her urged him to breathe, to pause for a moment and listen to what she had to say, but he could not think of a justification for the slaughterhouse that had greeted him.

The trust between them, precious and hard won, was not just broken, it had shattered into shards with edges that would rip and mutilate.

She called out his name, pleading for his understanding. But he could not look at her. From now on, it was work and nothing else. If they hadn't been running against the clock, he would have made his own way to the train station, but there was no time for that.

Blue called his name again, but Saul pulled on the motorbike helmet and ignored her. He did not hear her whispered explanation as the wind swept in from the bay, and the gulls descended in a flurry of feathers and greed, ripping the chicks to pieces with their beaks and claws until nothing was left.

15

Tickencote, Rutland: 1.03 p.m.

Missy kept her eyes closed but walked her fingers up the front of her coat to loosen the second and third buttons, just in case.

'Fox.' She breathed his name. The air temperature had dropped by a couple of degrees and it came out in a smoky puff. He did not move but let out the sigh of a sleeping man.

With a surreptitious glance through the window, Missy assessed the actions of the police officer. From what she could see, Missy deduced two facts: the uniformed constable was driving a marked patrol car and, more importantly, she was travelling alone.

The officer – a woman with curly hair and an open face – knocked on the glass.

Her movements were confident and unafraid, and Missy suspected she had stumbled across them rather than matched their number plate to the stolen car. But if their brutal crimes *had* been discovered, she would only need to run their registration through the system for all hell to break loose. Missy wound down the window. 'Hello.' A 1,000-kilowatt smile. 'Can I help you?'

'You're not supposed to park here. Didn't you see the signs?'

'What signs?' She was aware of Fox stirring, but she willed him to stay asleep. With a bit of luck, she could talk their way out of this.

'This is private property. You're trespassing, I'm afraid. The owner is a high-net-worth individual who has experienced multiple break-ins over the two last months and got a bit spooked when she saw your car, so if you'd kindly move on.'

'Of course.' Missy released the breath she had been holding, the tension easing from her shoulders. They were off the hook. She smiled again at the police officer and the officer smiled back. 'We're on holiday. We pulled over to eat our picnic.'

The officer jerked her head in Fox's direction. 'He looks like he's dead to the world.'

'Early start. I'll wake him up in a second.'

'Have a good day and enjoy the rest of your trip.'

Missy leaned forward to roll up the window, but as she did so, the neck of her coat fell open. The police officer's eyes widened in surprise. She took a step backwards, her hand at her hip, resting on her duty belt, the other hand on her police radio.

'What's your name?' All traces of friendliness had vanished.

Missy sighed. The woman had seemed nice enough. She considered giving her name. But it would be a delaying tactic, nothing more.

'I don't think that's going to help either of us.' She opened the car door and stepped into the cool air. It calmed her thudding heart.

'Stay back.' The officer's voice was strident but Missy detected the layers of fear beneath it and her confidence blossomed.

The road was a single-track country lane. In the hour they'd been sitting there, no more than two or three cars had driven past. Missy scanned the horizon, but the only movement was the rabble of crows in the branches of the trees, their nests stark against the sky.

She slid her hand into the inside pocket of her coat. The movement forced another button to pop undone, and then her coat was fully open, revealing the rust-stiffened fabric of her jumper. Part of her had wanted the police officer to see it. The wonky part. She'd understood there would be consequences and she was ready for them.

'Put your hands where I can see them.' The officer was fumbling for her baton but they both knew that even if time stopped, it wouldn't be enough.

The pistol was satisfyingly heavy. A Glock 17. Favoured by the police and military. And by her papa, an ex-cop who owned a gun shop in town. Difficult but not impossible to buy on the black market, according to him. Easier to steal. The trickiness of acquiring the correct ammunition without a Section Five certificate made it an unpopular choice. No revolving cylinder. Seventeen nine-millimetre bullets in each magazine. Aim and fire.

Missy pointed it at the police officer. She wasn't sure if she would have it in her when the moment came. But she shouldn't have doubted herself.

The police officer's face collapsed inwards. 'Please,' she said, 'I have a son. He's only four.'

Missy considered this. And found she didn't much care.

Something inside her had shifted during these last hours, an awareness that her purpose in life was at last becoming clear. Melissa Mary Smith had always wanted to leave her mark on the world. Her name up in lights that dazzled and awed. But it hadn't worked out in the way that she'd hoped. She consoled herself with the knowledge the events of today would lead to newspaper headlines, the fame that she craved. What happened in the next two minutes would cement her reputation – and prove to Fox she was as committed as he was.

'What's your name?'

'Penny Dunne.'

The police officer wasn't crying. She respected her for that. Even with a gun pointed at her face, she remained dignified, although when Missy studied her more closely, she noticed her lower lip was trembling. She didn't believe the woman had radioed her control room for back-up. But she couldn't be certain. Was there a secret method of communication that meant a battalion of police cars were on their way now like knights into battle? Missy tore a scrap of paper from the officer's notepad and helped herself to a pencil. 'Any last words, Penny Dunne?'

Penny Dunne – wife, mother, daughter, friend, and three weeks shy of her thirty-second birthday – opened her mouth to reply, and Missy shot her three times in the chest and neck.

The rat-a-tat of the discharged rounds forced the crows upwards, squawking in protest at the disturbance. Penny, who had been a police officer for less than two years after swapping her job as a baker for something more fulfilling, was thrown backwards, a look of surprise on her features.

The bullets tore through her left lung, spleen and oesophagus. She died one minute and twenty-five seconds after that first shot.

As Missy squeezed the trigger, a fire ignited within her, a sense of elation. Wielding the power of death over life. For the briefest of moments, she was aflame, fuelled by the resentments of her past, but soon they had burned up like pieces of tissue. When she pressed a little harder, she discovered that behind her euphoria was nothing at all. She probed herself for shock. Revulsion. Disgust at her actions and the sack of meat on the grass that had once been Penny Dunne, now emptied of humanity. But she felt numb. Disassociated from everything.

A hand closed around hers, encircling the gun. 'You're a dark horse.'

She leaned back against him, his reassuring solidity. He turned her around so she was facing him. His eyes were heavy-lidded from sleep but something sparked behind them, admiration and desire. He brushed her cheek with the back of his thumb. 'My brave girl.'

Fox crouched next to the body of the police officer. Her light brown hair was in a ponytail but some of it had come loose and the ends were stained with blood. He helped himself to the slim gold band that encircled the fourth finger of her left hand.

'We better make tracks.'

She nodded, jittery from the adrenaline. 'Do we need to swap cars again?'

'Soon. But not yet.'

Fox walked over to the edge of the fields where the last of the wildflowers were still in bloom before entering winter dormancy. He gathered as much common toadflax and autumn hawkbit as he could carry, and then tied them in a bundle with a lace he'd unpicked from the fallen officer's shoe.

He thrust them at Missy, a shyness to his actions. 'For you.'

She blushed with pleasure.

And then Fox was on the ground before her, his face upturned to the sky, resting on one knee.

'Missy Smith, will you do me the honour of becoming my wife?'

Missy's mouth fell open but she was lost to him. As she had been since the moment they'd first met. She flung her arms around his neck. 'Yes.' And again. 'Yes.'

Fox scooped her up and swung her around, both laughing for the joy of it. 'Hold on a minute,' he said. He ran back to the car for the cream silk scarf she'd stolen from the vicar's barn and when he returned, he covered her head with it. Then he asked her to hold out her hand.

She laid the gun on the grass and did as he'd requested. When he slid Penny Dunne's ring onto her finger, her heart skipped a beat.

He pressed the vicar's stolen platinum wedding band into her palm. 'My turn.'

With tenderness, she pushed it over his knuckle and kissed it. A simple ceremony. No need for pomp and circumstance. Two people in love. Bound by death.

In the still of the countryside, they stood hand in hand, knowing their marriage would be short-lived and that every moment from here on in would be coloured with the vivid certainty that their time together would be measured out in minutes and seconds rather than months and years.

Ride or die.

Fox unpicked the second lace from Penny Dunne's shoe. He strung it through the tabs of two fizzy drink cans and tied it to their tow-bar.

Their honeymoon would be a bloodbath.

PART TWO

SCOTLAND

16

Galen liked facts. Bottlenose dolphins belong to the order *odontocete cetaceans*. They have two stomachs, one to receive food and another to digest it. When they sleep, they rest one side of their brain at a time. These brains contain tiny amounts of magnetite, a naturally occurring mineral, which allows them to navigate vast oceans using the earth's magnetic fields. They do not drink water but absorb it from the fish they eat.

And her father had been dead for ten months and two days. Which was 306 days. Or 7,344 hours. Although that wasn't strictly true because she got muddled up when she tried to include his time of death – 12.41 p.m. – in the calculation. One of her mother's cousins had given her a notebook for her birthday. She updated it every day. *Sixty-five days since I last saw Dad. One hundred and three. Two hundred and seven.*

He'd been ill for a while. But it hadn't worried her. Feeling tired was something that every adult she knew complained about. She didn't want to get old because her mother was always tired and her teachers were always tired, and so was Auntie Carmen. The facial tremors were just a thing that

117

happened to him now and again, as much a part of him as his terrible jokes and fondness for fizzy cola bottles. Ditto his irritability. When he'd started to slur his speech one afternoon at a family barbecue, they'd teased him for drinking too many beers.

But, over time, his symptoms had become too intrusive to ignore. When she and her father had walked to the corner shop to buy a newspaper one Saturday afternoon, he'd stumbled and lost his balance, hitting his head on the pavement.

'Daddy,' she'd said, shaking his shoulder, trying to rouse him without success. 'Wake up.' She'd been worried about the proximity of dog mess and whether she should put her coat over or under him, and was it possible to die if there wasn't any blood?

An older man who was passing had insisted on waiting with her while she called her mother, and the sight of Christine running up the road in her heated rollers – her parents had been due to attend a fortieth birthday party that night – had mortified and comforted her in equal measure.

The sun had been shining that afternoon and there had been a traffic jam, the brittle light bouncing off each stacked-up car in a way that looked like falling glitter. She remembered the smell of the diesel fumes and the faces of the rubber-necking drivers as they inched past Charlie, and the feel of his hand, cold and dry and familiar, in hers. She remembered her mother repeating his name over and over again, as if her mantra might invoke the goodwill of Fate and make him wake up.

In the end, an ambulance had arrived and her father had spent the night in hospital. She never did get that Crunchie he'd promised to buy her.

Galen shifted, uncomfortable in the back seat of the car. They'd been driving for what seemed like hours. Her legs ached and she wanted to close her eyes again. She'd been sleeping a lot lately. Too much. She hadn't meant to listen but she'd overheard her mother on the phone a few days ago, her voice low, stretched thin with secrecy. 'I'm so worried about her. Do you think she's depressed?'

Well, Christine Hardwicke did not have the monopoly on worry.

Her mother had not spoken a word since they'd left their grandparents' house. After a perfunctory goodbye, she'd bundled Galen and her brother into the car, and had sat in the driving seat for all of ten seconds, her hands gripping the steering wheel until the skin of her knuckles appeared translucent. Then she'd marched back up the path before Daphne – unlike Tom, Galen had never called her Granny and it felt odd to start now – had even shut the front door.

Galen and Tom had watched them through the window. They couldn't hear their mother's voice but they recognized her anger in the shape of her body, and although Tom didn't understand it, Galen did. At one point, her mother held out her hands, imploring, and her grandmother shrugged, a gesture of such dismissal that it was akin to pouring petrol on Christine's anger, inflaming it. Her mother shouted something – her mother *never* shouted – and she'd thought about opening the window a crack, but her father had always told her that no good came from eavesdropping, and even though he wasn't here anymore, Galen wanted to do the right thing.

When Christine returned, her face was pinched and her eyes held a glassy sheen, two spots of colour on her cheeks.

She started the engine and drove off. Galen had been watching the odometer and they'd travelled for at least ten miles. Her mother still hadn't spoken a word.

'Mum?'

'Mmm.'

'Are you okay?'

'Sorry, yes, just a bit distracted.' A sigh slipped from her, full of something that Galen couldn't name but understood because she felt it too.

'Daphne doesn't care, does she?' The words tumbled from her before she could stop them. 'About me?'

Her mother didn't answer but her eyes filled with tears.

'When will we see Galen's dolphins?' Tom's fringe was sticking to his forehead. Her mother had turned up the heater and it was too warm in the car. His fingers turned in the palm of his hand although Galen couldn't see what he was playing with. She liked the idea of the dolphins belonging to her.

'Tomorrow, I expect. I want to go to the hotel first. We can check in and drop off our luggage.' Christine's voice was flat, like someone had ironed the emotion from it. Galen and Tom exchanged a glance.

'We stand the best chance of seeing them at rising tide when they're chasing the fish.' Galen held up her phone. 'Shall I check the times? In theory, we could look for them tonight.'

'Let's wait and see, shall we?' Her mother sounded weary. 'It's been a long drive and there's still a way to go.'

The sky was changing, the afternoon bruising it with rain. Galen watched the landscape change with it. The road had become less clogged with traffic, quieter now. The hills were voluptuous violet shapes in the closing light. She thought about how it might feel to roam across the fields, to breathe in the clean air and feel her legs – strong, steady – beneath her. To be freed from the shackles of grief and worry and fear. These were weighty burdens for a thirteen-year-old and she carried them without complaint, but some days she feared they'd collapse her.

Tom examined the contents of his palm. 'Did you know Daddy collected coins?'

'I didn't. Who told you that?' Christine's voice was even but Galen could tell she wanted to know more.

'Granny. She said he loved them when he was my age.'

'Numismatist.' The word presented itself to Galen from a corner of her brain.

'What?' Tom wrinkled his nose, his question a perfect note of sibling disdain for something he did not understand.

'It means a collector of coins.' She didn't know where she had first heard that term but it had stayed with her, the musicality of it. *Nu-miz-mah-tist.*

'Oh.' Tom considered this, his finger wandering to a speck of chocolate that had melted and hardened on his jeans. 'There's a big box of coins in Dad's bedroom. Lots and lots of them.'

'You saw Dad's room? At Daphne and Frank's?'

An expression of furtiveness crept across his face. 'Ye-es.'

The injustice of that burned in Galen's stomach. 'When?' That was the first question she'd asked Frank, if she could please have a look at her father's bedroom. He hadn't slept here as a boy – that had been another house, another life – but her grandparents had kept a room for him, a shrine of sorts, filled with keepsakes of the past. Galen hadn't explained why, but she'd wanted to see if she could find anything of herself in the trappings of his childhood.

'After we'd looked at Dad's tree. You and Mum were talking to Frank, and I needed the toilet and Daphne took me.' He held out the coin, a disc of silver. 'She gave me this, Dad's lucky sixpence. He took it everywhere with him when he was younger. When he had exams or played cricket. His driving test.' He beamed at his sister, no malice in his words but delivered with that lack of empathy common to younger children.

Tears coated the back of Galen's throat. 'Can I see?' He passed her the coin, the metal worn in places. She imagined her father tucking it into his pocket or inside his shoe, his fingers clasping this magic charm at life's moments of significance. Perhaps this was why he'd died. He hadn't had his lucky coin.

She passed it back to Tom. Her mother, who'd been silent during their exchange, caught her eye in the rear-view mirror, soft with sympathy.

Tom put the coin carefully in the front pocket of his rucksack. 'Did you get anything of Daddy's?' When he'd died, both children had been invited to choose what they'd wanted from his personal effects. Tom had picked out his old cricket bat and Galen the watch he'd received for his thirtieth birthday. But this was different. This was a part of her father she'd had no access to before; the boy he was, instead of the man he'd become.

'Nothing.'

'That's not true.' The lines around Christine's eyes deepened as she smiled at her daughter. 'You inherited his sense of humour and his stubbornness and his hair.' Her voice softened. 'His courage.'

Galen met her mother's gaze, her face unreadable. 'And what else, Mum?'

Tom, who disliked tension, noticed the charged atmosphere in the car, the sudden edge to his sister's tone, and unzipped his rucksack again. 'Here you are.' He held out the coin to Galen, earnest, loving. 'You have it.'

'No, Tom.' She folded his hand around the sixpence. 'You keep it. It's yours now. And I hope it brings you good luck.'

She dug an affectionate elbow into her younger brother's ribs and he leaned into her. He smelled of clean washing and heat and blackcurrant squash. A fierce rush of love for him claimed her. She rested her head on top of his.

But even her brother's kindness couldn't soothe her. Galen felt abandoned and ignored by her grandparents. She knew why her mother had shouted at them, even if Tom didn't. She couldn't put a name to it. It was too big. Too frightening. When she took it out and examined it, she found she could only stare at it obliquely because it was too much for her to contemplate all at once.

She couldn't call it by its name. She didn't know what to call it. Only that it was done now and couldn't be undone, however much she wished it.

17

Carter Bar, the Scottish Border: 4.47 p.m.

The sky took her breath away. Where she lived, the houses were pressed close to each other and the buildings were so high they cut shapes from it that hid the light. But here, everything was different.

It lacked colour but was not insipid, and held a majesty to it, the clouds hemmed with ermine and pearl. The sky was so wide it did not stop. There were no edges, no beginnings or endings, but a relentless expanse that dwarfed even the unspeakable deeds that she and Fox had committed. Missy gazed upwards, at the clouds and their shadows, and her mind was clear and her heart sang.

In the distance, the fields rolled away from her, packages of rust and green and the sludge-yellow of wheat stubble, blurred by dusk. She shivered, still wearing her blood-stiffened jumper. The air was sharper, and she was cold, the wedding ring she now wore loose on her finger, a spinning band of gold.

The vicar's car had been abandoned. Fox, with his new bride by his side, had decided she was deserving of something more stately – and with a little less heat attached to it.

He adored classic cars. They represented both his own

lack of material wealth and his ambition to acquire it. But if they wanted to finish what they had begun, it would take careful planning. Getting caught by the police before they were ready was something they could ill afford, and so they had driven on for a couple of hours without stopping.

In the end, luck found them. Or not so much luck as the strength of familial bonds. Fox's younger brother ran a car dealership close to a forgettable town 100 miles back from the Scottish border. He was in the forecourt when Fox drove in, overalls stained with oil, the same flaming hair as his sibling.

They didn't exchange words. Not at first. It had been three years since they'd seen each other but the time fell away, sloughing from them like dead skin. Fox looked at Buck. Buck looked at Fox. Then both men moved in tandem, their arms around each other in a lung-squashing embrace.

Buck let go first. He flicked a fingernail against his right incisor, and the sound of keratin hitting enamel reminded Missy of a woodpecker. His overbite – exaggerated by his narrow jaw – had earned him the nickname that had followed him into adulthood. His teeth had never been straight. His mother did not take him to the dentist until he was sixteen, and by then, he was so used to it that the idea of metal twisting in his mouth was more disturbing than the defect it was meant to put right.

It didn't matter. No one teased Buck about his teeth since the day he and Fox beat a boy into a coma.

'What are you doing here?' Buck glanced between Missy and Fox. Missy had never met his younger brother, but she had heard stories about him. Not from Fox, but at the whispered edges of conversations, behind hands or under breath.

If Fox was the outcast of the family, Buck had been excommunicated, expelled from the Lloyd clan in disgrace, never to return.

It was one thing to hurt a stranger but not one of your own.

'Thought we'd drop by.'

Buck's eyes narrowed. 'You never *drop by.*' His gaze flicked to his brother's hand and then to Missy's. 'You two are married. And you didn't invite me?' He clutched his chest in mock distress.

'We were the only guests,' Missy cut in, wanting to avoid upsetting him. 'Me and Fox, I mean. There wasn't anyone else.'

Buck's answering laugh was a rumble that started in his stomach and gained volume and breadth as it climbed through his chest and out of his mouth. 'I wouldn't have come, even if you'd asked me to. Don't want to give our mother a heart attack.' He dug his hands into his pockets, glanced sidelong at his brother. 'How is she?'

'I don't know. Haven't seen her in a while.'

'You should go and visit her then,' said Missy, frowning at the two men. 'Both of you.'

'I don't think she wants to see either of us.' Buck tapped his tooth again. 'Especially not me.'

The last time Buck had seen his mother, she was weeping over the body of her youngest daughter. Clarissa Lloyd had been walking home from school when she was abducted by a gang operating a rival protection racket to Buck's. His mother had begged him not to follow Fox down the unlit alleyway of crime, but he'd ignored her. Buck had revelled in the power, the lucrative line of work he'd chosen and excelled at. Business had been booming. The collateral damage that occurred at the fringes of his conscience was unfortunate but necessary. Until Clarissa. She was the price they'd all paid.

She was seventeen. Sweet as the sherbet pips she bought from the corner shop every week. The Bellamy gang – a family as familiar to the authorities as his own – had tortured and mutilated her. The police and pathologist had wanted to spare them the details but Buck had demanded to know. Her death had been slow and pain-filled. Ninety-seven of her body's two hundred and six bones had been broken. All her fingernails were missing. Across the instrument of her rib-cage, three words had been carved into her skin: *Fuck Buck Lloyd.*

Mrs Talitha Lloyd – their mother – had stayed awake for every second of the eighty-five hours Clarissa had been missing. As the fourth night slid towards dawn, she'd heard a noise outside and run to the front yard, a ghost of herself, haunting her own life. She'd found her girl in the violet half-light, dumped across their step like a sack of rubbish, already dead. Her cry of anguish woke the rest of the family.

But the Lloyd clan lived by a code of ethics. Nobody told the police who had killed Clarissa, although each of them knew, and the detective on the case had pushed them to reveal it as hard as he'd dared.

Talitha refused to let the undertakers touch her. She'd brushed Clarissa's hair and washed her skin and rubbed pink pigment into her lips and blusher onto her cheeks. And when she had buried her daughter in the dress she had chosen for her prom, she told Buck she never wanted to see him again.

'Come on, you don't mean it.' Fox had tried to change her mind, an arm around his mother's shoulders, shrunken down to the bone by grief. Despite her fragility, she had shaken him off, her fury lending her strength.

'What is wrong with both my sons that they willingly take the lives of others without thought or conscience?'

Buck left that night, away from Midtown-on-Sea, away from his family, away from the accusation in his mother's eyes. Fox stayed in the town, but he rarely saw Talitha. It was not a new state of being. His mother had given up on him long before Clarissa's death, focusing maternal hope on her daughter instead.

When they'd finished telling Missy their story, the brothers were quiet again. Missy didn't know what to say because there was nothing *to* say, so she busied herself by playing with her wedding ring.

'Why are you here?' The lines around Buck's mouth were faint, but she could see in them the man he'd become, a melange of sadness and arrogance. 'Are you in trouble?'

'The kind of trouble that only ends one way.' Fox dangled a car key in front of his brother. 'How about a swap?'

Buck eyed him, understanding at once without the need for specifics, a return to the language of their youth. 'Nice motor. Hide it in the body shop. I'll find you something else.'

That something else was a Rolls-Royce Silver Ghost, circa 1922. A classic beauty worth hundreds of thousands of pounds. Confiscated by Buck and his men in exchange for an unpaid debt they were still waiting on. 'Consider it a wedding gift.'

Fox tried his best, but he could not find the words to

articulate what this gesture meant to him. He knew he wouldn't see his brother again, and perhaps some part of Buck knew it too. Fox pulled his brother to him, buried his face in his shoulder. A rising scent of sweat and love and loss. The garage was quiet, but the sound of cars on the road outside filled the air with the hum of rubber on tarmac.

'You better go.' Buck's voice was earth and remembrance, a farewell.

Fox drove his bride north until they crept across the border at Carter Bar. *Fàilte gu Alba. Welcome to Scotland.* They had no route planned but the tree-flanked roads unfurled in front of them, and they did not falter. Through Jedburgh and St Boswells and Lauder, the kind of places that Missy had not seen before: houses gathered in close-knit communities, an invitation to linger amongst the buxom hills.

Her jumper was scratchy and smelled of iron. 'I need to change my clothes.'

'We can't go to the shops.'

'I know.' She rested her hand on his leg, felt his heat through the fabric. An intimacy had developed between them, the memory of the muscle and sinew of their earlier relationship. This connection – this *harmony* – was the reason that Fox found himself pulling into the rural village of Oxton and down a quiet lane off Main Street, left and right and right again.

The house chose them. It was tucked away on its own behind an overgrown hedge that would shield their car from prying eyes. A child's trike had been abandoned on the lawn. A slide, dribbled with rust, its plastic cracked and worn, stood under a tree. Across the garden a distinctive wooden tower, painted white, stood alone: a beehive.

In the fading light, a woman, youngish, her hair tied up in a colourful scarf, was unpegging washing and putting it in a basket, her back to them. The driveway was empty, which made Fox think her husband – if she had one – was most likely at work.

He drove slowly onto the sweep of gravel.

The woman turned towards them, a damp shirt in one hand, two wooden pegs in the other. She'd been singing a pop ballad that Missy didn't recognize, and that last note – high and jaunty – tailed off into silence.

Her accent was strong, flavoured with suspicion, but Missy noticed her mouth curved upwards in the manner of someone who spent a lot of time laughing. 'What do you want?'

Fox wound down the window. 'My wife, she's pregnant and she doesn't feel well. Could we beg a glass of water from you? Perhaps use your toilet?'

'Why don't you ask at the pub? They'll help you out.'

'She doesn't want to go anywhere public. She's . . .' – Fox gestured vaguely to an area below his waist – '. . . bleeding.'

The woman glanced, almost subconsciously, at the play-things and back to Missy, hunched in the passenger seat, arms folded across her stomach. Her face softened, trans-formed from wariness to warmth. 'Oh, poor thing. Let's get her inside.'

She dropped the shirt in the laundry basket and popped the pegs into the bag, and while her back was turned, Missy and Fox exited the car. The wind lifted the leaves in the trees, a murmuring, a warning.

Missy wondered if the owner of the trike was asleep upstairs or watching the television or at a friend's house, thinking about teatime, fish fingers and chips.

Was it a boy or a girl? Had they kissed their mother goodbye that morning or skipped into the playground without a backward glance, not knowing what lay ahead? Where were they now, in this pocket of peace, before everything in their world was about to change? Did they sense it? Not a vision or a premonition, but in the way the hairs on an arm might rise, or an unexpected pricking of their thumbs.

Fox nudged Missy in the hollow of her back. Their eyes locked and held in understanding.

By the time the woman turned back to them, a friendly welcome on her lips, Missy was pointing a gun at her, and Fox had slipped behind her, arm around her throat, as wily as his name.

18

Newcastle Central Station: 3.39 p.m.

Blue hated the smell of trains. The feel of them. Everything about them. When she leaned against the seat and the fabric pricked her skin through her shirt, she thought of all the passengers who had sat there before her. Their sweat, the particles of dead skin shed with every movement, and the dirt from their hands which had touched barriers and doors and countless other surfaces touched by other dirty hands.

She was first off, drawing in lungfuls of air tinged with the stink of the railway station. Talbot followed her onto the platform, almost missing his footing as he stepped off the train, and then Williams. Then Saul.

Saul had not spoken a word to any of them since the start of the journey. The train was busy and the four of them had shared a table, but Saul had jammed in his headphones, insisting he needed to work.

Talbot, exhausted by the morning's ordeal, had slept, his face as smooth as the jazz he'd loved since he was a boy. 'My father was a session musician for George Benson,' he'd told Blue earlier, over too-strong buffet-car tea. 'I didn't appreciate what a big deal that was.' He wasn't much younger than she was, but sleep turned him from a man into a boy,

132

erasing the light touch of early adulthood. Blue tried not to stare at him, but she envied him his ability to rest in public, free from fear or ridicule.

As for Williams, he had no time for her – he couldn't deal with women who spoke up and spoke out – and she didn't enjoy his company except for the sport of puncturing his pomposity. He was occupied with his phone, or following with his eyes any young woman who had the misfortune to walk past him down the aisle. When he complained that he could not 'partake' in a glass of red wine, she had rolled her eyes. Their conversation – intermittent, at best – was confined to work, mostly the note that Melissa Smith had left at her father's house.

She wasn't sure why O'Neill had sent her. She thought the investigation would be better served with her in Midtown instead of on this wild-goose chase. It wasn't procedure to send a forensic linguist into a live situation such as this, but O'Neill was ignoring procedure for reasons of his own. She'd considered arguing her point, insisting she stay down south for the good of the case, but for the first time in a long while, her heart had ruled her head. She was relieved to put distance between her and home for reasons she could hardly bear to think about. But that wasn't why she'd agreed to come. She wanted to be near to Saul.

For most of the journey, she'd watched the landscape slide past, every mile offering up the gift of something new: sheep polka-dotting the fields; a glimpse of a mirrored lake, edged with dying bulrushes; the alien form of a wind turbine; the undulation of hills shaped like bodies. It was easier to do that than spend time with her thoughts.

Every now and then, she sneaked a glance at Saul, but his

head was down, the skin across the bridge of his nose knotted into a frown. For a while, she'd even managed to sleep, which was not surprising, given she'd been awake for most of the night, but her dreams were haunted and a pain in her wrist woke her up. And now they were here and there was still no thaw in the coldness that had begun after that awful scene at the coastguard's lookout.

'Right,' said Williams. As the oldest and most experienced of the four, he moved to take charge. The others let him, although a muscle in Saul's cheek jumped, as if he was fighting against an impulse to speak up. 'Alex, you're with me.' He didn't need to spell it out. Saul and Clover. Clover and Saul.

She liked it best when he called her Blue, in the cloak of the night when he buried his face in her shoulder – 'You smell of cherries' – and cried out her name, but he wouldn't look at her. She waited for him to protest, to ask to be paired with Talbot, and defensive, bitter words corroded her tongue, but she did not need to use them. He was a professional and he didn't argue. Instead he said, 'I'll drive.'

She didn't know where to. There had been a sighting of Melissa Smith and Dashiell Lloyd in Cambridgeshire. A suspected one in Rutland. But that had been hours ago. Analysts whose job it was to plot their movements – to offer up potential scenarios – were throwing out ideas, but no one knew where they were. If they had an ounce of savvy – and she was certain they did – they'd have changed cars again. They could be anywhere. But they would leave a breadcrumb trail. And Saul was hungry. No, starving.

A conversation between Saul and Eliot – brief, to the point – on the platform edge, and the consensus was to drive north. O'Neill had said he'd call them, but there had been no word. They would liaise as soon as they had more information. Live sightings would be updated in real time, but they were playing a different game, although none of them was sure of the rules.

They walked through the station, beneath its roof of wrought-iron ribs and into the street outside. St Mary's Cathedral was awash with pigeons, which were using the window's stone tracery as a landing zone before rising as one entity into the sullen sky.

An officer from Northumbria Police was waiting in the short stay car park, the loaned vehicles parked in spaces reserved for taxis. Resentment leaked from him. 'You're late.'

'Yes, we asked the train driver to deliberately reduce his speed just so we wouldn't arrive on time,' said Blue before she could help herself. Saul's lips twitched and then he remembered himself, thanking the officer for his efforts.

They drove north.

He did not speak to her. Not a single word. She matched his stubbornness minute for minute, determined not to break first. This was a side to him she had not experienced before. It was like a switch had been flicked. He was a grey rock. Unresponsive. Impassive.

She imagined this was the face he'd presented to concerned teachers, social workers and police officers to deflect their interest while his mother drank herself to death and gave away her body for the price of a packet of cigarettes. He'd shared this glimpse into his past one night as they lay together in a darkness so complete she could not see him.

'Are you close to your parents?'

'They're dead.'

'I'm sorry.' She had rested her palm on his chest, felt his heart run faster than the beat of her own.

'Don't waste your pity. I was my mother's second greatest love. Her first was vodka.' He'd pressed the V between his thumb and forefinger around the hollow at the base of her throat, a wanton flirtation. His touch had aroused her, the arrector pili muscles at the follicle's root flexing to make each hair stand on end. She had closed her eyes, her senses intensified, listening for a softening, for the kink in his armour. It had come when she hadn't expected it.

He'd been talking about his father and the violence they'd experienced at his hands, and how the shadow cast over their lives by Solomon Anguish had disappeared with him on that summer night when the moon was high. They'd never seen him again.

'How do you know he's dead, though?'

Saul had stroked her neck with the tip of one finger. On the fourth word, his voice had splintered. 'Trust me, I know.' She had wondered then how he could be so certain. Her analytical brain had run several steps ahead in the only possible direction, and seized on the two ways he *could* know. Either he'd seen his father's body. Or he'd killed him.

But that intimacy – that sharing of secrets – seemed a lifetime away now.

After an hour of silence in the crawl of late afternoon traffic, she could endure it no longer. 'Please, Saul. Will you let me explain?'

At first, she thought he hadn't heard her. He was wearing that same impassive expression, the heel of his right hand resting against the steering wheel, his white-blond hair falling into his eyes, but then he cleared his throat, and she dug her nails into her palms, and there, at the join between England and Scotland, she waited for him to answer.

She waited as they crossed the border into a new and glorious country. She waited as the traffic cleared and the roads unfurled, full of possibility and danger and fear. She waited as the miles were lost to the horizon behind them and the afternoon drew its last breath.

But she never got the chance to hear what he was going to say.

As they were driving through the dusk, Detective Inspector Angus O'Neill called Saul's mobile phone, his voice sliding in and out as the signal dipped. For a few seconds, they could only catch the odd word between long moments of dead air, but the difficulty was short-lived, and soon they'd heard every heart-stopping detail of the inspector's message.

The hills were mauve in the slipping light, and Blue longed to be amongst them, pushing herself closer to the sky until her legs ached and her mouth was dry, and the last twenty-four hours were obliterated from her memory by the extremes of physical exertion.

She replayed to herself what O'Neill had just told them and she didn't know if she had the stomach for what lay ahead, concerned that if last night's nightmare did not consume her, the darkness of this case might.

Even O'Neill – a hard-nosed detective who'd witnessed all tragedy of human life – had struggled to contain his emotion when he'd explained to them what Smith and Lloyd had done.

'Get yourselves to Oxton,' he said. 'As soon as you can. But for Christ's sake, make Talbot wait outside.'

19

Christine was tired. She'd been driving for more hours than she cared to think about, and the strain of the day was taking its toll. Charlie had always done the driving. He'd hated being a passenger and she'd preferred to sit back and read, or watch the world flash by, so it had suited them both. A team with different strengths and weaknesses. But Charlie was dead, and she had to be mother and father now.

A streak of russet was illuminated in the headlights before it disappeared across the road and into the undergrowth. Christine, excited, called out to her daughter: 'Did you see that?' But there was no reply, and when she glanced behind her, both children were asleep, Tom resting his head on Galen's shoulder, his knitted blanket in his hand. 'A red squirrel,' she said, soft as the drizzle that had begun to fall, but there was no one awake to hear her.

On this empty road, she'd noticed several felled trees, bleached by the sun and wind, discarded like piles of animal bones. A place of brutality and beauty, watched over by the wooded hills.

Being the only adult was a lonely place to be.

The rain, although light, was the kind that made everything

wet. It covered the road and the leaves and the grass, nature's gloss. The windscreen wipers kicked into life, a rhythm that soothed her. Charlie would have drummed his hand against his thigh in time with their motion and she would have teased him for being annoying. He would have loved this trip.

On their first anniversary, Charlie had handed her a gift-wrapped notebook. She'd torn off the paper and inside was a record of their year together: ticket stubs from all the cinema trips and theatre visits, nightclubs and music concerts; battered flight and rail tickets for the places they'd travelled to; matchbooks from restaurants and bars and hotels they'd got drunk in together. Each entry had a date and a handwritten message, a memory. The history of their love story.

She'd been touched to discover he'd been saving these mementoes of their relationship, tucking the notebook into a storage box with old letters and cards. Every now and then, she took it out and looked at it, marvelling at how carefree they'd been.

Two months before he'd died, he'd handed her another gift-wrapped notebook. But this time, it wasn't a glimpse into their past, but her future.

With what little energy he'd had left, and with help from Galen and Tom, he'd created a path for her, a way to navigate her grief. Menus from fancy restaurants she'd talked about visiting, and open-ended tickets to tourist attractions, and photographs of Easter Island and the Rockies and Antarctica, places they had dreamed of travelling together. All accompanied by humorous notes and doodles, as if he'd be travelling by her side, a voice in her ear. Both children had chosen their own bucket list destinations: Tom, with typical enthusiasm, had drawn pictures of Disney World in Orlando, the M&M's store in New York, and the Sydney Harbour Bridge. Galen's choice was much simpler, the wild dolphins at Chanonry Point.

Even then, none of them were expecting him to die as quickly as he did.

Charlie was always late. Ever since he'd almost missed their wedding, it had been a standing joke. 'He'll be late for his own funeral,' her mother used to say. Except he wasn't. This time, he was early.

His downhill progression was rapid, but all of them were confident he had a few more weeks, even the nurses who came in every day with their masks and hand sanitizer. By then he spent many hours asleep and struggled to talk, but there were moments when he opened his eyes, and she could see the Charlie of old. *Her* Charlie.

In one of their last conversations, before conversations had become impossible, Charlie had asked her to make him a promise.

'I don't want to die alone,' he'd said. 'I know I'm supposed to be strong and all that bollocks, but I'm scared, Chrissy. I know it's a lot to ask of you, but I want my family with me at the end.'

'We're not going anywhere.' She had laid her head on his chest, listened to the slow march of his heart. 'We'll be there, I promise.'

With the help of Carmen's brother, Christine had moved his bed downstairs. Their dining room – the hub of many happy gatherings – became a sick room. The children popped in and out whenever they wanted to, their voices ringing through the house. Charlie liked to hear them bickering and laughing and calling up and down the stairs, the background noise of family life.

When the time came, she would keep them home from school, but only if that's what they wanted. 'Not if it's a Friday,' said Tom, pragmatic as ever. 'It's football.' But Galen was certain. 'I want to be with him.'

For her part, Christine had scaled down her hours and responsibilities at work, and was spending all her time caring for him, but it was relentless, watching the decline of the man she loved.

He died on a Wednesday afternoon in December with nothing remarkable about it. A leaden sky. No new Covid restrictions for Christmas in the news. One of those quiet sorts of days that pass the time until tomorrow.

Christine had sat by his bed, reading aloud from a novel so tedious it was difficult to keep her own eyes from closing, let alone Charlie's, but as she had no way of knowing if he was enjoying it or not, she didn't want to stop, just in case.

Just in case. Those words would come to haunt her.

Her bottom was numb from the hard wooden chair and she needed to use the toilet. In truth, she craved a few moments of solitude to stop being a carer and to feel free, however fleetingly. He was asleep – unconscious, although she didn't know it at the time. His chest was rising and falling, and his hands were warm, and she thought he'd be fine on his own for a few minutes. No more than five. She was meticulous about that. *Just in case.* She dropped a kiss on his forehead.

Looking back, she wasn't sure how she'd allowed time to slip away from her. She'd sat there, catching up on an agony uncle column she'd missed in the weekend newspaper, and laughing at an article Carmen had sent her about how to have more sex in your forties, and scouring the internet for recipes for a chicken chilli stew she'd wanted to try out. She'd sat there until the backs of her thighs were indented by the toilet seat and she had pins and needles in her left foot.

Ten minutes. A quarter of an hour. Twenty-four minutes on her phone. While she was reading about perimenopausal vaginal dryness, Charlie died alone.

As soon as she'd walked back into the room, she'd known he was gone. The air held a stillness to it. She went to him, pressed her palm against his cheek. 'I'm sorry.' Tears – the hot, unstoppable kind – leaked from her at the enormity of what his loss would mean for them all.

Outside, a dust-cart pulled up, its mechanical jaws swallowing the rubbish sacks lining the street. The wind lost its temper inside the chimney breast. A clock in the dining room measured out the seconds since his death in methodical, relentless ticks. The world kept turning, as she knew it must. She tucked the duvet over him and smoothed back his hair, so that when the children saw him, he looked as much like Daddy as he could. And guilt settled on her like a shroud.

No one tells a mother what to do when a father dies before his time and his children are at school.

Term had run a little later this year, closer to Christmas than usual. Should she collect them early? Break this world-upending news while they cry in the back of the car under the exposed glare of the outside world? Should she wait until they get home? The journey would be excruciating, forced to keep this knowledge from them as they chatted, unsuspecting, about the highs and lows of their day while she knew what lay ahead as soon as the front door closed. Send a friend? Too risky. Ask a teacher? Too impersonal. In any case, it seemed wrong to tell others before the children.

In the end, it was much worse than she could have imagined.

Galen had chosen this particular day – the last day of term – to leave Snapchat running, which depleted her already low phone battery to nothing, and so she missed her mother's message instructing her to wait for a lift instead of getting the bus.

Even now, ten months later, Christine lay awake in the hollow hours of the night, tormented by three things. She didn't say goodbye to Charlie, she didn't keep her promise to be with him at the end and she didn't protect her daughter.

Because while Christine collected Tom and waited outside the secondary school for her eldest, Galen let herself into the family home and found her father dead in his bed.

20

Oxton, near Lauder: 5.45 p.m.

Their first kiss as newly-weds happened on the bed of the woman they'd just killed.

Fox had always been shy. But Missy had enough front for both of them. It was up to her, she decided, to take the lead because he was handling her as if she might break. And who knew how long they might have left alive?

The gun was still warm when she wrapped her arms around him, pressed her mouth to his. He stiffened, surprised by her brazenness, but then he relaxed into the kiss, his desire for her climbing. She pulled her bloodied jumper over her head and slipped off her skirt so that she was naked except for her underwear.

Her skin was pale and stippled with rust where the blood had soaked through. He stared at her, her husband, and she stared back. It had been two years since he'd touched her body but he'd never forgotten what it had felt like to belong to her.

The woman – her name was Sally Brown, according to the driving licence in the wallet they'd emptied – lay on the carpet, one leg extended, the other tucked beneath her where she'd fallen when the bullet had entered her neck.

Fox had fired that one. Sally Brown was the first victim who'd resisted. He'd said she was like a wildcat in a sack, all teeth and claws. She'd bitten Fox on the fleshy underside of his forearm, and so he had shot her. He'd liked the feeling of power it had given him, to lift the gun and watch the fight fade from her.

Sally Brown's eyes were open. They were blue with a grey ring around them. Like her six-year-old son's.

Fox pulled down his trousers. Neither he nor Missy gave Sally Brown a second glance, although she watched them with her sightless eyes, head skewed, resting on one cheek.

On the bed Sally would never again share with her husband – Fox had nicknamed him the Birdman because in the photographs downstairs his nose was shaped like a beak – the newly-weds consummated their marriage. Quick and urgent. Missy cried out but Fox did not utter a sound.

Afterwards, they showered and dressed. Sally Brown's wardrobe was bursting with clothes. Missy chose a long-sleeved shift dress in pale yellow. She sprayed herself with perfume from a black ridged bottle. Fox chose a thick blue chambray shirt that belonged to the Birdman, whose real name was Martin.

Sally Brown was thirty-four with one child, a husband and a hive of honey-bees. She worked at an art college in Edinburgh two days a week, and enjoyed cooking and singing. When Fox had slipped his forearm around her throat, she had fought for her life with every part of her, bucking and biting and trying to scream with enough volume to alert her neighbours.

He'd dragged her inside, kicking open the front door which she'd left on the latch when she'd carried the laundry basket into the garden. Missy had followed them, the gun trained on Sally at all times.

Sally was slight, but stronger and faster than she looked. At one point, she almost succeeded in freeing herself from Fox's grip, twisting and wriggling like a fish, impossible to keep hold of. Once she was released, she would flee next door and call the police. As a former winner of the Scottish Schools Indoor Track & Field Championships, she still ran every day and could out-sprint them both with her eyes closed.

Except she hadn't bargained on Callum.

As Sally felt the power in Fox's forearm loosen and she prepared herself for a final burst of energy and defiance, a small boy wandered into the scene. He was wearing pyjamas, even though it was late afternoon, and his hair was standing on end. His eyes widened, cartoonish, and he looked at Missy and back to his mother again.

'What's happening?'

Without thinking, Missy swung the gun towards him. Sally cried out – 'No!' – and it cost her. Fox used her distract-edness to re-tighten his grip. All hope of an escape was lost in that flicker of time.

The boy – rarely ill, but home with a fever and a cough instead of at judo with his friend – turned to run, but Missy was expecting that and jerked him back by his pyjama collar. Following Fox's lead, they forced mother and son upstairs.

Fox dragged Sally to her bedroom. Fear for her son embold-ened her, and she tried harder than any mother could to free herself from her captor, scratching and biting and thrashing about. But Fox had the measure of her now. He held her against the flowered wallpaper by her throat, pressing down on her windpipe and squeezing the breath from her. 'If you don't stop, we'll kill him.'

She stopped struggling, but as soon as she could draw air into her lungs again, she spat at him. It slid down his face and onto the carpet. 'Callum.' His name stretched from her like a length of elastic. She called for him again and again until Fox struck her on the cheek to silence her. The skin reddened in the shape of a handprint.

Missy had taken the child to his room. A duvet covered with trains was thrown back, exposing the sheet. On the bedside table, a projector was switched on, spinning planets and stars and whole galaxies across the ceiling. He did not say a word, but followed her everywhere with his eyes. He could hear his mother's voice, urging him to her, and every now and then he opened his mouth to answer, but the expression on Missy's face stopped him.

'Are you scared of the dark?' She whispered the question to him, tickling his ear with her breath.

'No.'

'Are you scared of me?'

His eyes filled with tears. 'My mummy says if you allow someone to scare you, you're giving them all the power.'

She pressed the gun against his head. 'Are you scared of me?'

A tear rolled down his cheek. 'Yes.'

He reminded her of the children in her class, bug-eyed and full of reproach. Once upon a time, she might have bent at his fear; loosened, if not softened. But something inside her had switched off. If he had dread in his eyes, hers were unlimited pools of darkness. The usual mechanisms that governed most ordinary people had been altered in a way that was irreversible, a corridor of doors, each one slamming and locking behind her as she walked down it, no way back.

'Missy, bring him here.' Fox's voice made her jump. She jerked the gun in the direction of the door, and the boy walked in front of her, his head low. Sally held out her arms and Callum ran to her. Missy let him. Fox and Missy had guns. The Browns were unarmed.

Sally was crying. She bent to kiss him and whispered something in the boy's ear that neither Fox nor Missy caught. But the boy's eyes flicked towards the open doorway and gave him away.

After mother and son had embraced for a couple of minutes, Fox smiled at Missy, that lazy grin she loved so much. Callum's eyes had found the door again. Back and forth. His cheeks were flushed and his bare feet danced in readiness.

Fox's voice was pleasant, conversational, although the gun in his hand spoke another truth. 'Missy, would you mind fetching Callum a glass of water? He looks a little warm. Perhaps you could shut the door behind you when you go.'

Her eyebrow lifted, a question. But Fox nodded again and she acquiesced. She closed the bedroom door and had not even landed on the top stair when the first shot was fired.

Sally unleashed an inhuman sound of grief that seemed to travel beyond that room and fill all the spaces in the house. Missy stilled, listening to it. A second shot, less than five seconds later, and that noise stopped too.

The door opened, seemingly by itself. But then she realized Fox must have nudged it with his toe because he stood there with Callum in his arms.

Fox carried the boy back to his bed and pulled his duvet over him. It covered the wound in his stomach. It was the proper thing to do.

In the marital bedroom, Missy had found a zipped bag of lipsticks that belonged to Sally Brown. When Fox told her it was time for them to go, to continue their killing spree elsewhere, she pulled off their lids and examined the colours: Midnight Plum; Divine Wine; Bang-Bang. She pocketed the tube of scarlet and, with the purple lipstick, wrote on the sheet in the bed they had fucked in. When that ran out, she used the burgundy one: *I know that some day they will get me but it won't be without resistance.*

A fire had kindled inside them both. Their craving for infamy was no longer satisfied by the act of murder alone: they desired something greater, something that would carve out their place in history. The thrill of firing a gun had already deadened into a cartoon-like facsimile of violence. Something more was required to immortalize their crimes, and Fox had an idea, seeded when they'd arrived, that had now begun to flower.

Outside, the street was quiet. He crossed the lawn and beckoned to Missy. 'Give me a hand.'

Missy wasn't certain she liked Fox telling her what to do. She was capable of making her own decisions – today had proved that to her – but she did as he requested because she was curious.

The hive was quiet. No guard bees to knock against him and warn him off. His grandfather had kept bees and Fox knew they clustered together for warmth during winter, although they still made the occasional cleansing flight or foraging trip. But all was calm, in preparation for the colder months. In this state, bees were vulnerable to predators like mice and green woodpeckers.

And humans.

Fox slid his fingers beneath the hive and lifted it. As it started to tip, unbalanced, Missy ran to it and hefted the other side.

'What are we doing?'

Fox's mouth curved into that lazy grin again.

They carried the hive back into the house and placed it in the centre of the hallway 'Get ready to run, okay?'

She had scarcely registered what he'd said when Fox began to shake the hive, not with the gentle oscillations of a flag in the breeze, but short, violent bursts of movement.

He threw the hive onto the floor and kicked it, splitting the wood apart, destroying their stores for the colder months and the resin-like substance the bees had produced to make their environment watertight, condemning them to death.

'Now.'

Fox grabbed Missy by the hand and they sprinted as 5,000 bees rose together in an agitated state. He flung the front door shut as the first bees crashed against the glass, one or two escaping into the cold day, but the rest remaining inside the house, their humming audible from outside.

Laughing from exhilaration, from the primal fear engendered by these insects with their deadly stings, they climbed back into their car, kissed for longer than they should have, and then fled further north to wreak their particular brand of havoc elsewhere.

21

Oxton, near Lauder: 6.10 p.m.

It had been a bad day and it was about to get worse. DC Saul Anguish pulled up outside the house in Oxton, blue lights flashing, but he had no desire to go in.

A neighbour had raised the alarm after Sally Brown had failed to collect her elderly father-in-law's prescription as expected. A small detail, but a significant one. To avoid the risk of serious complications, it was important Mr Brown Senior did not miss a dose of his Parkinson's medication, and the pharmacist, knowing village business as he did, had calculated the bed-bound pensioner was about to run out. He'd phoned Mrs Brown an hour before closing time to remind her, but received no reply. Callum Brown hadn't been in school that day either, according to his teacher, who'd popped in for some corn plasters on her way home.

The pharmacist, who was due to shut his shop at 6.30 p.m. because Mondays meant late-night opening, enquired of his customers whether anyone had seen Mrs Brown. When it emerged they had not, Mrs Augustine from next-door-but-one was summoned to check on the family.

A woman – presumably Mrs Augustine herself – was

standing outside the gates, speaking to an officer from Lauder police station. According to O'Neill, she'd looked through the letter box and seen the broken beehive in the hallway, and assumed there'd been some kind of accident.

But she hadn't been the only one to alert the authorities. A dog-walker, who'd been in the fields across from the house, had reported hearing two gunshots. She'd dismissed them at first, used to the sounds of the countryside. It was hunting season for feathered game and some types of deer. But then she'd glimpsed a couple running out of the property and driving off. She'd had the presence of mind to take a photograph of the fleeing pair, hand-in-hand, a flash of distinctive red hair. Thanks to the electronic circular on the PNC, it had taken the police moments to identify them as Melissa Smith and Dashiell Lloyd.

Liveried cars lined the lane from the top of the village and all the way down, past the fields of sheep and the tumble-down hotel. It would be a bureaucratic nightmare to speak to witnesses, but that wasn't why Saul felt sick.

O'Neill said there was a child in there, and Saul had an issue with those who hurt children.

Blue ignored everyone and marched across the gravel driveway. Pebbles crunched underfoot. A second police officer, standing halfway towards the house, put out his hand to stop her. 'You cannae go in, I'm afraid.'

'I'm part of an investigating team from Essex,' she said, bristling, reaching for her identification. 'Or do you have a problem with that?'

'Calm down.' The officer had an accent like running water. 'I meant you literally can't go in.'

'Why?' Saul held out his hand and introduced himself.

The officer shook it with a genial enthusiasm. 'Bees. We're waiting for an apiarist to come and round them up.'

Saul was intrigued. His insect collection was full of dead specimens but it would be fascinating to confront a colony of live bees. 'They're still loose?'

'Aye. Thousands of them. We might be waiting a fair while too. The beekeeper is on another job just now. He's on his way, but won't be here until the back of seven.'

Saul frowned. 'So we have no idea whether Mrs Brown or her son are still alive?'

'Have Lloyd and Smith left any of their victims alive?' Blue was terse.

'Even so.' Saul was vexed. He understood the need for caution but Callum Brown was six years old. If there was a chance he – or his mother – was alive, they had to act as soon as possible. 'I'll go in.'

The officer laughed. 'Nice try and very commendable. But my SIO would never allow it.'

'Call the Fire and Rescue Service, if you haven't already,' said Saul. 'And get them to bring a carbon dioxide extinguisher.'

Saul Anguish had an affinity with bees. He still remembered his joy at finding a queen on the path to his flat when he was a teenager, the white flare at her tip. He remembered, too, being stung more than 200 times protecting a swarm from a gang of boys with a death wish, shrieking and poking at it with a stick.

It was the height of summer and they'd surrounded the bees – 40,000 of them, he'd later found out – clustered around the trunk of a willow. But they were too stupid to know the difference between an established colony and a displaced one.

He'd been older then, on the cusp of turning twenty-one. He knew that bees became aggressive when provoked, releasing alarm pheromones that encouraged the others to attack. Everyone – whether it was the boys or him or an unsuspecting bystander – was fair game.

He'd shouted at the boys for tormenting the swarm, and they'd run from him without challenge. He'd thought it was because he'd done an excellent job of scaring them away, but when he'd turned around, the mass of bees was upon him.

Under normal circumstances, the swarm would be docile, their bellies full as they waited for the scout bees to find a new home. A hand enclosed by the swarm might feel the soft beating of wings, a drumming of feet. But they were angered, and Saul Anguish, who by the simple act of breathing smelled of threat, was the focus of their ire.

The bees became his shroud, covering his body, crawling into his mouth and inside his nose, stinging the exposed skin on his arms and his neck and his eyelids. He forgot about himself and could focus only on the pain, the dozens of simultaneous prickings that became a fire, inside and out. Each time he cried out, more bees found their way into the soft parts of him, sacrificing themselves to protect the colony. As he was overwhelmed by venom, his skin swelled and tightened, restricting him. He collapsed to the grass.

His life was saved by a woman on a picnic with her three children, who did not run like the others, but called the emergency services and directed them to his location. The fire fighters had no time to don protective clothing but used a carbon dioxide extinguisher to subdue, then suffocate the bees.

Saul spent two days in hospital. When the medical team ran tests later, his antibody levels had rocketed to offer him a level of protection against bee stings. It didn't mean he would always be immune, but of the three of them standing outside the house on that October evening, Saul decided he was the least at risk.

While the officer confirmed the fire service *was* on its way, Saul started towards the house.

'Wait.' Blue called out to him. 'Your body armour. Just in case.' She was right, of course. Witnesses made mistakes. There was an outside possibility Smith and Lloyd were still inside.

It almost broke him, her show of concern. That even now, despite his coldness, she cared enough to put her own pride aside to protect him. He wanted to touch her, to feel her yield to him. But then he remembered the dead chicks in his house, and his heart hardened. A voice in his head told him he should at least hear her out. But he was a stubborn man and he blocked out the whispers.

The house was still. He paused in the hallway, listening for bees. The remains of the hive were strewn across the floorboards, bits of splintered wood and damaged honey stores. A handful of dead bees was scattered nearby but not enough to neutralize the threat. Even a colony depleted in preparation for the winter months would be made up of many thousands.

With spare, efficient movements, Saul checked each of the rooms downstairs, but they were undisturbed. In the kitchen, a drawing was laid out on the table, *Mummy, Daddy and Me* written in a rainbow of wax crayons. Saul's heart clenched.

He climbed the stairs.

The bathroom was empty and so was the study, a room with a desk, full of books, the walls plastered with more of

Callum's illustrations. Saul opened the door to the master bedroom.

He recognized no hope when he saw it.

Sally Brown was lying on the carpet and there was a hole in her neck. Her eyes were open, that fixed look that confirmed death. Her socks had hearts on them. When she'd pulled them on that morning, she'd had no idea what lay ahead. Was she thinking about breakfast? Putting a load of washing into the machine? The early-morning sex she'd enjoyed with her husband? Whatever had been on her mind, he'd bet his life it wasn't her death. That thought always undid him.

Saul kneeled beside her like an attending priest too late to administer last rites. 'I'm sorry this happened to you. But we'll find them and make them pay.' The carpet was saturated with blood and the burden of his knees against the pile caused it to rise to the surface, soaking through his trousers. It was cold against his skin. He removed the scissors he carried in a neat case in his pocket, cut a lock of her hair and placed it in an evidence bag.

The room smelled of old keys and two-pence pieces, and a hint of perfume. The bed was unmade which struck him as odd, as the rest of the house was neat and tidy. He took a closer look. Written on the sheet in imprecise letters was this message: *I know that some day they will get me but it won't be without resistance.* Saul frowned, wondering. He photographed it with his mobile phone to show to Blue.

He searched the room, its wardrobes and en-suite bathroom. Every now and then, his gaze fell on the body by the foot of the bed. Sally Brown's hair was the colour of cinnamon. Her teeth were bared, as if she was a lioness protecting her young.

Callum Brown was not in the master bedroom.

'I'll be back for you,' he said, 'but I need to find your boy.'

The house was squat but wide, an old shepherd's hut that had been modernized with an extra storey but had retained its shape. At the far end of the upstairs landing, Saul noticed a door was ajar. Brightly coloured magnetic letters spelled out a little boy's name. As he approached, he heard a distinctive hum.

He opened the door wide enough to press an eye to the crack.

The humming increased in volume but Saul couldn't see the bees. When the colony had calmed, instinct would drive them to cluster together, but it was impossible to gauge their whereabouts from his vantage point. He drew in a breath to steady himself and went in.

Callum was not on the floor or the bean bag slouched next to his bookcase. He was not by his toy-box or the wooden train track that filled one corner of the room. He was not sitting at his desk or playing with his Lego bricks or racing cars across the carpet, as a boy of six should.

Saul was a young man of restraint. He had learned to suppress physical pain or vulnerability until he'd become so numbed that his feelings for Blue were the first he'd felt in years. He was a killer, and a seeker of justice. Hardened by his childhood, let down by those in positions of power, he was a loner and a survivor. He was used to seeing broken things and people. But when DC Anguish found that boy, he let out a sound that echoed his name.

Callum Brown was lying in his bed. The duvet had been pulled up to his chin but the cover was dirty with blood. A glimpse of his neckline told Saul he was wearing pyjamas.

His hair was the same shade of cinnamon as his mother's. But the detective couldn't see the boy's face because the honey-bees had formed their cluster on it.

The swarm covered Callum's ears, eyes, nose and mouth. Not an inch of skin was visible. Saul wondered if he had died from his gunshot wound or if he had been stung to death or if the bees in his nostrils had suffocated him.

The bees seemed docile now, crawling over the boy's body. Saul's instinct was to swipe them away but he recognized the futility of that. There was no point in antagonizing them. His anger was aimed at Lloyd and Smith, not the colony. Saul hoped Callum had died before his mother, and that his death had been swift, if not painless.

The detective had not cried for many years, and even now, in the face of such tragedy, his eyes remained dry. But a stone lodged itself in the back of his throat. It would not loosen and fall away until these killers were brought to justice.

Callum was small for his age. The bees crawled down his chest in symbiosis, part human, part hymenoptera, a mass that pulsed and vibrated with a life of its own. If Saul watched them for too long, he could almost convince himself the boy was still breathing.

He crouched by the single bed and lifted Callum's hand with the tenderness he was owed. With his scissors, Saul took a fingernail clipping for his crime scene tableau. When he returned home, he imagined building a miniature bed, painting a bee no bigger than the head of a pin.

He squeezed the boy's hand. 'I'm sorry this happened to you and your mother.' He was still holding Callum Brown's hand when the boy squeezed back.

22

At night, whenever she closed her eyes, Galen saw her dead father's face.

In the daytime, it was easier. The light chased away the hollows beneath his eyes and that odd twist of his mouth and the mottling that created jigsaw patterns on his skin. She could distract herself with homework or television, forgetting for an hour or two.

But in the dark, those haunted hours that stretched from here to there, she could not hide from the memories of that day. She could not hide from the monster that death had made of her daddy.

Evening had crept up on them while they'd stopped for a quick bite to eat at a pub in Pitlochry – although Tom had refused dinner – and now a dense blackness surrounded their car. Galen tried to blink away the past but her mind wouldn't let her. She gazed out of the car window, unseeing, and let it claim her.

The house had been too warm. Her mother had turned up the heating because she was worried about Charlie getting cold during those never-ending December days. In her distress, she'd forgotten to turn down the thermostat. When

Galen had let herself in, she'd felt as though she was step-ping into another country.

She'd shrugged off her coat, blazer and jumper, but even then, she was still too hot. The air was uncomfortable, suffo-cating. She would make a cold drink, she decided. Fill it with ice. And wash her hands. But first she would check on her father, as she did every afternoon when she got home from school.

Galen had known for thirteen weeks, five days and twenty-one hours that her father was dying. Her mother had broken this news to her while Tom was at a birthday sleepover.

'When's Dad going to tighten my skates?' Galen was helping her mother lay the table for dinner, a Friday night treat of a takeaway. 'Isla wants to go to Roller Kingdom tomorrow and I said I'd go with her.'

Christine had put down a plate, an odd expression on her face. 'Sweetheart, I can help you with that. Dad isn't going to be able to do that sort of thing again.'

Galen, who had been reaching into the cupboard for glasses, turned to her mother, one in each hand. She'd known her father was seriously ill, but she'd always expected him to recover.

'What do you mean?'

Christine's voice was gentle. 'Dad isn't going to get better.'

'But he won't get worse, right?' Galen could feel her panic rising.

'I'm afraid that's the only thing the doctor *is* sure of. I'm sorry, honey. I know it's difficult to hear.'

'Is he going to die?'

'Yes.'

'Soon?'

'We don't know how long he's got. A few months, probably.' Christine held out her arms to her daughter but Galen
did not – could not – move.

The panic building inside her reached its apex and tipped
into the kind of free-falling descent that snatched her breath
from her. Galen dropped the two glasses she was holding and
they hit the kitchen floor, splintering into dozens of pieces.

Christine moved towards her daughter, to comfort her,
but Galen shook her off, bolting to her bedroom, consumed
by a compulsion to be alone. As she fled the kitchen, shards
of glass cut into her bare feet, marking the stairs with bloody
footprints.

While Galen lost herself in grief, her mother scrubbed
the carpet on her hands and knees until most of the blood
had disappeared apart from a stain in the shape of Italy.
Every time she climbed the stairs, twelve-year-old Galen was
reminded of the moment she discovered her father was
going to die before her thirteenth birthday.

In the days that followed, her mother promised, at her
father's request, that Galen could be with him at the end of
his life, whenever that may be.

'You won't be alone, I promise you, Dad.' She'd held his
hand as she'd said that. 'You don't need to be afraid. I'll be with
you, keeping you company for as long as you need me to.'

The girl had found that thought sustaining, a last act of
love she could bestow on him. Galen had always had a special
relationship with Charlie; their shared sense of humour and
love of American comedies the superficial manifestation of
a love that ran deeper than most.

But her father's death was the last thing that Galen was
thinking about when she let herself into the overheated

house three days before Christmas. The brain was a sophisticated machine. Once the shock had worn off, she'd adjusted to the reality of his impending death in the way that children do. Or perhaps it was the opposite of that. Perhaps it was a kind of low-level but long-running shock that cushioned her from dwelling on it for every minute of every day, and the cost would become apparent once he had left them. Either way, there was nothing about that afternoon that suggested it would be any different from the last few weeks and months.

'Dad.' Her voice was soft as she pushed against the door. 'Are you awake?'

She knew it was unlikely he would answer but she liked to include him in conversation. She'd heard one of the nurses talking to her mother, telling her that hearing was the last sense to go.

His room was in the half-light. Her mother insisted on keeping the curtains shut to protect his eyes, but Galen felt certain he would prefer to follow the natural cycle of the day, to watch the progress of the shadows that shifted with each hour that passed.

His eyes were open.

This was not unusual. But there was an odd cast to them, as if they'd been stuck into his sockets with glue. His skin looked strange too. She couldn't find the words to describe it, but they had learned about tallow on a school trip to a museum last summer and his face was the same colour as the candles that had been on display there. His arm, which was lying on top of the blanket, was discoloured, the hue of a deepening bruise.

But it was his mouth that caused her the most concern.

His tongue protruded from lips that didn't fit together as they should.

Forgetting about Covid and germs and her mother's strict rules on cleanliness around Dad, she pressed her palm to his chest like she'd seen done in films. He was cooler than she'd expected. His hand, which she'd held a thousand times, was a lead weight in her own.

The knowledge of his death was something that came upon her in the way a leaf might unfurl. It happened in increments, tiny but inexorable, and once the process had been put in motion, there was no going back.

His eyes. His mouth. His skin. And now her hand, the one she had placed in the hollow above his rib-cage, had been still for more than two minutes.

No rise and fall.

A gasp rose inside her. Her head began to swim. Because she knew – with the same certainty she knew she was allergic to watermelon or that yellow didn't suit her or that Sara Lisle in Year Nine was a bully – that her father had gone.

She pulled away from him, as if his death might infect her. He did not look like Charlie Hardwicke anymore. He was a dummy from the department store, a blank-faced bogeyman. Whatever he was, he wasn't her daddy.

A dozen thoughts fought for her attention. *Should she call the police? Her mother? What was supposed to happen when somebody died? Where was her mother? Did she know he was dead? Why didn't she collect her from school early if her father was getting worse? What did it feel like to die? Where was her mother? Did her father call out for her? For any of them? Where would his body go? Would he stay in that bed all night?*

She shivered, repelled by the idea of trying to sleep with a dead body downstairs, then felt a stab of guilt, as if she'd betrayed her father. She could not bring herself to look at him but felt an obligation to stay, so he wasn't alone.

There was a chair by his bed and she turned it around so it faced the wall and the dresser that had been pushed against it. To distract herself, she pulled open one of the drawers, wondering if her father's mobile phone was inside because her own had run out of battery at lunchtime, and she knew her mother kept his charged up in case old friends and colleagues tried to contact him.

Medication. A book of crossword puzzles. Some dressings and tape. A thermometer. Her father's mobile.

She picked it up to call her mother, realized that she could not remember his passcode – and noticed a letter tucked underneath addressed to the *Parent/Guardian of Galen Hardwicke*.

She hadn't seen this letter before but it looked official, a long white envelope with a postmark printed in pastel blue ink. It had been opened and a piece of paper was folded inside.

The letter was typed in black ink with four lines of handwriting under the signature, a personal message to her parents. The paper trembled as she read and reread it.

When she had absorbed its contents, she folded it and put it back in the drawer, exactly where she'd found it. She placed her father's phone on top of it.

Then she left the room and closed the door behind her. She didn't look at Charlie once.

It was only when she'd called her mother from the landline, drunk a glass of water and taken herself upstairs, to the safety of her bed and Bear, that she allowed herself to cry. For her father, yes. But mostly for herself.

23

Loch Tummel: 7.55 p.m.

For a woman who had never travelled further than London, Missy devoured the landscape with a hunger matched only by her desire for Fox.

As they'd driven towards the Highlands, the colours of autumn had enthralled her at every bend and turn. The moors were aflame with deer-grass that had turned a deep shade of russet. Some trees were evergreens, dark and fresh, but her favourites were those that were tall and straight and looked as if they'd been plucked from the ground and turned on their heads, their uppermost branches dipped in amber.

A bank of woody shrubs caught in their headlights was dressed in violet, the colour of a damaged sky. The air smelled of pine. It cut through everything until she could taste it on her tongue. Ahead of them, a tantalizing glimpse of mirror-glass glittered through the woodland.

She did not know the names of all the trees and plants she saw, but she felt a kinship with this place, and felt certain she would learn every one of them if this became her home. A longing stirred within her to make a life in this corner of paradise. If they had made a baby at Sally Brown's house, the meadows would be filled with summer flowers and birdsong by the time it was born.

But then the truth hit her. There would be no future after what they'd done. While they had evaded the police for several hours, both of them knew their luck would not hold.

As they wended their way through the trees, they rounded a corner which opened up into their first view of the loch, a vast body of water that dominated the landscape, six miles west of a town called Pitlochry.

'Look,' she said, thrilled by it, craning in her seat for a better view. Fox yawned, tired of driving and the constant drip of adrenaline that came from being hyper-vigilant for the police. She looked at him and then back out across the loch. 'Shall we stop here?'

Fox's reply was a low whistle. She tore her gaze away from the passenger window to see what had prompted such an expression of admiration, and when she glimpsed what lay ahead, her own words caught in her throat like tangled strings.

Although it was dark now, the moon was bright, illuminating the scene before her.

The hotel was set against a backdrop that blazed with autumn fire, trees that dripped gold and burnt orange heather spread across the bank. It was imposing, constructed of wood and stone and slate that was weathered but not scruffy, its windows iced by the cool breath of moonrise. A carved sign proclaimed that visitors had arrived at *The Lodge on the Loch* and a handful of expensive cars were parked on the sweeping driveway. With its twin turrets, it had the feel of a French chateau, storybook-pretty and inviting, but even then, it was outshone by the majesty of its surroundings.

In the still air, its facade was mirrored by the loch, the edges blurred like a watercolour painting. A stag emerged from the undergrowth and stood at the shoreline, its antlers bold and powerful. It scented the air, dipped its head to the loch to drink, and then disappeared as quickly as it had arrived. Missy let out a breath. It was the most perfect place she had ever seen.

Fox was watching her, that smile playing around his lips. 'You like it here, don't you?'

Missy turned to him, her eyes shining. In that moment, she was not a thief of life, an in-cold-blood killer, but a young bride entranced by the scene in front of her. 'I love it.'

For a few minutes, Fox drove further around the loch and then, without warning, he pulled off the road, bumping them over fallen branches and dirt until the car was hidden in the undergrowth.

'What are you doing?' Missy was laughing, holding onto the sides of her seat.

'Wait and see.'

When the car had come to a standstill, Fox got out of the driver's seat and headed to the boot. He packed all the guns and ammunition he could fit into one holdall and then he slung the bag over his shoulder. He opened Missy's door, mock-bowed and held out his hand. 'Mrs Lloyd?'

Missy stepped out, playing along. 'Mr Lloyd.'

Hand in hand, they stumbled through the dark undergrowth until they hit the road. Five minutes later, they were standing outside the Lodge on the Loch.

A telegraph pole stood at the point where the pavement intersected the entrance to the hotel. Fox removed a pair of pliers from his holdall and cut the telephone wires at the base of the pole. These served a few houses within the remote community as well as the main switchboard within the lodge. The guest telephone system was unaffected, although he didn't know that then.

Fox started across the driveway but she resisted, tugging him back towards her. 'What are you doing?' It was a question she had asked him several times that day but this felt loaded, the most important one of all.

His lips brushed hers. 'It's our honeymoon. I thought we could lie low for a bit, spend the night here.' A shy look. 'If you want to.'

She flung her arms around his neck and kissed him back, a lover's kiss. 'I want to.'

The concierge was dressed in a suit that belonged to his father. His name was James Robertson, he was twenty-one and it was his third week in the job. His mother had told everyone he'd got 'an important job at the big hotel' and she made him a packed lunch every day, even though he'd explained that his meals were catered for. He liked gaming and was an excellent rower. He was forbidden from watching television or checking his phone during working hours. If his employers hadn't been such sticklers for the rules, Mr Robertson might have recognized Missy and Fox, whose names and faces had been plastered across all major news channels for the last three hours. He might have lived.

But his future was decided when Fox pushed against the heavy doors of the lodge and stepped into the wood-panelled lobby, leading a giggling Missy behind him.

A curved staircase with an ornate wooden bannister swept upwards to the hotel's bedrooms. Sofas and armchairs in opulent fabrics were positioned around a vast stone fireplace. Lamps with low lighting invited guests to stop for a drink and stay for the night. Everywhere smelled of woodsmoke and luxury.

'Good afternoon, sir. Can I help you?'

Fox, unused to this type of place and form of address, was awkward, ill at ease. 'We'd like a room for the night.'

'Have you booked?'

'Nope.'

The concierge's smile faltered but did not disappear. 'Well.' He pressed some buttons on his keyboard and scanned the screen.

'It's our honeymoon.' Missy put her hands on the desk to show off Penny Dunne's wedding ring. 'We've just got married.'

The young man clapped his hands together. 'That's wonderful news. Congratulations.' If he'd noticed their clothes didn't quite fit and they carried one battered-looking bag between them, he didn't comment. Neither did he express surprise they had not pre-booked their accommodation for such an auspicious occasion. James Robertson wanted to make his guests happy. He scanned the online booking system again, and then he made a decision because he could.

'I'm delighted to say our honeymoon suite is available tonight.'

Missy shot a glance at Fox, an unspoken question. *Do we have enough money?* They had what they'd stolen from the vicar's house but they might need that later. But Fox had that look on his face. He wasn't thinking about practicalities. She willed him to exercise the self-control that would allow her a wedding night, at least.

'Excellent, thank you.' He was courteous, less nervy now. Missy squeezed his hand.

There was no one on reception – the hotel was quieter on Monday nights after the weekend rush – and the concierge gestured at them to follow him.

'Let me check you in. May I take a copy of your credit card?'

Fourteen words. Simple ones. And just like that, James Robertson sealed his fate.

Fox put the holdall on the floor, the movement restrained and deliberate. 'I don't have a credit card.'

The concierge's face did not betray his surprise. 'Would sir prefer to pay in cash?'

A woman in a red woollen coat walked into the lobby, talking loudly on her phone. 'What did you say? I can't hear you. The signal's terrible.' She tutted, her irritation evident. 'I'll call you from my room later. Michael? Michael?' When it was clear there was to be no further response from Michael, she tossed her phone into her handbag.

The woman – in her early fifties, blonde bob, glossy finger-nails – unbuttoned her coat and slung it across one of the armchairs. She had a silver crucifix around her throat.

Ignoring Missy and Fox, she clicked her fingers at the concierge. 'A gin and tonic. No ice.'

'Bar's that way.' Fox, with his slow drawl, pointed through the archway that led into a separate drinking area he'd noticed a few moments earlier.

The woman's lip curled as if she had stepped in something unpleasant. Her eyes flicked to Fox's blue shirt and unkempt hair. He might have let that slide, but then the woman laughed in a way that confirmed she was afflicted with delusions of grandeur.

The gun was in his hand before the last note of her mirth had died away.

'Shut the fuck up.'

Missy, who had recognized the inevitability of this as soon as the woman had demanded her drink, ducked down and plucked her papa's pistol from the holdall. She pointed it at the concierge, who was lifting the receiver of the hotel's telephone to his ear. 'Put it down.'

James Robertson did as he was told.

Missy scanned the lodge's lobby. It was quiet, but if a guest or member of staff arrived now, they'd have time to run and raise the alarm. Missy couldn't allow that.

Stairs. Bar. Entrance. Restaurant. Missy's gaze flicked over them all, dismissing them. But then a locked door tucked away to the left of the reception desk caught her eye. Its bronze signage spelled out a word in italics: *Ballroom*.

She motioned to Fox. 'Let's take them in here.'

The ballroom was vast and overlooked the lodge's stunning grounds. It smelled musty – when the concierge unlocked the doors, motes of dust rose in the disturbed air – but there was no mistaking its grandeur. She glimpsed the loch through the windows, lit by the moon, and her heart stirred. It was unlikely she would see another dawn. In the next few hours, she was going to die. But Missy found she didn't care as much as she might. Everyone had to die at some point. If it had to happen to her, in this lodge by the loch, there were worse places to spend her last hours.

A pang of wistfulness surprised her. When she was younger, she had imagined a wedding night – a future – with a lover who revered her. Motherhood. A kinship with friends and family that seemed to elude her, however hard she tried.

But, like so much in her life, the things that came naturally to others were out of her reach. Her brain was too crooked for her to be anything close to ordinary.

When she had fired a bullet into her papa's head that morning, she had known as soon as her finger had pressed down on the trigger that this act of brutality would cost her everything. *Almost* everything. He had wrecked her childhood and, in turn, she had taken his life. But it wasn't all noble sacrifice. That single act of violence had served as an entry point to this new beginning. *John Saint. Penny Dunne. Sally and Callum Brown.* With every dead body, Melissa Mary Smith was also gaining something that she had always craved. Notoriety.

'If you want money, I have it. Lots of it.' The woman with the red coat wasn't so superior now. Her eyes glistened with tears and they darted towards the swing doors and back again. 'We won't tell anyone, will we?' She appealed to the concierge. 'Let us go and we won't say a word. Neither of us. Will we? *Will we?*' Panic made her desperation feel aggressive.

The concierge did not speak. He had never seen a gun before. He came from a family of tailors, of sewing machines and bolts of fabric. His uncle hunted grouse at the weekend but his father did not approve of bloodsports. A voice in his brain told him this was a different kind of bloodsport, with humans as the prey.

'How much do you want?' The woman was still talking. 'My husband will pay you whatever it is.'

Fox ignored her, his attention on James. 'How many people are staying here?'

The concierge's mouth moved but no sound emerged.

Fear had rendered him mute. Fox dug the barrel of the gun into the young man's chest. Tears spilled from him, a stain darkening his father's suit trousers.

'Not many,' said the woman. 'Lots of people were checking out this morning. I think there's twenty-one rooms. Is that right?' She stared at the concierge and repeated her question. 'Answer the man, for God's sake.' But she didn't give him a chance to do as she bid before rattling on. 'I'm sure it's twenty-one. But I don't know if any of the staff stay on site. They do that sometimes, don't they? Although the night manager probably wouldn't sleep, would he? He'd have to stay awake. Did you know there's an island called Inner Farne in Northumberland where you can see puffins and the volunteers stay there when the visitors go home and the boys have to sleep in separate buildings to the girls and sometimes they don't shower for days until they go back to the mainland and—'

The bullet tore through her pectoralis major, the fan-shaped muscle that stretched from her armpit to her collarbone, and exited through her shoulder. The wound was ragged because she'd turned towards Missy as she'd discharged the gun and the entry point was not clean.

Missy pressed her index finger to her lips. 'Hush now.'

The woman's voice had seemed to scratch the air – the katydids were at their most raucous while she'd been talking – and Missy had heard enough. If the concierge would not tell them what they wanted to know, she would find out another way. But first she'd had to silence the noise.

Despite its poor acoustics, the gunshot reverberated around the ballroom and beyond, bouncing off the walls and ceiling. Fox whooped and clapped his hands. Then he stilled, like his namesake, poised for flight or fight, depending on what happened next.

The woman fell forward onto her knees, as if in prayer. No amount of money would save her now. The concierge staggered against Fox, staring at her in appalled fascination.

A bubble of blood appeared at the corner of her mouth. Missy wanted to pop it, but it burst of its own accord and left an imprint in the shape of a flower on her skin.

Fox rubbed the back of his head with the palm of his hand, forehead corrugated, eyebrows raised into his hairline. 'I wasn't expecting that.'

As a rebuke, it was mild, but Missy prickled. 'What else did you want me to do?' And then, 'If it was up to you, she'd have talked us all to death.'

It was the first hint of discord between the newly-weds. But Missy couldn't help herself. The taste of disappointment was on her tongue, and it was bitter.

Fox's shoulders twitched, less pronounced than a shrug but greater than indifference, and she remembered his tendency to bury his head in the dirt to avoid confrontation. It was one of the reasons they had parted ways.

The woman was face down on the parquet, blood spilling from her as her words had done earlier. Fox nudged his boot against the hollow at the base of her spine and turned her on her back.

At the sight of her face, the concierge began to cry again.

'How many people are staying here?' Fox was softly spoken and polite.

'I don't know. I can't remember. Maybe ten. Most of our weekend guests have gone. A few rooms are occupied but not many.' When he'd finished speaking, he looked at Fox with an expression of such hope in his eyes that it was almost painful for Missy to watch.

'Thank you.' Fox smiled his wily smile. 'That wasn't so difficult, was it?'

'What about staff?' Missy was more pragmatic. She knew they wouldn't be able to operate under the radar for long but she didn't wish to be blindsided.

'Mondays are quiet. There's only me and one receptionist. A barman. The kitchen team – a chef and a couple of others. Two or three waiting staff.' He looked from Missy to Fox and back again, trying to gauge who held the power. 'I'll give you a head start, I promise. You'll have time to get away.'

Missy cocked her head and stared at the young man.

'Have you ever been in the newspaper?'

'Once. After I won a rowing competition at school.'

'Congratulations.'

He looked confused. 'It was a long time ago.'

'Everyone will know your name soon.'

Although he'd taken his Highers four years earlier, the concierge did not look much older than seventeen. His father's oversized suit might have been plucked from a dressing-up box. His mother, with her determined person- ality and dressmaking scissors, had insisted on cutting his hair. He was on the cusp of manhood but with a boy's innocence.

That's why it took so long for the penny to drop.

At first, he tried to pretend he didn't understand what Missy was getting at, but he couldn't hold his feelings in. He shook his head, a denial. His face – his whole body – crumpled. It reminded Missy of standing on the beach as a child, watching the smokestacks across the bay implode during a series of controlled demolitions.

When he had gathered himself, the concierge spoke again. His voice cracked almost as soon as he began. 'Rory, that's my little brother, he died three years ago. In a bike accident. It was awful. Worst day of my life. Dad was on the way home from work, drove right past it. He saw Rory's helmet – it was so distinctive, flames painted on the side – and he tried to get to him but they wouldn't let him through the cordon. We buried him in a St Johnstone shirt.' A tearful, shuddering breath. 'They've only got me now. My mum, she'll be devast—'

Two shots. One to his lower back. One between his shoulder blades. The report was so loud that Missy put her hands over her ears. The concierge hadn't seen the bullets coming. A small act of mercy from Fox. As his body jerked, his mouth and eyes widened in surprise. His grandmother had been born on Skye, and although he could not say how or why, in the dying moments of his life, he remembered one of the Gaelic words she had taught him as a young boy. He breathed it out. 'Máthair.'

A fine spray of blood covered the hem of Missy's borrowed dress. She inspected it with scientific interest and took a step backwards from the slick now spreading across the floorboards.

It was fascinating how people bargained for their lives in all sorts of ways when confronted with death.

Fox bent over the concierge and retrieved the keys the young man had used to unlock the door to the ballroom. He bounced them in his hand.

'Let's see what's happening in the rest of the hotel, shall we?'

'I'm hungry,' said Missy. 'Can we find something to eat?'

Fox kissed her. 'As you wish, Mrs Lloyd.'

Before they left, Missy took a last glance at the bodies on the floor. From the woman's neck, she unclasped a thin silver chain with a crucifix, and placed it around her own.

24

Detective Inspector Angus O'Neill shut the office door behind him and buried his face in his hands.

An ambulance had taken Callum Brown to hospital. The bullet had grazed his stomach, a flesh wound rather than the cataclysm of a deeply embedded bullet, and although he'd lost a fair amount of blood, O'Neill was praying the boy would survive. The bees had been collected by an apiarist. Sally Brown's body was still in situ and would remain that way until the Scenes of Crime team had finished their painstaking work.

Five minutes ago, he'd received an unofficial complaint from his colleagues north of the border about DC Anguish breaking protocol, but the young officer's actions had potentially saved the life of a child. He had smoothed it over. For now. There had been no fresh sightings of Smith and Lloyd. He didn't know how to feel about that.

O'Neill drew in a lungful of stale office air. He'd done an impressive job of directing his part of the operation so far, holding everything together since the discovery of Graham Baxter, but the past was about to catch up with him.

Throughout his stellar career at Essex Police, he'd done

178

his best to be a good detective, a mentor and a friend. He knew that some of his officers disliked him – their egos cut to ribbons by his sharp tongue – but all of them respected him. They wouldn't respect him after this.

He pulled out his wallet – the leather was worn and cracked in places, but it had been an anniversary gift from his late wife – and smiled at the photograph of her he kept in its plastic sleeve. He brushed his thumb over her face, wishing she wasn't a two-dimensional snapshot in time, but was waiting for him at home, as she'd always been.

Lydia had been his wife for eleven glorious years. He'd met her at the library in those lonely months after his first marriage had broken down. Every fortnight, he'd borrow three new cookbooks in a quest to teach himself how to master the basics. As she'd stood behind the desk and checked them out, they'd chatted about *al dente* pasta, bread-making, home-made versus shop-bought pastry and red velvet cupcakes, and she made him laugh with stories of her own culinary inadequacies: 'I can only make sandwiches.' After a while, he'd started going in just to see her. One day, he'd plucked up the courage to ask if she'd like to join him for dinner. 'At a restaurant, naturally.' From that moment on, she'd never left his side.

Their wedding was a low-key affair and the best day of his life. They had no children together but their lives were enriched by their union in a way neither had experienced before. His first marriage – he'd been young and stupid and selfish – became a memory, still painful but the kind that softened over time until it became more pliable, easier to handle. He recognized the mistakes he had made, and there had been many, but as he'd grown older, he'd started to think about putting them right. Happiness had gifted him freedom from the chains of his past. But happiness always has its price.

Lydia died from meningococcal meningitis when she was fifty-two. A swift and brutal end. One night, she'd gone to bed complaining of a headache, seventy-two hours later she was gone, septicaemia ravaging her circulatory system and shutting down the major organs in her body.

It had been almost two years since he'd kissed her goodbye for the last time. 'Let go now, sweetheart.' O'Neill still couldn't believe it. Sometimes it felt like a lifetime ago, and sometimes it felt like five minutes. If she were alive, he would talk everything through with Lydia. She would know what to do. He, on the other hand, was at the centre of a self-created career-ending mess.

Tucked at the back of his wallet was another photograph, taken fourteen years ago when his only child – a daughter – was nine. She was standing in the back garden, wearing a ballet leotard and holding a flower, her acid eyes squinting at the camera. He'd cut the rose for her a few minutes earlier because she'd told him they were her favourite. He remembered when it was taken because it was the day his first wife told him she was reverting to her maiden name and moving in with another man. For years he'd carried two copies. One for him and one for his girl.

At first, he had tried to see his daughter every weekend. But his shift patterns and the unpredictability of police work made it awkward. He'd considered changing his job and taking his case to the family court, but the child told the court-appointed social worker she didn't want to see him. To his shame, he channelled his hurt into his career and promotion. He sent money on her birthday and wrote the occasional letter, but she never replied. One drunken night, he'd argued with her mother and she had threatened to ruin him. 'Fuck off, Angus, or I'll report you for harassment. We don't want you. We've moved on. I suggest you do the same.' He loved his daughter, though. He always would. But as the years rolled by, he gave up on her and she became a stranger. Until now.

A knock at his office door. He took off his glasses and polished them. He rarely cried but the lenses were mottled with salt. He barked a reply. 'Come in.'

By the time the detective sergeant entered, Detective Inspector O'Neill had put away his sorrow, his rangy frame folded into his chair, that hard set to his mouth.

'Sorry to interrupt, sir, but we knew you'd want to be kept informed.'

DI O'Neill leaned forward, his elbows on the desk. 'Spit it out. What's happening?'

'There have been reports of multiple shots fired, sir. At a hotel near Pitlochry.'

25

'I'm not tired, Mum.'

'Neither am I.'

'Well, I am. I've been driving since stupid o'clock this morning. I'm ready for a bath.'

Galen and Tom exchanged a look, both in agreement it was worth another try. 'It says on Google Maps that it's one hour and fifty-six minutes to Chanonry Point from here,' said Galen.

'We can find a place to stay when we get there.' Tom rested his palms on either side of the driver's seat headrest. 'Please, Mama.'

'It will be too dark to see anything.'

'There's a full moon tonight. Think how beautiful it will be.' Galen sounded wistful. 'The dolphins and the light hitting the Moray Firth.'

'Don't dolphins go to bed?' Tom stuck a finger into his back tooth to dig out the remains of a jelly sweet. 'How do they sleep without drowning?'

Galen smiled at her younger brother. 'They manage. A mother dolphin doesn't stop swimming for the first few weeks of a newborn's life. Otherwise her calf will sink. She sleeps while she's on the move.'

ALL OF US ARE BROKEN

'Did you sleep when I was born, Mum?'

Christine laughed. 'Not very much. You were a bit of a night owl, like your dad. Your sister, on the other hand, has always loved her bed.' She turned on the full beam. 'Would you two really want to spend another couple of hours in the car?'

Galen reached for Tom's hand and squeezed it, triumphant. Excitement lit his face. Their response was unanimous. 'Yes.'

Christine rubbed the bridge of her nose. In truth, she found it difficult to refuse her children anything since Charlie had died, but the idea of driving for another two hours exhausted her.

She knew how much Galen wanted to see the dolphins, and since the trauma of her father's death and the way her poor girl had found out, she'd tried to put things right in as many ways as she could. Briefly, she considered driving on to Fortrose. It was feasible, she supposed. And the romance of it appealed to her. Why shouldn't Galen get what she wanted? But she dismissed the devil in her ear. What if she had an accident on the way? She had to draw the line somewhere.

'I'm so tired, guys.'

Galen's eyes flashed and she bit down on her lip. Tom's dismay was more pronounced. He aimed a kick at the base of his mother's seat but there was no commitment to it. She did not chastise him. They had been driving for a long time and she understood his disappointment.

'Tomorrow,' she said. 'We'll check the morning tides in a bit and spend as long there as you like.'

Shadows had claimed the interior of the car by now. The

air had a textured quality to it that belonged to the night. According to the satnav, the hotel was five minutes away. Her mouth watered at the prospect of a glass of wine she hadn't poured herself and the fresh sheets of a bed she hadn't made.

At their first glimpse of the loch, the children perked up, although Galen seemed pale, smudges under her eyes. And too quiet. In the past, she'd spent her evenings chatting to friends, finishing their homework together and planning weekend trips into town. For months, she'd been surgically attached to her mobile phone. But it had been a long time since Christine had heard laughter coming from her bedroom. She wondered if it was grief or something deeper.

'Look,' said Galen, pointing to the water's edge, lit by the shimmer of moonshine. Four or five deer were poised on the shoreline, their heads dipped as they drank. 'Deer are specialized herbivores. There are forty-three species. All of them lack a gallbladder and some have scent glands in their legs. Their antlers are warm to the touch.'

Christine marvelled at the way her daughter retained facts. But it had its downsides. Galen recalled the name of every medication her father had taken, and every mechanical and biological process that had failed his body on the route to his death.

And every word of that damn letter she had found.

Christine swallowed, trying to dislodge the thickening in her throat that had become a permanent fixture since Charlie had died. She'd been worried there was something wrong with her, that she too would become ill and die, leaving her children without parents, but her doctor found nothing except the twin malignancies of anxiety and grief. 'It will

184

ease in time,' he'd said. But it was still there, suffocating her. She swallowed again and tried to focus on the road.

They turned a corner and, without warning, the hotel was in front of them, rising from the wall of trees, a welcome sight after their long drive.

The lights spilling across the frontage were warm and inviting. The Lodge on the Loch. Christine had wanted to stay here ever since she'd heard a programme about it on the radio. The renovation had been costly but the owners were determined to give back to the community, using local materials and produce, and employing those who lived within a thirty-mile radius. It had won prizes for its commitment to ecotourism, for its back-to-nature ethos, and for its architectural majesty, and had featured in several films and television dramas, including Galen's current favourite, *The Karma Hotel*, about three sisters brought up in a fictional hotel.

When she saw where they were, her daughter squealed, clapping her hands in childish delight. 'I didn't know we were staying here.'

Christine flushed with pleasure. 'Surprise!'

At last she had done something right.

26

Saul was on the phone to DI O'Neill. That was her first conscious thought. Blue kept her eyes closed, listening to the rise and fall of his voice, seduced by the lulling motion of the car. Her tongue felt thick. She needed water. A proper bed.

After their motorbike accident last year, she had promised Saul, and her mother, she would restart her medication. She was a danger to others and herself without it. *A dextroamphetamine a day keeps the narcoleptics at bay.* But she hated the way it made her feel. A restless energy that had no outlet. Weight loss from a frame that was already spare. And it didn't always work. Her sleep attacks had reduced for a while, but they were becoming more frequent again, and she'd been warned she might develop a tolerance to her drugs. She couldn't bear to think about that. She checked her watch. Fuck. With the events of last night and today, she'd forgotten to take her lunchtime dose. God, she was tired.

She tuned Saul back in.

'I understand. What do you need me to do, sir?'

A pause. The rumble of the tyres on the surface of the road. She looked sideways at him. His profile was serious.

'Are you sure? Do you think she'll listen?' Silence. 'No, I don't either. But there are trained negotiators who'll do a better job than me.'

He was quiet for a long time then, listening. He was wearing Bluetooth headphones and so she could only hear his half of the conversation, but he sounded troubled, shocked even.

'I didn't know that, sir.' His fingers tapped against the steering wheel, betraying his agitation. 'You should have told me before.'

Another silence for O'Neill to reply. Then Saul hit the steering wheel and made her jump. 'You could lose your job.' She sensed the anger radiating from him. 'So could I.'

Saul was listening again, and then his face softened along with his voice. 'It's a risk, but I'll take it because you've asked me to. I understand your motives but I don't agree with your methods. At all. It's not fair to the others.' A muscle in his cheek twitched. 'Yes, sir. I will keep you informed.'

The car was dark and quiet. He was brooding on whatever O'Neill had said to him, holding himself in that stiff, defensive way of his. Blue wanted to touch him, to ease from him whatever was troubling him. She sensed in him a great conflict.

From the window, the hills were bodies hidden beneath the blanket of the sky. She bit her lip.

'Did you know that shadows are not wholly black? The dark centre, when all light is blocked, is called the umbra, but the paler shadow at the edge is called the penumbra.'

She thought he wouldn't answer but he surprised her, his voice catching on the silence. 'Why are you telling me this?'

'Because even when it feels like everything is darkness, the light will find a way around it.'

Unconsciously, her fingers found the bruises on her neck. Even though her touch was light, she winced. He caught the movement. Something indefinable but as charged as the attraction between them clicked into place.

'What happened, Blue?'

'I can't tell you.'

'Why not?'

'Because I'm scared of what you'll do.'

She thought he would shut her down again then, that she had ruined things between them in a way that could not be resolved. But his expression was thoughtful, more open than she had seen all day.

'I'm sorry I've made you feel as if you can't tell me.'

'It's not that. I—'

Tears threatened to leak from beneath her eyelashes. She brushed them away, furious with herself.

'Please tell me you didn't hurt yourself.'

'No.' Her denial was sharp. 'Of course not.'

'But someone did.'

It wasn't a question. And she didn't have the energy for rebuttals or half-truths. She'd wanted to lean into him, to loosen her armour and rage over every humiliating detail. She almost had. But now she couldn't. Or wouldn't. Because she knew what kind of man Saul Anguish was. She had seen inside him, and he was cut through with vengefulness and ambiguity, the slider of his moral scale set closer to darkness than any hope of light.

His knuckles whitened on the steering wheel. He was right to read her silence as assent. She wouldn't deny him that.

To divert him, she said, 'Where are Talbot and Williams?'

'O'Neill wanted them to stay at the hospital in case Callum Brown wakes up. But he's changed his mind. They're meeting us at the hotel.'

'And what will we do when we get there? They've got firearms, Saul. We can't go anywhere near them. This is a wild-goose chase. I don't know what O'Neill is thinking.'

Saul turned to her, his pale hair almost silver in the dimly lit car. 'He has his reasons.'

'Are you going to tell me what they are?'

'Are you going to tell me how you got those bruises?'

His quicksilver tongue was a match for hers. She liked that about him. But she couldn't answer and neither would he. Relief, though, that they were communicating again.

'Do you think that boy is going to survive?'

'No.'

A syllable. But there was pain in it, a leaden grief that hinted at the futility of his actions. She didn't know much about his past but she wondered what might drive a man to risk his life, knowing almost all hope had already been lost.

'You did a brave thing.'

'It was stupid.'

'A bit. But he's still alive. The paramedics said if he'd been left for even a few more minutes, he'd have died. There's a chance for him, at least. That's down to you.'

He didn't respond, his eyes fixed on the road. On instinct, she reached for him, as she had done so many times before. Her hand brushed the warm skin of his neck, the collar of his shirt, grazing against something that felt both familiar and alien. Her fingers closed around it. A dead bee.

It sat in her palm, its plumose hairs without imperfection,

even in death. Without asking, she wrapped it in a tissue from her bag. In case he wanted to examine it later or keep it for his insect collection. 'Why do bees die when they sting you?'

'Their stingers are barbed. When they strike, the stinger becomes lodged in the skin of their victim. The bee cannot remove it and is forced to leave behind part of its digestive tract, muscles and nerves. This abdominal rupture kills it.'

'So it attacks, even though its own death is inevitable?'

'It seems they're not the only living creatures compelled to behave in that way.'

'Why are they doing this?' That question had haunted her since the discovery of that first body. Every hour. Every minute. The blood they had spilled stained her own hands too. She cast around for the right word. Outlaws. That's what they were. And for every bullet fired, for every life taken, she felt responsible, as if they should have been able to stop them by now.

'Why does anyone do anything?' He shook his head. 'But they must realize there will be serious consequences for them both.'

'*I know that some day they will get me but it won't be without resistance.*' Blue's voice was soft in the intimacy of the car. Now they had started talking, she did not want them to stop. 'It *was* Melissa Smith. She wrote that on the bedsheet. The way she forms her Ls and the imprecise circle of the Os. It's her handwriting, but . . .'

She frowned, puzzled by something that was troubling her. 'But what?'

'But I don't think those words belong to her. The cadence is wrong, and stylistically, it feels old-fashioned.'

'But why did she write it?' Saul fed the wheel through his hand, his eyes on the shadowing roads. 'What is she trying to say?'

Blue picked at the ragged skin around her thumbnail. 'That they won't go down without a fight?'

Saul's face was grim. 'That's what I'm afraid of.'

27

The Lodge on the Loch: 8.08 p.m.

The three kitchen staff were shot one after the other before they'd had time to register that a man and a woman who didn't belong amongst the piles of potatoes, the marinating venison, the shallots and redcurrants were firing weapons. It took thirteen seconds.

Afterwards, Missy cut herself a still-warm slice of tarte Tatin. She opened the vast commercial fridge and poured a generous helping of cream over the apple dessert. Her face was flecked with blood.

'This is delicious,' she said.

Fox tore apart a bread roll and cut himself a wedge of cheese. Poppy seeds fell over one of the dead, a twenty-nine-year-old woman called Fern Duncan in her fifth job since leaving catering college. She lived with her boyfriend, who'd been planning to propose on her milestone birthday the following week. They'd been trying for a baby for eighteen months. In four days' time, the coroner's office would inform her family that she'd been pregnant when she died.

'Someone is going to call the police, if they haven't already.' Fox was agitated, stepping over the bodies on the tiled floor. Their chef's whites were dark, sodden. One of them had been hulling out-of-season strawberries for a compote, and when Fox popped one into his mouth, it twisted at its sourness.

Missy spooned up another mouthful, eyes closed in pleasure. 'What shall we do now?'

Fox could not settle, pacing back and forth across the hotel kitchen, the bag of guns and ammunition slung across his shoulder.

'We're rats in a trap in here,' he said. 'Let's move out into the open.'

She laid a hand on his arm. 'We could run again. If you want to. Go back to the car and drive through the night.'

'Is that what you want?'

Life on the run: looking over her shoulder; an unrelenting state of hyper-vigilance. That was not a life at all.

'I don't want to go to prison, Fox.'

'You're sure about that? Because the alternative . . .' He let it hang in the air, unspoken.

'I want to be remembered.'

She pulled him to her, kissed him, fierce and unafraid. Skin against skin. Time was suspended for a few minutes. Fox and Missy, witnessed by their dead.

When they were finished, she pulled down her dress. 'What about you, though?'

He ran his hand across his face. A day's worth of stubble made a rasping sound. 'There's nothing for me in this life except you.' He opened the holdall and put a magazine of ammunition in each of his pockets. 'I've been in prison. I don't want to go back there. But what choices are there for a man like me, except a life of crime?' He shook his head, resigned to his fate. 'To the rest of the world, I'm damaged goods. Not worth the dirt on their shoes. Even if I wanted to start again, I couldn't.' His smile was gentle. 'I don't want to spend my life pinballing from this job to that. I want to take care of my wife, but we can't live on fresh air.'

It was the longest speech Missy had ever heard from him.

Neither spoke of those they had injured or killed in the last twelve hours. Katie Andrews. Graham Baxter. John Saint. Penny Dunne. Sally and Callum Brown. The woman in the red coat whose name was Anita Singer. James Robertson. Fern Duncan. Her two kitchen colleagues, twins Iain and Russ MacGregor.

Even when he was a boy, Fox had learned how to absolve himself of responsibility. Those he had killed were unknown to him, an obstruction or a means to an end. He did not feel sorrow or empathy. He was devoid of those things. He did not consider himself a psychopath, although he was one.

Missy was different. She had never committed a crime before, not even shoplifting. But she had a tendency towards the dark and was embracing her time in the shadows. On an intellectual level, she knew what they had done was brutal and sadistic and horrific in a multiplicity of ways. But she did not care.

'We don't have anything to lose because we have each other.' She held out her hand to Fox. 'Until the end.' He kissed it and repeated her words. 'Until the end.'

The lobby was empty. When the first shots were fired, a handful of the hotel's guests were in their bedrooms, resting before dinner. Adrian Restorick, a businessman whose room was on the ground floor, had made the first call to the emergency services on the hotel's landline before escaping to safety through the front doors and into the car park.

He was not the only one.

Eleanor and Roger Kennedy in Room 17 had also called the police. The 999 operator had informed them help was on its way, but it might take a while due to the hotel's remote location, and urged them to barricade themselves in using furniture. Roger wanted to take a chance and leave the room, to escape to their car which was parked outside, but Eleanor favoured following official advice.

Their bedroom was the first on the left at the top of the hotel's sweeping staircase. The rooms were tastefully decorated in shades of moss and earth and terracotta. When Fox tried the handle, found it locked and used his sawn-off shotgun to blow it open, they were sitting on the carpet next to the bed, still arguing in furious whispers.

He shot Roger Kennedy first, because he looked like a geography teacher who had written in his end-of-year report: *Dashiell claims he wants to travel but is currently on the road to failure.* The bullet ruptured Mr Kennedy's spleen but his cause of death was a cardiac arrest.

His wife Eleanor screamed and would not stop. The blood from his wound strafed the wall, the duvet and her open mouth. She died from a single shot between the eyes and the taste of her husband's murder on her tongue.

Missy bent over their bodies while Fox trained his gun on the door in case of surprises. She removed the gold watch that Mrs Kennedy had received on her retirement from the Civil Service and put it around her own wrist. In the woman's handbag, she found some strawberry bonbons and helped herself to one, offering the packet to Fox, who declined.

Together, they stood in the doorway, listening for movement, for the wail of approaching police sirens. But there was no sound at all except for a ringing in their ears and the drip of ruined flesh.

'Where next?' His breath was warm against her neck.

She pointed down the corridor, and Fox and Missy headed for the next bedroom.

28

The Lodge on the Loch: 8.17 p.m.

Galen stepped out of the car, yawned and shivered. The autumn air had bite. Her mobile buzzed once in her pocket. She froze, afraid to check her messages but compelled to do so. The screen was dark. Her body relaxed. The phone had run out of battery and powered itself down, that was all.

In the last six weeks, this was a taste of the messages Galen had received from Gabrielle.

> Why don't you kill yourself?

> Are you dead yet?

> No one will go to your funeral when you die.

Galen could not bring herself to tell her mother about the cruelty that had begun in the months after her father had passed away, as if death was somehow catching. At first, she had pleaded with Gabrielle to stop. Then she had tried to ignore her. As a final solution, she had blocked her number, but she still found a way to torment her.

The others weren't unkind in the same way. Isla smiled at her in the corridor if the others weren't around. Lily, who sat next to her in Maths, shared her scientific calculator when Galen forgot hers. But Gabrielle was the ringleader, which meant her circle of friends had fallen away until Galen had become socially isolated. In the beginning, she had agonized over it, this absence of sympathy and kindness, the comfort of friendship. But, in the end, she had recognized it for what it was: a childish response to a situation none of them knew how to handle. She supposed it was because she was different now. Tainted by something beyond her control.

It sounded spiteful, but she hoped the memory of her cruelty would haunt Gabrielle for the rest of her life.

Her head swam from being cooped up in the car, and she staggered, unsteady on her feet. Her mother was busy with the luggage, but Tom, who loved anything with wheels, was asking to pull one of the suitcases, and she watched them both, her thirteen-year-old heart swollen with love.

The hotel was exactly how it looked on the television. Once upon a time, she would have messaged her friends in a state of excitement but she allowed it to fill her up instead, a balloon of joy. For once, it was enough.

Christine turned to her, smiled and held out her hand. 'Ready?' Tom did the same. She stood between them, her mother and brother, both dragging a suitcase with one hand and holding hers with the other, and what was left of the Hardwicke family walked into a nightmare.

* * *

The fire in the grate had almost gone out and the armchairs were empty; the reception desk was unmanned.

Christine waited for a minute or two, but when no one came, she rang the service bell. She had not stayed in many places as luxurious as this before, but even she sensed it was unusual for the hotel to feel so deserted.

Tom was examining a shelf in the seating area, bulging with board games. Galen was perched on the edge of a sofa, eyes to the ceiling, which was painted with a mural of the loch and trees in autumnal colours of silver, gold, amber and rose. 'I don't know where everyone is,' Christine said to no one in particular.

She pulled her phone from her handbag, to make sure the hotel hadn't emailed a cancellation at the last minute, but the signal was patchy, flickering in and out before disappearing. She sighed. It was to be expected. On its website, the Lodge on the Loch prided itself on being cut off from the rest of the country.

'You two stay here. I'm going to see if I can find anybody who can check us in,' she said. Tom didn't acknowledge her. Galen murmured her assent. Christine wandered off in the direction of the bar.

She'd been gone for less than three minutes when she heard a sound in the distance, a muffled *pop-pop-pop* of an exhaust backfiring. She was beyond the bar, in the dining area, which had been laid for evening service but was devoid of staff. She stilled, to listen. When the noise did not come again, she called out a greeting to the empty room.

'Hello? Is anyone there?'

It was odd to be standing next to the pristine table-cloths and wine glasses that shone in the white glare of the chandelier's light. She felt like an imposter. It had been such a long time since Christine had dressed up, been wined and dined. But she didn't have room in her life, her heart, for someone new.

Every now and then, she burned for sex, the distilled physicality of it. At first, she did not understand why. Distressed, she'd poured her heart out to a friend who had lost her husband a few years earlier. The friend had explained it was a documented phenomenon known as Widow's Fire, a frantic and unquenchable need following the bereavement of a spouse or partner. But Christine had not yet sought out those faceless connections, although she knew she could not freeze-frame her life in perpetuity.

She glanced around her. She'd have expected the restaurant to have seated several diners by now, the hustle and bustle of the first sitting to be well underway. The lack of activity was unsettling.

It took another sixty seconds for Christine to recognize that someone was screaming.

Her head jerked towards the archway that led back towards the bar and lobby, but her brain told her she must have imagined it. She swung around, hoping to see another guest standing there, so she could say to them, 'Did you hear that?' But there were only shadows pressing against the windows.

Silence.

She laughed at herself for getting spooked. It was a child misbehaving. Or some kind of horse-play between friends. Nothing for her to worry about.

The second scream was unmistakeable.

Acting on a mother's instinct, she ran through the restaurant and back into the bar, towards the lobby where she had left her children. She did not think about what the scream might have meant or whether that *pop-pop-pop* sound was not a car, but the report of a gun.

Christine ran past the tables set for diners who were not there, and past the empty stools in the bar. She heard raised voices, the sound of crying – not a child, but an adult – and she was still running when a hand closed around her ankle and she fell, face-forward, to the floor.

29

The Lodge on the Loch: 8.21 p.m.

DC Saul Anguish killed the lights and drove into the hotel car park. A handful of cars, no more than eight or nine, were parked in the stillness. A moon was rising.

'We're the first here,' he said. His leg jumped, a repetitive movement that told Blue he was keen to get to work. He opened the car door and shut it softly behind him. He listened, but the only sound was the fluting call of a male tawny owl. He did not tell Blue some believed its presence to be a portent of misfortune.

Blue stepped into the night, following suit. It was colder now the sun had gone down. Her voice was low, not much louder than a whisper. 'We should wait.'

'For who?'

'For back-up. There's two active shooters in that hotel. You can't go in there.'

He didn't answer but his body leaned towards the hotel like a jachelt tree, contorted not by the wind, but by his compulsion to act.

Another vehicle slid into the car park, its lights off, tyres crunching slowly over the gravel. In the distance, the sound of sirens could be heard, the cavalry announcing its arrival.

'You're a bit of a hero, aren't you?' PC Alex Talbot grinned at Saul, clapped him on the back. 'That little lad.'

'How is he?'

Talbot's tired face creased further still. 'Holding on.'

DC Williams joined the throng. 'Are we having a party?'

'As sensitive and empathetic as always.' Blue rolled her eyes.

'Just a joke, love.'

Saul could almost hear her unspoken response. *I know you are.* He addressed Williams. 'Have you spoken to O'Neill yet?'

'Not properly. He's up to his eyes.'

This was news to Saul, but signalled a useful fact he hadn't known previously. That O'Neill didn't trust DC Williams in the way he trusted Saul.

'So what now?' Williams was appraising the hotel. 'Can't do much with two cars and four of us. Do you think we should try and put a cordon in place?' Armed Response Vehicles had been despatched from Perth, Dundee and Edinburgh, but it would take at least forty minutes for the first of these to arrive, following that initial emergency call from a hotel resident. 'And where the hell are the locals?'

As if they'd heard his sniping, a convoy of four marked police cars swung into the car park, sirens off but blue lights flashing. 'Do you reckon they were all down the pub together?'

Saul ignored Williams's sarcasm but Blue could not. 'Shut up, Eliot. Not everyone's a piss-head like you.' He didn't have a chance to respond because two of the officers were walking towards them. The rest were either on their radios or busying themselves with setting up the on-scene control room and installing floodlights.

After brief introductions, Chief Inspector Shona McGill of Police Scotland's North division took command. An outer cordon policed by unarmed officers to prevent entry by traffic and the public was established. On their arrival, authorized firearms officers would implement and guard an inner cordon. Home Office authorization had also been sought for the deployment of specialist firearms officers from Edinburgh, a highly skilled team with more training and expertise than AFOs. Westminster still wielded power when it came to firearms legislation.

'We're unaware of the current situation inside the hotel,' said the chief inspector. 'We know several shots have been fired and witnesses have reported sounds of distress. Melissa Smith and Dashiell Lloyd were picked up on traffic cameras two miles from here, but the vehicle they were travelling in has not been recovered.'

Saul glanced around him. Her officers were intent and focused, their faces pale in the moonshine.

'The situation is complicated by inconsistent mobile phone coverage in this vicinity. Some of the hotel bedroom landlines are operational but the main switchboard is down. We've had four emergency calls alerting us to gunshots. We've been communicating with a man in Room 5, who says there are two armed perpetrators, one male, one female, whom we believe to be Lloyd and Smith, but he is fearful of being overheard and has taken his receiver off the hook.' She looked around the car park. 'He was going to make a run for it.'

She went on to explain they did not yet know how many guests were in the hotel or whether they were being held hostage, hiding or dead.

'You'll appreciate this is a fluid and developing situation but I'm expecting a major incident to be declared shortly. Our focus is on containing the suspects, getting the hostages out as quickly and safely as possible, and protecting the public.'

Saul knew the drill. As the chief inspector was talking, more police cars, marked and unmarked, arrived. Shona McGill was the operational firearms commander or Bronze Command, up as close to the incident as safety allowed. The on-scene control room – the tactical side – would be run by a Silver Commander. Gold Command, responsible for the whole incident strategy, would work out of a nearby police station. He didn't know where that left O'Neill or them.

While McGill was directing her team, Saul drew Blue towards the periphery of the police activity. Williams and Talbot were talking to a young constable from Pitlochry, who had found a traumatized hotel guest wandering around the car park, and he recognized it as the diversion he'd been waiting for. If he tarried for too long, the window would close.

It hurt him to say it, but he did so because he felt he owed it to her. 'I'm going to go in.'

'No.' Blue's face twisted. 'That's stupid.'

'I have to.'

'No, you don't. That's machismo talking, not you. You don't need to impress O'Neill. It takes far greater courage to wait until it's safe. Do you know why? Because it's the opposite of what you want to do.' Agitated, she ran her fingers through her hair. The moon had turned it grey, and her eyes with it. A wraith in the night. 'You could die, Saul. Have you thought about that?'

An expression of longing shadowed his face. He'd never been afraid of dying. He'd watched the light fade from the eyes of others, and had come to believe there was a freedom in losing oneself to the dark. Some fought against it. But Saul understood a fundamental truth about death, the thought drifting from him into the evening air. *We are all the same in the end.*

'I'm sorry you don't agree. But I've made up my mind.'

'Please don't.' Softer now. Her hand slipped into his, not caring who might see. Letting go of her then was one of the most difficult decisions he'd taken in his lifetime, but he extricated himself. Blue watched him lope across the car park before he was rubbed out by darkness.

She ran after him. He'd rounded the corner of the hotel, heading down its western flank, intending to enter through a back door or fire escape before the Strategic Firearms Unit stationed its officers at every point of exit and entry. Before the arrival of police marksmen and observation points and strict protocols. 'Wait.'

He turned to her then, told her to go back to the others.

But Blue stood her ground beneath the graveyard of stars. 'I'll tell you how I got these bruises. If you still want to know.'

He was a reserved man but emotion played across him, the four seasons of hope, respect, frustration and dismay. He knew then that she was desperate, trying to buy time that wasn't for sale. With a loss of control that was rare for him, Saul gripped her hands until they were white, bloodless. 'Of course I want to know. But not now. Now I have to do this.'

She was crying, this young woman, as hard and as brittle

as he was. Saul cupped her face and wiped away her tears with his thumbs. 'Go back now.'

She bowed her head, accepting the inevitability of his decision and wondering if she would see him again. She watched him edge along the perimeter until he was almost out of sight, and then he was back, kissing her until she had no breath.

It lasted no longer than fifteen seconds but she was bereft when he pulled away.

He didn't speak again until he was almost too far from her to hear, but then he stopped, and because he was a man of his word, he called to her, his voice low and clear in the night.

'She's his daughter, Blue. Melissa Smith is O'Neill's daughter, and I promised him I'd get her out.'

30

The Lodge on the Loch: 8.26 p.m.

When she was nine, Missy's mother told her that her father didn't love her anymore. She was too difficult, too head-strong, too *Missy*. That because of this unfortunate fact, Missy had to change her surname from O'Neill to Smith, and leave the house she had known all her life, her school, her friends, and all her toys and stuffed animals. Because of her father, they had to move into a smaller house with Mummy's friend Graham, who smacked her when she didn't eat her peas and tickled her at bedtime and whispered that he liked it when she sat on his lap.

Missy had asked her mother several times if she could see her father. She waited by the letter box on her birthday, and, instead of presents, she asked Father Christmas if he could make Daddy love her again. But her mother didn't like it when she talked about her old life. Over time, Missy forgot about her primrose-yellow bedroom, and the way her father's silly voices made her belly ache with laughter, and her mother married Graham, who insisted she called him Papa.

In the hotel corridor, Missy blinked twice, surprised by the assault from her past. It was the wallpaper, she decided.

The precise shade of her childhood bedroom. She was glad Graham Baxter was dead. He'd done things to her he shouldn't have, and her mother had turned a blind eye. Even now, she could never understand why her stepfather had told her over and over again that she was a bad girl when he was a policeman and supposed to be good.

Two bodies lay on the carpet, dressed in hotel uniforms. The men had been running in the wrong direction – straight into the path of Fox's gun. He'd considered letting them go for the sport of it, but decided against it. He did not like loose ends.

A neon light swept across the wall and was gone.

'Did you see that?'

Fox had not. He followed Missy to the arched window that overlooked the courtyard at the front of the lodge. A tent had been erected in the farthest corner of the car park. Floodlights had been installed. Police officers scurried below them like ants.

'It took them longer than I thought.'

'Why haven't they tried to come in yet?'

Fox smiled. 'Too rural. They're waiting for officers who know how to shoot.'

Strange as it might sound, she hadn't thought about the mechanics of her own death until Fox said that. She'd watched on television the aftermath of shootings in America – in schools and churches and supermarkets – and understood that those who committed these atrocities did not survive. She expected to die at the hands of the police. But it was the first time she had thought about the feel of a bullet in her breast or temple, and what shape that pain might take.

The katydids began their chorus again.

Missy and Fox descended the sweeping staircase that took them back into the lobby. 'Imagine if this was your house.' Fox was jangling the keys to the front doors. 'Shall I lock us in? Barricade the entrances and exits?'

'I don't know,' she said. She didn't. There was no rulebook for the execution of strangers, for writing oneself into history with the blood of innocents. *No one is innocent.* She thought about the children in her class at Midtown Primary. Even at their young ages, she could see those with a cruel streak, the pushovers and the leaders. *'You're a bad girl, Melissa Smith.'* Isn't that what Papa had told her when she was nine?

Fox did not waste time trying to locate the correct key, aware he was a target. Instead he bolted the doors while Missy drew thick curtains across the windows that framed the lobby's seating area. The embers of the fire flickered in the grate. She wondered how it would feel to be the kind of woman who spent nights in places like this, ordering goblets of wine and wearing a laundered robe that wasn't her own.

'Come away from the windows,' he said.

He was right. She stepped away, aware of her vulnerability, and moved towards the centre of the hotel lobby. Two suitcases on wheels, their handles extended, were abandoned by the reception desk.

'Where did these come from?' Missy turned in a full circle, her eyes scanning the shadows for interlopers. A ceiling beam creaked and she startled, lifting her weapon to her chest.

'What do you mean?'

'These suitcases. They weren't here before.'

While Fox examined them, she walked across the lobby,

her heels clicking on the parquet floor. She bent over one of the armchairs, next to a shelf filled with games and books. When she returned, she was holding a hand-knitted blanket with a hole at its centre and edges that had unravelled like strands of woollen spaghetti.

'Someone was here while we were upstairs,' she said.

Fox shrugged, seemingly ambivalent, but he tightened his grip on his gun. 'Does it matter?'

Missy, infuriated, threw the blanket onto the wooden counter where guests checked in. 'Of course it does.' She paced up and down the lobby. Her cheeks were flushed and Fox moved to kiss her again, but she pushed him away. 'It means that somebody is making a fool of us.'

'And what do you propose we do about that?'

There was only one answer she could give. She cocked her gun.

31

The Lodge on the Loch: 8.31 p.m.

Tom had thought it was the start of a fireworks display. He left his blanket on the sofa and wandered over to a hotel window, expecting to see rockets and silver rain falling from the sky. He hoped there'd be hot dogs with ketchup and fried onions, and candy floss, and fairground rides that made his head whirl. He hoped there'd be sparklers to spell out his father's name, and a guy stuffed with newspaper to toss on the bonfire. But there was nothing except a few clouds and a bright moon.

His stomach rumbled. He was hungry, and although he would rather die than admit it, he was tired too. When he was younger and half asleep after a long car journey, his father would carry him upstairs to bed. Tom would rest his cheek on his shoulder, his father's jumper scratching his skin, legs hanging long and loose. Charlie would joke that Tom was growing so fast he would overtake him by morning.

He didn't want to tell Galen or his mother, but he couldn't remember what being carried by his father felt like anymore, and, once or twice, he'd forgotten the sound of Charlie's voice until he'd watched a video on his sister's phone and reminded himself.

Sometimes it upset him. Sometimes he thought his father wouldn't have minded at all.

The fireworks went off again but the sky was still empty. He glanced behind him, puzzled by its blankness, intending to ask his sister if he could go outside for a better look, but she was stumbling towards him, a stricken expression on her face.

She grabbed him by his left wrist, dragging him away from the window, past the sofas and armchairs. 'Stop it,' he said. 'That hurts.' She pressed her fingers against his mouth to silence him. He pushed them off. 'What is it?' She shook her head and mimed firing a gun.

Tom was eight years old. He had no experience of violence. He did not watch the news and his mother said he was too young to play shooting games on his console. To him, guns were a vague and shadowy threat but not one he considered. He did not understand what Galen meant.

'Leave me alone.' He was tired and wanted to watch the fireworks. His mouth set in a stubborn line.

Galen crouched next to him, the words whispering from her like autumn leaf-fall. 'We need to get out of here, okay? It's important.'

In the distance, somebody screamed. Both children stilled but it was muffled, a long way away. Tom studied his sister's face. Her bottom lip was trembling, but she kept biting it, as if one act of physical sabotage would stop the other. He hadn't seen her do that since the day their father died, and he and his mother found her hiding in her bed, her lips raw and bleeding. She was frightened, he could tell.

'What about Mum? She told us to wait here.'

'We'll find her in a bit.'

Tom let his sister take his hand. The entrance to the hotel was around thirty paces from where they were standing. A grand staircase swept down to a set of double doors that led into the night. Galen pointed at them, to show Tom where they were headed. As noiselessly as they could, brother and sister stole across the parquet.

They were about halfway to the outside world, to the gathering police and a place of safety, when voices at the top of the stairs froze them in their tracks.

A woman was speaking, rude and impatient. A man's voice, indistinct, replied. Galen's gaze moved upwards, and quick as lightning, she pressed herself into the alcove under the stairs, pulling Tom with her. She placed her fingers on her lips.

She had seven seconds to make a decision before the man and the woman reached the bottom step.

On the turn of the fourth second, she squeezed Tom's hand and they made a beeline for a door opposite them that was ajar. She pushed Tom through it first, careful not to let it shut and alert the couple to their presence.

Tom's heart was racing and he thought he might cry. Galen was already halfway across the room, but she was limping. His new trainers had caused a blister on his heel that was beginning to hurt. He wondered if she had one too.

He looked around to see where they were. Books filled every shelf and cabinet, thousands of them. Tall windows overlooked woodland beyond, lit by solar-powered lamps that spotlighted a fountain in the centre of manicured lawns. A vase of flowers stood on top of a piano. Some of the books had edges that were sprayed gold. Some were fat and some were thin. But there was no mistaking what this place was: a library.

Galen made for a door that opened up onto an outside terrace. She tried the handle, once, twice, but it was locked. In any number of Hollywood films, she might have picked up the vase and smashed the glass, escaping to safety. But it was tempered, designed to withstand pressure and shatter inwards, and she lacked the power to break it, even if the thought had occurred to her. Tom was frightened and had no idea what to do next, but he trusted his sister. She was older than him. She would make them safe.

'What shall we do now?' Without thinking, his small hands traced the ivory and black keys of the piano. It sounded unnaturally loud in the silence of the room.

'For God's sake, Tom.' Galen could not contain her irritation and his eyes filled. He snatched his hands away and dug them into his pockets. 'I'm sorry,' she said, immediately contrite. 'But you have to be quiet.'

Voices outside the door.

Galen's face turned the colour of milk. Tom felt a pressing need to go to the toilet. He looked miserably at his sister as the front of his trousers darkened. She hugged him to her.

Then she beckoned to him to follow her, and she was moving through the library, past the neat shelves and glass-fronted cabinets until she reached the far corner of the room. Her mouth was moving, as if she was talking to herself, and Tom realized she was counting. She stopped in front of a particular section of the library. These shelves were a bespoke design, nine rows high and framed in wood, and set beneath a watercolour of Loch Tummel that held a magical quality to it, as if stepping through the canvas might lead them to Narnia.

Galen was pressing the spines of every book on the fifth

shelf. Tom watched her, puzzled. Until there was an audible click and the bookshelf swung open to reveal the mouth of a staircase.

Despite everything, she grinned. 'Come on.' He followed her into the dark, frightened of the unknown but more frightened of the voices outside the library door. 'Shut it behind you.' She waited for him to close the false door and began to descend the steps.

'How did you know?' Tom's voice was small. 'You're smart, Galen.'

She laughed. 'Not really. It was in episode six, season three of *The Karma Hotel*. I didn't know if it was a real thing but turns out it is.'

The steps took them down to the basement, close to the staff eating quarters and the laundry room. But they couldn't get out. The door at the bottom was locked from the outside and no amount of pushing or pulling would open it.

'What shall we do?'

'Sit tight for now.'

The walls were made from stone, and the stairwell smelled like their garage at home, of mildew and damp. One light was working but it was faint, as if the bulb was about to die.

'I want Mum.' Tom's voice wobbled. Galen sat on the bottom step and drew him onto her lap. 'Don't worry, we'll find her.' Together, the children huddled in the shadows, more lost than they had ever been.

Christine's nose was bleeding. She was on her hands and knees, and a face with a beard and eyes that were almost black was closer than either of them was comfortable with.

'They're upstairs,' he said. 'Two of them. With guns. You can't be out in the open like this. You need to hide.'

He was lying on his stomach, trying to keep low and out of sight. He gestured at her to join him, but she shook her head, decisive. Two or three droplets of blood fell onto the floorboards like rubied jewels. 'No. I need to find my children.'

'Did you hear what I said?' A fierce whisper. 'I've just seen three dead bodies in the kitchen. If you don't hide, your children won't have a mother to find them.'

Because leaving her children without either of their parents terrified Christine more than anything else, she did as the stranger suggested. Her body was bruised where he'd caught her ankle and caused her to fall, a bolus of fear in her stomach. But she saw the sense in what he said, however painful it was to hear.

'I can't leave them out there by themselves.' Her voice broke apart and she buried her face in her hands, smearing them with blood.

'I know,' he said. 'But you're more help to them alive than dead.'

They crawled back through the bar area and the deserted restaurant until they reached the kitchen. The man stood and Christine did the same. He was taller than her, broad, and was wearing chef's whites. A lilt in his voice and a glint in his eye. His beard was flecked with grey, but it was neatly trimmed, and there was a steadiness to him she found appealing. A sense that he was in control, he had a plan. 'Don't look anywhere but ahead of you.' He moved quickly, navigating his familiar space with ease.

Christine kept her gaze fixed on the sleek metal counter-tops, the commercial oven, the vast sink, but the tiles were awash with blood and the place smelled like a butchery.

She staggered against a cupboard, her heart running hard and fast. How could this be happening to them? To those who were already lost? A noise spilled from her, a primal exhalation of fear and shock.

The man – he'd introduced himself as Al – turned around, his face creased with compassion. He opened the pantry and withdrew an expensive bottle of brandy. Despite his air of calm, his hands were trembling as he uncapped it, and as he poured, amber liquid ran down the outside of the glass he'd found on the side. As Christine drank, the fumes burned her eyes, mixing with the tears. He watched her, empathy in his expression. Then he picked up the bottle and knocked back a generous mouthful.

'I was in the toilet. "I'll be back in five minutes," I said. We were prepping for evening service, but I'd missed a call from my brother – he struggles a bit – and I wanted to ring him back.'

He couldn't look at her. 'I shouldn't have left them. It's my kitchen. We were so busy, and I left them, and if I hadn't, maybe we could have overpowered them and they'd still be—' Al wiped the back of his hand across his mouth. He couldn't say it.

Christine hardly knew this man but she felt a compulsion to comfort him. As a gesture of solidarity, coupled with her own need for human connection, she rested her hand on his shoulder. He touched it once in return, an acknowledgement, and then composed himself.

'Are you here on holiday?'

'Sort of. Not exactly.'

He smiled then, lines creasing his face like leather that is worn but comfortable. 'Sounds complicated.'

'I'm a widow.' She blurted it out. It was the first time in six months she'd told someone she didn't know. It was different with her friends – no explanation required – but the idea of having to field questions about Charlie from a disinterested acquaintance made her squirm. Something about Al told her he would understand.

'That's rough.'

She waited for the inevitable slew of questions. *How did it happen? Was it expected? How are you all coping?* But he didn't pry. Instead he said, 'My brother lost his wife a couple of years ago. Because they were in the process of getting divorced, everyone thinks he's over it, but he's a fucking mess.'

'It's not easy, even when things weren't perfect.' She smiled. 'Although Charlie was pretty perfect. I was lucky.'

Al rubbed his beard, his gaze fixed on a point somewhere between the hob and the extractor fan. 'Seems to me you were both pretty lucky.'

She looked at him askance, a bubble of laughter building inside her, despite the horror of everything around them. 'Are you *flirting* with me?'

'God, no,' he said, embarrassed, and then he caught her eye and laughed too. 'I didn't mean to sound quite so emphatic.'

'Flattery is clearly your superpower,' she said, and they both laughed again, recognizing a kinship that warmed them. Al held out the bottle to her, and she shook her head. *It's important to keep a clear head when you're about to die.* He allowed himself another swig and replaced the cap. *Or drink until oblivion, whatever floats your boat.* He gripped the tops of her arms, suddenly serious.

'There's a cold store,' he said. 'We can lock ourselves in it until the police come.'

'I can't do that, I'm afraid.'

'They'll kill you.'

She closed her eyes then, unable to articulate a truth that every parent understood. If her children were dead, she would not – could not – want to live.

'I can't,' she said again. 'You stay here, honestly. But I can't hide away and leave them out there on their own, fending for themselves.' She swallowed down the lump in her throat. 'They only lost their father ten months ago. I can't let them think I've abandoned them too.'

Al possessed enough grace not to say what both of them were thinking. Her children might already be dead.

Christine did not begrudge him his instinct for survival and she could not argue with his logic. Locking themselves away until this was over made sense. But her instinct to protect was stronger than her will to survive. Now she'd done as he'd asked and followed him to a place of safety, she realized she couldn't stay here, and nothing he could say would deter her. His eyes flicked to the cold store at the back of the kitchen and back to her. They were hard and bright and determined.

'What are their names? Your children?'

'Tom and Galen.' *My loves, my life.*

'So what are we waiting for? Let's go and find them.'

32

The Lodge on the Loch: 8.40 p.m.

The team of specialist firearms officers had arrived from Edinburgh. They were clad in their standard-issue uniform of black shirts and trousers, fire-retardant overalls and balaclavas, goggles, ballistic vests and helmets.

Each of them carried two radios – one to communicate with operational command and a secure one to talk with other firearms officers on the ground. All of them carried primary and secondary weapons – a Heckler & Koch MP5SF semi-automatic carbine and a Glock 17 pistol – and ammunition pouches, stun grenades, tear gas, tasers and pepper spray. Their point man carried a ballistic shield to protect the team if they were being fired on.

Four BMW X5 Armed Response Vehicles were also in the car park, manned by authorized firearms officers and distinguished by a circular yellow sticker on their bodywork. Two teams of rifle officers, trained to fire through glass with precision, were armed with bolt-action sniper rifles and had been allocated observation points, front and back, in case Dashiell Lloyd and Melissa Smith came into view through the hotel windows.

But they still had no idea how many guests or staff were inside.

As they prepared for their tactical assault, Blue watched from the sidelines and wondered what had happened to Saul, and whether he would live or die.

She should have told him the truth. As soon as it had happened. Even though she could barely face it herself, could only scrape the surface of it in her memory, because if she examined it too closely, it would dismantle her, and she would not allow him to take that from her too.

She found a bush and vomited behind it, purging herself – momentarily, at least – of the complex cocktail of distress, revulsion and self-hatred she'd been carrying inside her for the last twenty-four hours. She wiped her mouth with the back of her hand, tasted its bitterness on her tongue, and finally gave herself permission to relive what had happened, determined to stoke her fury instead of allowing the horrors of what she'd endured to swallow her up, to suffocate her.

Her flat had been in darkness when she'd arrived home the previous night, which had surprised her because the lights were timed to switch on as soon as the sun went down, but she assumed there had been a glitch or a power cut, a mistake she would bitterly regret.

Still fizzing from dinner with her sister, the kind of joy that comes from spending time with a loved one, her cheeks pinked from cold and laughter, Blue called out to Miss Meow, but there was no answering cry. But still, she wasn't worried. Her cat often disappeared in the evenings, prowling the nearby streets and gardens. She would come home when she was ready.

Her mouth dry from too much Chinese food, Blue

wandered into the kitchen for a glass of water. She had intended to pick up a change of clothes and head straight to the coastguard's lookout but Douglas Lynch, the detective constable who had sexually assaulted her the previous year, was sitting at her table, wearing gloves, his baton in his lap.

'I know about the birds,' he said.

His voice was low in the autumn evening, his expression hard, devoid of emotion. Blue had turned from him, to run, but he was expecting that and he hit her once, in the stomach, to stop her. She bent over, winded, adrenaline blunting the pain. Last year, she and Saul, aware he suffered from orni-thophobia, had filled his house with dozens of birds by way of revenge. She'd heard on the grapevine that he'd applied for – and been granted – a transfer from Kent Police to Midtown-on-Sea, and now here he was, seeking vengeance of his own.

He grabbed her, one hand around her neck, the other rough around her breasts, and then between her legs. She screamed once, kicking and twisting, and he laughed and punched her, and his face blurred before her, cut into little stars.

Detective Constable Douglas Lynch forced Blue through the hallway and onto her bed.

He tied her wrists together with a pair of her tights, his gloved hand across her nose and mouth. Blue had felt like she was suffocating then, the air pressed from her by a thief. A minute, perhaps two, and her lungs would have stopped inflating altogether and stilled. That's what had scared her most of all.

She'd given up fighting then and had lain there, the moon-rise visible through a gap in the blinds, and she had counted the pinpricks of light in the sky above until she was lost amongst the galaxies and stars, some distant place that carried her away from herself.

At times, she was aware of him, but her brain had allowed her to disassociate her body from her mind, and she found herself wandering the memories of her childhood, the warm summers of sticky cherry brandy ice lollies and sand between her toes, the sound of her mother laughing at a quiz show on the radio, the feel of her younger sister when she was a baby, a compact weight on her shoulder, scented with talcum powder and sweetness, and her jumper drawer lined with brown paper and lavender bags. These bright spots of memory worked as talismans against the horror that was unfolding, and she clung to them.

For ten hours, he took what did not belong to him, stopping for brief periods to doze or use the bathroom, and he whispered to her that if she told anyone, if she tried to report him or make a formal complaint, he would kill Saul Anguish and come back for her.

And when the sun had risen on her darkest night, he had driven her to the coastguard's lookout and they had watched Saul, unsuspecting, make his way across the salt marshes on his journey to work. Then Lynch had forced her to show him where Saul kept his spare key, hidden beneath the anchor, scraps of rust flaking onto the grass. He left the dead chicks – as he had the blue egg – as a warning to them both.

A leaden weight sat inside Blue, made heavier still by the tension of the day, the unfolding horror of it all. It would not dislodge; it was a part of her now. But she was good at pretending. She packed her feelings into a box and put them away, and when DC Eliot Williams and PC Alex Talbot joined her on the periphery of the police activity, she was Dr Clover March again, professional and focused.

Williams had just come off the phone to Detective Inspector O'Neill, and he was not happy, his impatient feet scuffing the concrete as he walked towards her.

'Where's Anguish?' He was brusque, almost aggressive.

'How should I know?'

Williams rolled his eyes. 'Because you two are as thick as thieves.' He waited for her to answer, as if she was his subordinate, but when it became apparent she had no intention of doing so, he said, 'This isn't a joke, March. Where is he? I need to talk to him.'

'No one's laughing, *Williams*.' She wouldn't be spoken to in that way, especially not by a man as condescending as he was.

From across the car park, Chief Inspector Shona McGill signalled to Williams, a gesture that smacked of urgency. According to Talbot, O'Neill had promised her a verbal update on Smith and Lloyd's backgrounds, but their DI was proving elusive while McGill needed to gather as much intelligence as she could, as quickly as possible. Williams went off without another word.

'*Do* you know where Saul is?' Talbot was curious, but she sensed he was not the kind to betray a confidence, although she couldn't be certain. She swallowed and took a gamble on him.

'Yes.'

'Where?' He threw a glance behind him. 'Williams is going to lose his shit if he doesn't show up in a minute.'

She hesitated, not sure if she should trust him but needing to talk it through with someone. 'He's gone into the hotel.'

Talbot's mouth dropped open. Even an officer as inexperienced as he was recognized the foolhardiness of such an action. 'What for? Why didn't he wait for the firearms team?'

She shrugged, reluctant to break the confidences Saul had shared with her. 'He has his reasons.'

'Must be bloody good ones.'

'They are.'

'He'll be all right, though, won't he?' Talbot sounded as if he was trying to convince himself. 'I mean, he's Saul Anguish. He's always all right.'

But before Blue had a chance to respond, a burst of gunfire exploded from the hotel.

33

The Lodge on the Loch: 8.41 p.m.

Missy held the semi-automatic pistol above her head and fired once, twice, three times. Fox ducked out of the way as plaster fell from the ceiling. 'What are you doing?' Missy had changed since he'd picked her up in Midtown that morning. She was no longer the meek girl of her childhood, or the teenager at society's edges, or the young woman who did as others asked without thinking of herself. She was a loose cannon. He liked it.

'It's a warning to anyone who thinks they can hide from us.'

Fox flattened himself against the wall and edged towards the windows. He whistled through his teeth. 'The big guns are here. They'll be making a move soon.'

Missy arched an eyebrow. 'Then it's time to get ourselves together, Mr Lloyd.'

'And what do you propose, Mrs Lloyd?'

She slid her arms around his neck. 'Would you care for a dance, my love?'

He understood what she meant as soon as she'd said it because they'd discussed what they'd both named The Last Dance earlier. When the time came – and they'd know when it had – they would gather the surviving hostages in the ballroom, barricade themselves in and go violently into the night.

Fox and Missy had systematically checked every room on the first floor of the hotel and now they would check every room on the ground floor, swift and focused. Whoever they found from this point onwards would have the misfortune of knowing they were going to be murdered but being forced to wait for it to happen.

Fox laughed and gathered his bride into his arms. He murmured a song in her ear and kissed her neck. Missy closed her eyes and swayed against him. Then they reloaded their weapons and began to hunt.

34

The Lodge on the Loch: 8.41 p.m.

Saul Anguish had always been more comfortable in the dark. After he'd said goodbye to Blue, he'd allowed himself to fold into the night, chasing the shadows and avoiding the moon's spotlight.

Gaining access to the hotel was much easier than he'd anticipated. He thought he'd have to break a window or scale a wall, but when it came to it, he'd crossed the wide terrace then run alongside the back of two thirds of the building, and tried one of the doors to find it unlocked.

He'd found himself in a snug with two armchairs, a low table, and a fireplace that was unlit. He listened to the sounds of the hotel, but everything was quiet.

He wondered how many people were inside. As a police officer, it was his duty to find out, and to relay this information to Chief Inspector McGill's team. But Saul did not intend to focus on the victims. His purpose was to get to Melissa Smith and arrest her, both of them unharmed. O'Neill had asked him to pass on a message to his daughter, and he intended to do so, even though it was at great personal risk to himself.

Saul didn't care what happened to Dashiell Lloyd. Except that he wanted him dead.

Did it matter which of them had fired the gun that had wounded Callum Brown? Smith was in Lloyd's thrall, he was sure of it. Before this morning, her record had been clean. No previous convictions. No run-ins with the police. But he'd read Lloyd's file, and the world would hail Saul a hero for switching him off. He just had to be careful about the way he did it.

Saul walked through the snug and into a larger lounge. Through the doors, he could see the hotel corridor, and beyond that, some kind of reception area. The lights had come on automatically and they made him squint after being outside. He searched for the switches, to put them out. It was easier to disappear into darkness than evade the light.

His first task was clear-cut. He would need to separate Melissa from Lloyd. A few minutes alone with her, that's all he wanted. He'd convince her to listen, see sense and come home.

Three gunshots tore through the hotel.

Instinctively, he cowered, scrambling to the floor. His ears rang with noise, the explosive pressure of bullets exiting the barrel. It was loud, closer than he'd expected. Much closer.

He crouched behind an armoire stacked with antiques, waiting.

A few minutes later, a woman's voice caught his attention. *Melissa?* Her words were indistinct, too muffled for him to hear what she was saying, but there was amusement in them. A laugh, the lower timbre of a man. The exchange of two or three sentences. Their voices were growing louder until he became convinced they were standing outside the lounge door. Saul's tongue felt thick in his mouth. Although he did not fear death, he did not wish to bleed out like a stuck pig at the hands of Smith and Lloyd.

The door opened, a sliver of light spilling across the wooden floor. He closed his hand around his baton. His heart rate accelerated. It was possible he could disarm one of them. But not both. He was no match for a gun fired at point-blank range. *Blue, I'm sorry I didn't listen to you.*

The shape of a woman was haloed in the door frame. She was slight, dark-haired, with the same arched eyebrows as O'Neill, and wearing a dress that was too big for her. She was holding a gun, a Glock 17, standard police issue, probably the one stolen from her stepfather. He'd seen the mess she had made with it. It was raised to chest height, pointing in front of her, steady and true.

She was looking in the opposite direction, towards the far end of the lounge and the woodland beyond. But if she turned her head and stepped forward a few paces, she could not fail to see him, tucked in a dark corner like the coward he was.

Saul tried to form his first sentence – an appeal of sorts to her – but the words dried on his lips. O'Neill had decided not to make the journey north because he didn't think Melissa would listen to him. Too late, Saul realized he'd fallen victim to his own arrogance. He was a believer in second chances and he'd wanted to help them both, to lay to rest the ghosts of his own past by helping others to fix theirs. He'd convinced himself he'd be able to connect with her on some level, as he often did with the misfits and lost souls who found their way into the police station. For the first time – stupid as that sounded – he realized that she might not listen to him, but shoot before he'd uttered a word. She was armed and dangerous, and he was as exposed and vulnerable as a newborn. *Stupid, stupid, stupid.*

She took a step further into the room, her head beginning to turn. Saul lifted his baton.

'Missy.'

A man – he assumed it was Lloyd – called to her.

'Yes.' She didn't turn around but she stilled. Saul held his breath.

'Come and see what I've found.'

35

The Lodge on the Loch: 8.44 p.m.

'We'll still get to see the dolphins tomorrow, won't we?'

Tom had wriggled off Galen's lap and was sitting next to her on the bottom step of the hidden stairwell. Galen's eyes were closed and she was leaning her head against the wall, exhausted.

'Absolutely.'

She thought about telling him the truth. That there was no *absolutely* about it. If yesterday felt like home, tomorrow was an alien planet. *But which one? Pluto? Dimidium? It doesn't matter, Galen.* They might all be dead by then. Tom. Her mother. Herself. Her ex-schoolfriends would be pleased about that. For some reason, this thought tickled her and she laughed to herself. She couldn't stop laughing. In the end, Tom put his hand over her mouth until the urge had subsided and she'd regained some semblance of control.

Galen stretched out her legs in the cramped space. They felt stiff, as if they'd been encased in layers of mud that had dried in the sun. Her hands were shaking too. Tom was picking at a scab on his elbow. His stomach rumbled. It had been hours since lunchtime and he hadn't eaten his dinner.

As if on cue, 'I'm hungry.'

She stroked his head, a gesture of comfort she repeated again and again until she felt his body relax into hers. 'I know, captain.' She slid a hand into her pocket and found a half-eaten packet of Polos. 'Here you go.'

He tore off the foil and crunched one. The smell of peppermint filled the air. 'Do you think Mum's safe now?'

Tom was seeking reassurance, she was old enough to realize that, but Galen was trying her hardest not to think about their mother. She'd heard five gunshots since they'd been inside the hotel. Five chances for their mother to be struck by a bullet. Five chances for their mother to die.

'I hope so.'

'That means you're not sure.'

'What do you think? About Mum?'

He popped another sweet into his mouth and offered the tube to his sister. 'Shall we have a competition? To see whose lasts the longest?'

Galen eased one from the packet. She rolled the mint between her thumb and forefinger, and pressed her eye against the hole in the middle, a one-eyed Polo-mint monster, coming for her brother. 'Shall we start the clock now?'

'Not fair,' said Tom, giggling, crunching his second sweet as quickly as he could. 'I've already started mine.'

'Hurry up,' she said. 'We haven't got all night.'

Tom took a third Polo and for a few moments, he and Galen forgot about their ordeal. They stuck out their tongues to compare how thin each ring of mint had become. When Tom's snapped first, Galen teased him and gave him the last sweet in the packet. 'That's how much I love you.'

They were playing their third game of Rock Paper Scissors

when a man's voice spoke from a place somewhere above them.

'Come and see what I've found.'

A rush of vomit burned the back of Galen's throat but she swallowed it down. She whispered to Tom. 'Did you shut the door properly?'

Tom bit his lip. 'Ye-es.' But Galen could tell from the look on his face he wasn't certain. Neither was she now. It wasn't his fault. She should have checked.

She turned the handle of the door at the bottom of the stairs again and again, even though she knew it was hopeless. Footsteps crossed the floorboards above them, slow and deliberate. Tom began to cry.

From above, a light filled the stairwell, as if God Himself was present. Galen didn't believe in divine refulgence or in a spiritual explanation for the light at the end of the tunnel reported by those in near-death experiences. Just as she understood that was a neurological phenomenon caused, in part, by loss of blood flow and oxygen, she knew the light coming from the top of the stairs meant the false door had been discovered, and the shadow that came with it was a man with a gun.

Tom reached for her, a look of fear on his face so pure she thought he might die from fright before the man had a chance to shoot them. But she remembered the words of her father when she was scared of the dark, or afraid of falling from the monkey bars, or shaking with nerves on the high ropes strung between trees taller than her imagination: *Bravery is knowing when to turn back and when to face your fears.*

If the Hardwicke siblings were going to die here, at the bottom of these stairs, Galen would not let them see her cry or let herself be cowed. *I love you, Mum.* A last hug for her brother.

'Stand behind me,' she said.

And then they came.

36

The Lodge on the Loch: 8.52 p.m.

There had been no gunshots for eleven minutes.

The Strategic Firearms Unit and Gold Command had agreed between them to wait no later than 2100 hours for the arrival of a trained negotiator who would attempt to communicate with the shooters via a WhatsApp call. This decision to hold back was a matter of some controversy. Gold Command favoured a watch-and-wait approach, especially as civilian hostages were involved, but the SFU knew time was of the essence with active shooters. The firearms officers, poised and in position, were itching to go in.

Like them, Chief Inspector Shona McGill did not want more blood than was necessary on her hands. She favoured launching a tactical assault with immediate effect and was locked in animated discussion with the Silver Commander, who, in the absence of further gunshots or an exchange of fire, agreed with Gold Command and advocated gathering more intelligence. No one knew how many victims were inside or whether the shooters had turned their weapons on themselves.

Beneath the floodlights, PC Alex Talbot watched the manoeuvrings with interest. The SFOs didn't pay much attention to him, a lowly police constable who still looked like a boy, but he was fascinated by their body armour and weaponry. Their bravery too. In a live and fluid situation such as this, trust between each officer was paramount. Every action and reaction could mean the difference between death and life.

He didn't trust anyone at Midtown Police Station except perhaps Saul Anguish. He barely knew the man and yet Saul had covered his back in multiple ways that day, asking nothing in return. Talbot respected that about him. Admired him, if truth be told. A part of him wanted to be like Saul, although he'd probably deny it if anyone cared enough to ask.

Dr March was standing a short distance away. She was talking to someone on the telephone and her face – all hollows and planes in the artificial light – was creased as she scribbled on a notepad. When she'd finished, she lost her footing and stumbled across the car park. By the time he reached her, she'd regained her balance, but her eyes looked heavy, as if she was about to fall asleep, and then she tipped forward, a collapsing puppet.

He caught her beneath her arms as she fell, and lowered her to the ground. She was insubstantial, a wisp of a woman. Talbot hadn't had a girlfriend for a couple of years and it felt odd to touch her, a relative stranger, in this intimate way. Her lips were slightly open and her hair had fallen to one side, shielding her face with a pastel curtain. A ring of bruises circled her neck.

He cast around for help but everyone was busy, and, from what little he knew of her, he didn't think she was the type who'd like a fuss. Talbot took off his jacket and placed it under her head. For a couple of minutes he dithered, uncertain, and then she opened her eyes, which turned silver as the light hit them. When she noticed him watching her, she sat up, although he could tell the effort cost her.

He looked away, not wanting to embarrass her. 'Do you need anything?'

'Some water. There's a bottle in my bag.' She pointed to her rucksack, which had slipped from her shoulder when she'd blacked out. He wasn't sure whether to pass it to her or retrieve the bottle himself. Would it be patronizing or gentlemanly? While he spent an agonizing sixty seconds deciding on the best course of action, she had grown bored with waiting, grabbed her bag and was now unscrewing the cap. She looked tired, he thought. Violet shadows beneath her eyes. 'What happened? Shall we get you to a doctor?'

She shook her head, dismissing his question. 'Just felt a bit light-headed. It happens sometimes.' Her gaze slid away from him, as if she was concealing a more fundamental truth, but he didn't want to press her and instead changed the subject. 'Was that O'Neill on the phone?'

'No, it was a friend of mine from an auction house in Boston.'

He whistled, putting on his impressed face. 'Are you buying or selling?'

A barely-there smile in acknowledgement of his weak attempt at humour. 'Neither.' She took a long swig of her water, fingers picking at the peeling label. 'Did you get a chance to see the sheet on Sally Brown's bed?'

Talbot looked away, the teasing words drying on his lips. 'No, but I heard them talking about it when I went to Callum's room to fetch his pyjamas and teddy. Why do you ask?'

Dr March rubbed a hand across her face. Forget tired, she looked exhausted. 'I think I've got a good idea why Melissa Smith wrote what she did.'

'Go on.'

'It's a quote from a letter.'

Dr Clover March was sitting on the cold concrete, cross-legged. Although they were similar in age, she seemed older to Talbot, more worldly. Her eyes had turned from silver to dark grey and he glimpsed hidden depths behind them.

'What letter?' His curiosity was piqued.

'It was for sale. Lot 1,005. The successful bidder paid $23,750 for it.'

He whistled. 'That's a lot of money for a piece of paper.'

'Not as much as his gun. His .38 revolver, a Colt Army Special, sold for almost $50,000.'

Talbot wasn't sure if he was being stupid or if she was being oblique. He ran his hand across his jaw, aware of a day's growth of stubble. 'Whose letter? Whose gun?'

She uncrossed her legs and stretched them out in front of her. Her biker boots seemed too big for her, as if she was a child who had borrowed her mother's clothes. 'Clyde Barrow. Do you know who he was?'

He considered the question but came up blank. 'I don't think so.'

'What about Bonnie Parker?'

The penny dropped then. He remembered a long-ago Sunday afternoon when his father had persuaded him to watch the film, rain lashing against the windows. 'As in Bonnie and Clyde?'

'Bonnie wrote the letter to one of their former gang in prison. On behalf of Clyde. He dictated it to her, but it was

in her handwriting, that beautiful cursive style, full of extravagant loops. The poor grammar was his.' She scratched
a patch of eczema on her wrist. 'Saul doesn't know this.'

'Would it make a difference if he did?'

'Don't you see?' Her sea-mist eyes were clouded now. 'He
thinks he can talk to her, persuade her to give herself up.'

All at once, Talbot understood. Those infamous outlaws died
in a hail of bullets after a bloody confrontation with police. If
Melissa Smith wasn't coming out alive, neither was Saul.

'You have to let him know.' He was urgent, insistent. 'Can
you radio him?'

She opened her rucksack to show him Saul's radio. 'He
gave it to me; he was worried about it giving him away.'

'His phone?'

'I've tried but the message hasn't gone through.'

'Keep trying.'

'I'm going to tell McGill. She needs to know who they're
dealing with before sending in the SFOs. Smith and Lloyd
want to die. They'll be walking into a trap.'

'What about Saul? Are you going to tell her about him
too?'

The agonized expression on her face suggested she was
still tussling with that dilemma.

Talbot watched Dr March run across the car park. All
around him was the bustle of activity, a sense of purpose
that he sometimes felt he lacked. He always knew he wouldn't
be the kind of officer to be garlanded with police commen-
dations or fast-tracked for promotion, and he'd made his
peace with that. But now and then, he wondered how it
might feel to be as noble or courageous as others before
him. To do something brave.

A murder squad detective with a phobia of dead bodies was not exactly someone his superiors could be proud of.

At a loose end, he wandered to the edge of the car park, hiding in the shadows the floodlights couldn't reach. Dr March was trying to get McGill's attention, her face lively with intent. He knew the forensic linguist wouldn't want to land Saul in trouble. He'd seen the way she'd looked at the young officer – and the way he'd sneaked glances back as soon as she'd turned away. But if someone didn't let Saul know what Smith and Lloyd's endgame was, his chances of survival were bleak.

Talbot held his face up to the sky and let the rain glaze it. It was the kind of rain that soaked everything. When he was a boy, he'd gone swimming with friends during weather like this, in the river that ran along the bottom of his garden. Joe, Taylor, Frankie and him. Frankie, the boldest of their gang, had stripped off his shirt and jeans, playing the fool and making them laugh. Before Talbot could tell him to stop, he'd thrown himself backwards from the wooden jetty, crossing his eyes and pursing his lips in a comical way. The other boys – no more than fourteen or fifteen – had laughed at Frankie's antics and waved at him from the river bank.

'Come and join me,' he had shouted to them through chattering teeth. 'It's not cold.' But Talbot had not laughed. 'Get out,' he'd said, standing at the water's edge. 'It's dangerous.'

Joe noticed first. Frankie was there and then he was gone. Talbot knew the current was merciless. Ever since he'd been old enough to walk, his parents had taught him to respect the river. But Frankie – who had only ever lived in the city – wasn't used to it. Talbot caught a glimpse of his pale skin against the reeds, his flailing arms, and then the river closed over him.

He had shouted for Frankie until his throat was sore and tears stung his eyes, but his feet were glued to the damp wood. Even though Frankie was his best friend, Talbot knew enough not to follow him in. Taylor, though, who was captain of their school swimming team, dived into the river without thinking. They watched, helpless, as the current took him too, and swept him around the bend and out of view.

By now, Talbot and Joe were crying and screaming, clutching each other. Talbot longed for his father, a reassuring bear of a man who would know what to do, but his parents were away for the weekend. This was the first time they'd left him alone.

His mobile phone was out of battery, so they'd used Joe's to call the emergency services. They were still waiting for them to arrive when a small boat appeared at the bend, making for the jetty. As the vessel moved closer, Talbot's heart leapt. Frankie and Taylor were inside. Shivering but alive.

Later, when the boys were warming themselves with mugs of soup around Talbot's kitchen table, Frankie had explained how Taylor's act of bravery had saved his life. His friend had untangled his ankle from the reeds, and kept him afloat until the boat had appeared like a gift from God.

'If it wasn't for Taylor, I'd have drowned,' he'd said. 'He came after me, even though he almost drowned himself.' He'd spoken these words with a quiet awe.

Talbot had never forgotten that day, not only because Frankie and Taylor did everything together after that, but because of one simple truth: despite the great personal risk to himself, Taylor had deliberately chosen to do something stupid and reckless for little more than an outside chance of saving his friend's life.

Talbot wondered what Saul would have done if he had been in the same situation, and realized he already knew the answer to that.

The hotel lights mocked him in the darkness. He could die if he went inside. Not an outside chance, but a distinct possibility, even if he was wearing body armour. Even if he was careful. It would be stupid. Reckless.

The rain continued to fall. As a little boy, he'd been scared of the dark. As a teenager, the river. Now, as a young man, he was frightened of death in all its guises. But he was terrified of something else too, something that had tormented him throughout the years. His own cowardice.

The officer stood motionless under the rain-dirty sky, the pendulum of free will swinging back and forth. A minute later, he pulled his mobile from his pocket. Sent a message to his family WhatsApp group. *Love you all xxx*

Then PC Alex Talbot turned off his phone and slipped into the night.

37

The Lodge on the Loch: 8.52 p.m.

Christine heard her children before she saw them. The relief was so intense that her knees went from beneath her, and Al steadied her, his finger to her lips to remind her not to cry out.

It was a long time since she'd been touched by a man who was not in her family, and the solidity, the warmth of him, surprised her. Their eyes met, and then she pulled away, embarrassed. Even with their lives at risk, she still had the capacity to blush. Charlie would have teased her about that.

In that moment, she missed her husband more than she had ever done in the ten months since his death. He'd been a calm, practical presence for them all, and if there was ever a time she needed him, it was now. But Charlie was gone, and the safety of Tom and Galen was her responsibility, and hers alone.

Her relief turned out to be short-lived.

Christine and Al had crept from the kitchen, past the restaurant and bar, to one of the guest lounges, which is where they were hiding now, crouched behind a sofa.

The voice she'd heard in the corridor was Tom's. Six joyous

words. 'I need to use the toilet.' She almost went to him then, not waiting for Galen's reply, driven by a need to touch her children, to reassure herself that they were safe. But Al had pulled her back down in time for a woman to reply, 'No dice, Tommy.'

The room spun.

Al sat so still she couldn't tell if he was breathing or not until his fingers found hers, and they became entwined, an instinctual and mutual comfort. She squeezed shut her eyes. All she could hear was the thunder of her pulse and the metronomic consistency of the clock on the wall.

Christine willed Galen to speak, a confirmation that she, too, was unharmed. But the clock ticked on, and her daughter remained silent.

'I don't know what to do.' She was so quiet that Al had to lean forward to hear what she said. By chance, she shifted position at the same moment, and the ends of her hair brushed against his face, tickling the tiny hairlike paddles in his nose called cilia. It wasn't that she needed his advice or approval, but she was paralysed by indecision, by fear of taking the wrong path.

In the end, the choice between hiding or defending her children was taken out of her hands. That seemingly innocuous physical interaction had devastating consequences neither of them could have predicted. With almost no time to warn her, Al turned to Christine, an agonized apology in his eyes.

For the briefest of moments, Christine convinced herself it was going to be fine. By pinching his nostrils together and clamping his hand across his mouth, Al managed to stifle that first sneeze.

But then time slowed into a series of tableaux, reminding her of a game she used to play with the children when they held themselves motionless at her command. *Freeze*. Al inhaled, his chest inflating with air. *Freeze*. His mouth opened, his respiratory system alerting itself to the need to expel irritants, an involuntary biological process beyond his control. *Freeze*. Al's head tipped backwards. *Freeze*. His eyes half closed.

In a detached manner, which she recognized as a form of shock, Christine recalled a newspaper story about an A&E patient who had ruptured his throat after attempting to suppress an explosive release of air, and that an average man's sneeze peaks at ninety decibels. She remembered these facts because one summer's afternoon, she'd tried to persuade a hayfever-stricken Charlie to compare his sneezes to the roar of a lawnmower, and he'd laughed so much, he'd accidentally run over the electric cable.

Freeze.

Al sneezed again. This time, he couldn't contain it. It took Fox seventeen seconds to sniff them out.

38

The Lodge on the Loch: 8.54 p.m.

Four hostages. Missy rolled the word on her tongue. *Hos-tuh-juhz*. Fox's finger itched on the trigger of his pistol, but she surprised herself by relishing the power that came from making them wait for their own deaths. In this world of online immediacy, there was something to be said for delayed gratification.

'Line up, single file,' she said. It turned out that children did what they were told when threatened with a gun.

A part of her was concerned about the inherent risk in being outnumbered. Keeping an eye on the man and the woman would need to be a priority. But being armed meant she and Fox held all the trump cards.

For fun, she pressed the muzzle of her weapon into the man's Adam's apple. His breathing quickened. 'Are you a chef here?' He swallowed. 'Answer me.'

'Yes.'

'Did you bump into your friends in the kitchen?'

When he refused to respond to her taunt, she laughed. 'Your apple tart was nice but it needed more sugar.'

Fox and Missy marched their hostages through the hotel lobby, past the library and the guest lounges, the reception desk and the locked front doors until they reached the battle-field of the ballroom again.

The concierge and the woman with the red coat were still on the parquet floor at the centre of a lake of blood.

'Barricade the doors,' said Missy.

Fox acknowledged her by lifting his fingers in a salute but instead of doing as she asked, he placed the holdall of guns on the far side of the room. One by one, he removed the weapons and laid them side by side on the floor, checking each of them was loaded.

While he was at work, Missy pulled heavy drapes across the ceiling-height windows that overlooked the hotel's twenty-five-acre grounds.

The children were silent. This surprised her. In Missy's experience, children were rarely silent.

'How old are you, Tommy?'

The boy looked at the girl, who nodded. 'Eight.'

'And this is your family?'

'My mum and my sister.'

'And where's your daddy hiding?' She kneeled before him, her voice low and dangerous. 'Is he somewhere in the hotel?'

'No.'

'Are you sure about that?'

She pressed her gun to his abdomen. He smelled of ammonia and fear. His mother cried out and Fox hit her across her face. His hand left a print on her cheek.

The girl spoke. 'He's dead.'

Missy did not turn around but caressed the boy under his chin. He flinched, but she was generous enough to pretend not to notice.

'Poor Tommy. I lost my father when I wasn't much older

than you.' She considered telling him he would survive that loss, as she had done, but the absurdity of such a statement made her laugh.

The ballroom radiated an old-fashioned grandeur she wasn't used to. The rest of the lodge was contemporary, decorated in earthy shades that suited the natural environment. But this place held an opulence to it that both awed and impressed her.

Five crystal chandeliers were suspended from the gilded ceiling. The parquet had been polished until it shone. Luxurious wallpaper was threaded with gold. Stately yet romantic.

She waved her gun at the four hostages. 'Stand by that wall.'

The girl was limping, she noticed. She could be thirteen or sixteen, it was difficult to say. And pretty. Like the shiny girls who'd ignored her all her life. Missy also noticed that Fox seemed to be paying her a lot of attention, glancing in her direction every now and then. Something about that made her burn.

The katydids began to sing again.

Her footsteps echoed as she walked across the floor and came to a halt in front of the girl. Missy did not speak. Instead she stared at her, her gun cocked. But if she thought that behaviour would intimidate her, she'd misjudged the situation. The girl stared back, her chin up, gaze steady.

Missy ran the muzzle of her gun along the girl's collarbone.

'Have you got a boyfriend?'

'No.'

'A girlfriend?'

'No.'

'Do you want one? I bet you do.'

'Leave my sister alone.'

Missy swivelled with an almost balletic grace to the source of those last four words. She sighed once, regretful. This insubordination would not be tolerated. She would not allow it in her classroom and she would not allow it here.

Gun pointing at the centre of the young boy's head, her finger danced on the trigger.

The blow came from nowhere, to the hollow at the base of her throat. Missy fell into the black hole of it, the pain sucking her into its core and dragging her to the edge of consciousness, its pull so intense that her vision blurred.

Gagging and clutching at her throat, she dropped to her knees, the pistol slipping from her hand, all but forgotten. She'd never been struck with such force before. Tiny stars filled her vision, spinning and twisting, a kaleidoscope of suffering. The swelling had already begun, closing up her airway and making it hard for her to breathe. On her hands and knees, she gasped, panicked.

The first slug hit Alun 'Al' Hunter near his groin, but it was a surface wound, shearing off towards the wall, where it ricocheted and embedded itself in a chair to the left of a window. The second tore open his femoral artery, causing such trauma that he died within two and a half minutes.

Fox, who had fired the shotgun from his position on the floor, helped Missy to her feet, pressing her gun back into her hand.

'It's like being winded,' he said. 'A punch to the throat. The sensation will pass in a few minutes.'

Missy coughed a couple of times, the pain already starting

to ease. Her voice didn't sound like her own. 'That was too close.'

The mother was crouched over the body of the chef. His trousers were soaked through with blood and bodily fluids, and it reminded Missy of those absorbent pads found in packets of raw meat. The sound of weeping irritated her. Stupid man.

'Such a waste,' she said.

Suddenly furious, she pressed the gun to the boy's head and pulled the trigger. It clicked once. The chamber was – had been – empty all along.

39

The Lodge on the Loch: 8.56 p.m.

The air ambulance was on standby and could land in the hotel grounds within three minutes. Six ambulances and two paramedic cars were parked in the far corner of the car park, close to Silver Command's pop-up control room. The three nearest hospitals had been alerted to the ongoing situation, and had called in extra personnel, including two military field trauma surgeons, experienced in treating gunshot wounds.

Through binoculars trained on the front windows of the hotel, a firearms officer had witnessed Melissa Smith and Dashiell Lloyd, together with an unidentified man, woman and two children, moving east through the lobby, but then they'd vanished from sight. A blueprint of the hotel's layout suggested they would be either inside the ballroom or some kind of guest lounge opposite.

As soon as they'd heard a further two shots, Bronze, Silver and Gold Command were in unanimous agreement to begin negotiations with the hostage-takers while authorizing the firearms team to begin their tactical assault.

Inside the hotel, Detective Constable Saul Anguish knew exactly where the gunfire had come from.

In an attempt at covert surveillance, he'd been lying on his stomach in a cocktail lounge that faced the ballroom when both shots were fired. A woman screamed, but he could tell it wasn't from physical pain, which suggested the man or the children had been executed. A duet of bullets. Two out of three.

A short while earlier, tiny hairs pricking at the back of his neck, he'd listened, helpless, as Lloyd and Smith had discovered each of the hostages and their hiding places before shepherding them to their current location. He'd seen three bodies in the kitchen, two in a bedroom upstairs and another two in a nearby corridor. He did not believe in a higher power, neither God nor Fate, although sometimes he felt the breath of something darker at his shoulder, a fetid presence, an apostate of evil. By some miracle, he was not dead yet. And yet he had never felt so adrift. He was a man used to working alone, to making difficult decisions, but he was standing at a fork in the road.

Raise the alarm now and face being expelled from the police force for gross misconduct before his career had properly begun. Fail O'Neill. And himself.

Or stay and risk death. Risk everything. His future with Blue, if he had one after this. His reputation. And his life.

Saul was stuck. He did not like to be stuck.

In the weeks that had followed his rescue of Clara Foyle, a five-year-old abducted by notorious serial killer Mr Silver, they'd tried to make teenage him talk to a child psychologist. Her name was Dr Elizabeth Winterson. Dr Winterson had invited him to open up and trust her, but he'd resisted, suspicious of her motives, of anyone in a position of authority paid to exploit the minds of the vulnerable and young.

But she'd said one thing that had resonated with him then, and he remembered it now. 'Whenever you're unsure about what to do next, always make the choice you can live with afterwards.'

Saul knew he could not live without trying, whatever the outcome. Not only had he made a promise to O'Neill, but he owed it to the hostages – especially the children. And every time he had found himself in a situation such as this, luck or ill fortune had rolled up like a silver sixpence or a bad penny. What happened next was about the toss of that coin.

At that moment, as if by some alchemy, PC Alex Talbot ran across the lobby at a half-crouch and skidded in next to him. His face – naive and open – broke into a relieved grin. 'There you are. Thank God for that.'

'Get down.' Saul was terse. A whisper. 'What the hell are you doing here? It's not safe.'

The police officer lay on his front next to the detective, a crestfallen expression narrowing his features. 'I came to warn you.'

'About what?'

In as few words as possible, Talbot relayed what Blue had discovered. If Saul was planning to confront Melissa Smith, he would not survive their encounter. 'You've done the best you can, but now you need to get out.'

Saul's face hardened. He didn't like being told what to do. 'I don't think I asked you to follow me here, did I?' He shook his head, emphatic. 'I'm not leaving until I've spoken to her.'

He could tell Talbot didn't wish to argue, but from the look on his face, Saul suspected his colleague was convinced he had right on his side. He wondered what Talbot would say next to convince him. He didn't have to wait long.

'Even if Dr March wants you to?'

Saul stilled, aware that Talbot was pressing on his Achilles heel. He stared at Talbot, trying to gauge him, not sure if he was telling the truth. If he knew one thing about Blue, it was that she wasn't the type to issue demands. But while the young officer was eloquent and persuasive, Saul was stubborn. 'I have to talk to Smith first.'

'Are you insane? She'll kill you.' Talbot tugged on Saul's shirtsleeve. 'Come on, let's go before the big guns come in.'

Saul was not one for regrets. But in years to come, he would often look back on this moment and wish he had answered differently. 'Go and tell Williams there are four hostages in the ballroom, including two children, with two possible casualties. There are two armed perpetrators with at least four guns between them, possibly more. I've seen seven bodies so far, but I'm certain there are others.'

'What are you going to do?'

'Try and draw her out.'

'How?'

'Go, Alex.'

'Tell me.'

Saul had no intention of telling Talbot anything, and that was his mistake. While he, Saul, did not know another way to live, haunting the grey spaces of moral ambiguity, he did not expect it of others. He'd believed, wrongly, he had the measure of PC Alex Talbot, twenty-three years old, scared of his own shadow and with a phobia of death. But Talbot, inexperienced and impulsive, desirous of earning Saul's respect, had his own ideas.

40

The Lodge on the Loch: 8.59 p.m.

The woman with the gun wanted to punish them.

Christine could see it in the set of her mouth and the way she'd taunted Galen and Tom. It was in every movement of her body, and in her contempt for the dead as she stepped over them to reload, to replace the magazine. Her laugh. Her lipstick. The blood on the hem of her dress. It was in the way she rubbed at her throat, a reminder of what Al had sacrificed to protect her son.

The tears welled. He was a stranger, and he'd done that for them.

She had liked him. Not like that. At least, not yet. But he was funny and kind, and he'd saved her from herself, and now he was gone, and any future possibilities with him. She thought she might be sick.

'You.' The woman jerked her gun at Christine, and pointed in the direction of the man. 'Over there.' The man, whose shotgun was propped against his shoulder, grinned at her. His blue chambray shirt had circles of sweat beneath his arms and his hair was greasy, but with his russet colouring and narrow face, he had a vulpine look about him that reminded her of the fox she'd spotted that morning.

When she'd seen her children that first time, just after their hiding place had been discovered, she'd thought she might burst from it. She'd run to them, not caring about the consequences, and pulled them to her, relishing the feel of them, the familiar scent of their hair, of home. They'd hugged for a few seconds before the woman had slid her gun between them and ordered them apart.

The man pressed his gun against Christine's temple. The metal was still warm from the shots that had killed Al, and she closed her eyes, hot tears trickling from beneath them.

And then Charlie was with her. Her rational brain told her that was impossible, but she caught the scent of his favourite aftershave, pine and sandalwood, although it might have been from the trees outside. A sense of serenity enveloped her, patching up the broken bits of her heart.

She'd read somewhere that fear could sharpen the senses, and Christine was aware of an odd metallic taste in her mouth, and the pinch of her shoe at the heel, and the wet sound of blood still leaking from the wound on Al's thigh. Charlie's voice was murmuring in her ear, telling her to keep breathing and to open her eyes. She did not believe in an afterlife, or the imprint left by souls on the earthly world, or spiritual presences. She knew Charlie's body was in the dirt and the dark. But he was right. If she was to die now, the last faces she would want to see would be those of their children. And so she forced herself to open her eyes.

Galen was shining, a kind of radiance lighting her face. But when she looked more closely, Christine realized it was a trick of the light, and her daughter's skin was sheened with sweat. Tom had cried so much his eyes were swollen. Even now, his bottom lip was wobbling and he began to sob again. Galen's arm was around her brother, although Christine could tell she was leaning on him, and they were standing by a set of heavy drapes drawn across double-height windows.

The woman touched her throat again, her fingers grazing the crucifix she wore, and then pointed her gun at Galen's stomach.

'Tell him to shut his fucking mouth or I'll do it for him.'

'Hush now, Tom. Pretend it's a game.' He cried louder still, and Galen squeezed the boy's shoulder and put her hand across his mouth. 'Stop crying. It's making her cross.'

A wash of blue and red spilled across the flocking on the wall. Christine's heart was running in her chest, harder and faster with every electronic pulse of sound that drifted from the sweeping drive outside. The police were here. She willed them to act.

The woman jerked her weapon at Galen, gesturing at her to move. With her free hand, she dragged Tom by his wrist, tearing a cry from him.

'They'll try to negotiate.' The man's gaze slid to the window, his voice wet and warm, as if his mouth was filled with too much saliva. 'Missy, did you hear me?'

'I heard you.'

Missy. That was her name. It held a femininity that contrasted with her deeds. Christine watched her, incapable of tearing her gaze from this monster in female form. Missy glanced towards the drapes. Those blue and red lights pulsed again, a neon heartbeat. She turned back towards the man. He was talking in short bursts, the machine-gun fire of his words bouncing around the high ceilings and alcoves. Panicked. Agitated. Out of control.

'Calm down.' Missy's voice was amplified in the still of the room but he carried on talking, the vowels and consonants like bullets, ricocheting between the walls, directionless and dangerous. She raised it a notch. 'Fox.' At the sound of his name, the man stopped mid-sentence. The pressure of the gun against Christine's temple eased. The metal had cooled now, and she drew in a breath, grateful for the reprieve, however brief.

'We always knew how this would end.'

Fox staggered forward, a wild light in his eyes. 'Of course we did. But it feels—' He gestured towards the bodies on the floor. 'Not enough.' His eyes travelled to the children. 'Remember what we said? We need something more.' Flicked back towards Missy. 'So they never forget us.'

Missy smiled at Fox, lips shaped like a bent pin, transforming her face into something sly and hard. Christine and the children watched this interplay, fear swelling their lungs.

Tom began to cry again, quiet sobs he tried to muffle with his fist. Galen pressed her own hand against his mouth but it was not enough to evade the spotlight of Missy's attention, a feverish, searching thing.

Missy signalled to Fox, and in one synchronized movement, they'd each flanked a child, their guns bruising the tender hollows of Tom and Galen's cheeks with a dark symmetry.

Charlie was with her again, whispering in her ear to keep calm and breathe. *No heroics, Chrissy, love. Look what happened to Al.*

'Do you *want* to live?' Missy was gazing at Christine, head cocked to one side. The smattering of acne on Galen's face was obscured by the gun. Her daughter's eyes met hers.

'Yes.' Christine was abrupt. Urgent. She buttoned down the panic that was rising in her and tried again, softer this time. 'Yes. Of course I do. We all do.'

Yes. Missy imitated her and Fox laughed. He tried it. *Yes.* With his free hand, he mimed firing a gun at Christine. 'Boom.' His eyes darted back to the window again and he ran his fingers around his collar. A sheen of perspiration gilded his forehead. In contrast, Missy looked cool and fresh in her long-sleeved shift dress.

'At least your mother doesn't have to wash the sweat out of your shirts anymore.' Missy laughed as she said this, and Fox laughed too. 'I wonder if they'll give it back to her, full of bloodstains and bullet holes.' She eyed the drapes. 'Do you think the police marksmen have arrived?'

Christine stilled, drawing in a sharp breath. Her mind raced faster than her heart. Missy and Fox had resigned themselves to death. And she understood what that meant, even as she prayed her children did not.

'Do you want to live?' Missy again. Quizzical. Mocking.

'Yes. Please. *Yes.*'

'Then choose a child to die.'

Tom stiffened as Missy spelled out her demand. Galen squeezed his shoulder to comfort him, to communicate what she knew in her head and her heart. Her mother would never choose between them.

Missy's gun was digging into her cheek. She supposed it must hurt, but she could not feel it. She could not feel very much at all. Galen felt as if she was floating, somewhere distant from here. With dolphins and the cold kiss of the moon, salt spray coating her lips.

Her mother was standing on her own across the ballroom, three dead bodies between them. Death had been between them for months now. Her face looked the same way it had on the day their father died, the same colour as chalk or that disgusting medicine Charlie had taken for all his infections. Christine stumbled, as if she'd lost her balance. 'What do you mean?'

'One child lives. One dies. You decide.' Missy giggled, and Galen wanted to force the gun from her fingers and kill her with it.

Her mother bent at the waist, one hand pressed against her chest, head bowed, and Galen was worried she was about to collapse or suffer a heart attack. Then Christine lifted her face, her gaze flitting between Tom and Galen, and there was something in her expression that Galen was trying to read, trying to understand, but it eluded her.

Tom leaned into her, and God forgive her, she did not want to, but she tried to push him away with her hip, as subtly as she could, because she dare not risk antagonizing them. She didn't want to give them an excuse, no matter how small, to shoot him as they'd shot that man for defending Tom, who'd been defending her. Both of them had been so brave. Galen stuck out her chin, defiant even now. She could be brave too. A single tear tracked down her cheek.

Her mother would never choose.

'Oh, I forgot to say,' said Missy, still smiling. 'If you can't choose between them, we'll kill all three of you instead.'

The ballroom was freezing. Galen's head spun, as if she was buckled into a carousel rotating at vertiginous speed, her mind flitting from one isolated thought to another. Part of her wondered if she was in shock. *Symptoms include feeling cold, clammy skin, weak and rapid pulse, dizziness, shallow breathing and low blood pressure.* She'd learned that during a First Aid class in PSHE with Miss McKenna. Miss McKenna was the head of pastoral care for the lower school. She'd tried to persuade Galen to talk about her grief and loss and fear of the future, but Galen did not like missing her Textiles classes to attend these sessions. She loved sewing and crocheting, and Missy had said she would kill them all if her mother did not choose.

Galen could feel her pulse in her neck. Faster and faster, the beat of a stick on a tin drum. Her mind danced with it, trying to find an answer to this heartbreaking dilemma, swooping and gliding through all permutations until she arrived at the only possible one.

Her mother would never choose between them unless she had to.

Fox cocked his gun and pointed it at her mother. Missy followed suit, directing hers at Tom. A cry spilled from Galen before she could stop it.

At the sound of her daughter's voice, Christine's gaze whipped towards Galen, and they fell into each other's eyes. Galen's lips moved in a soundless plea to her mother, repeating a single syllable over and over again.

Tom wouldn't look at either of them. His palms were flattened across his eyes, the laces of one of his trainers untied, his body wracked with sobs.

God, she loved them both, her mother and her brother.

From the inside pocket of the concierge's suit jacket, a mobile phone began to ring.

From outside, a disembodied voice identifying herself as

Chief Inspector Shona McGill implored them through a tannoy to answer it.

The sounds echoed around the ballroom, silencing them all. Fox gave a shiver of excitement and bent forward, grinning at Missy. 'It's started.'

Missy readjusted her grip on the gun she was holding, slid her free hand into the bag she had stolen from Sally Brown and now wore across her body, and removed the lid of her lipstick before reapplying a coat. She inspected the bottom of the gold tube, where the shade was printed on a perfect scarlet disc. *Bang-Bang*.

Her finger tightened on the trigger and she smiled with her blood-red mouth, eyes half closed in a sort of ecstasy at the prospect of another kill.

'Three.'

Galen, defiant but trembling, flicked her gaze between her brother and mother: Tom, his eyes screwed up now and a thin mewl escaping from him; Christine, shoulders hunched, horrified.

'Two.'

An impossible choice. Unthinkable. But Galen was brave. She was a superhero.

'Wait.'

Her mother's voice sounded too thin, like a piece of Tom's over-stretched plasticine. 'Turn them around. Please. So they're facing the wall.'

Missy considered ignoring the mother's request. But she was not a monster. She grabbed the girl – Galen – and spun her around. Fox did the same to Tommy.

The mobile phone was still ringing.

'Shall we answer it?' said Fox.

Missy considered the question. It would be fun to taunt the police officers, to lead them on a merry dance. But they might distract her with their weasel words, and she was busy here.

'No.'

The children were holding hands, their bond unbreakable even in the face of this ultimate test of sibling rivalry. A flicker of envy surprised her.

Missy had wanted a baby sister. To dress up and cuddle and play with. Her mother and Graham had tried, but it was not to be. She had one stepbrother, who was seven years older than she was, and she was lonely.

One spring evening, when she was almost fourteen, her mother had marched into her bedroom, grimacing like one of those ugly stone statues by her stepfather's pond. Papa was on a night shift. Missy was lying on her bed, watching television.

'Have you had sex with a boy?' No preamble at all.

She sat up, pulling her knees into her chest. 'No. Of course not.'

'You haven't had a period for three months.'

She'd known it had been a while, but not that long. She'd also known it was a bad thing, but she'd buried her head so deeply her mouth was full of sand. 'I know.'

In the humiliating sequence of events that followed, Aurelia had forced her into the toilet and insisted on shoving the pregnancy test stick between her legs. Two lines. Positive.

Missy had never forgotten the sting of her mother's slap across her cheek.

Three weeks later, she had opened her legs again as the

doctor at the clinic had scraped her baby from her. In bed that night, she'd soaked her pillow with tears.

For months afterwards, her mother's lips were thin and white with fury, and she refused to leave Missy unchaperoned in the house. She was forbidden from closing her bedroom door or from leaving the bathroom door unlocked. Her mother reduced her hours at work so she was at home when Missy got in from school, and she declined all evening shifts. She never spoke to her daughter about what happened that day, and, six months later, Graham Baxter moved out. He never touched Missy again.

The boy was crying for what felt like the tenth time. The mobile phone was still ringing. The katydids were almost deafening.

She fired at the floor in front of the children's mother. The children screamed, but Missy did not flinch. 'If you don't choose now, I'll do it for you.'

The woman bowed her head. A few grey hairs were dusting her roots. Missy was close enough to notice she had freckles across her cheekbones, as if one of her Reception pupils had drawn them on her with crayons. The skin around her eyes reminded Missy of scrunched-up paper. She looked old, Missy thought. Defeated.

'What's your name?'

'Christine.'

Both children were crying now as Christine crossed the ballroom floor. She moved awkwardly, as if she was in pain, as if each step cost her, knives to her feet like the mermaid in the fairy tale.

When she was within touching distance, Christine stopped abruptly, both children with their backs to her, their shoulder blades protruding like the angel wings one of them was about to gain.

Their mother turned to Missy in desperation, one last try. 'Will you take me instead?'

Missy shook her head and cocked her gun.

The woman raised her hands in a gesture of surrender. Tears were streaming down her face. She turned back to her children, stood equidistant between the boy and the girl. She closed her eyes. Opened them. Whispered something to herself that Missy and Fox could not hear. Then she lifted her hand and pointed to the back of the head of the child she'd chosen to die.

Missy nodded once, a gesture of grudging respect. She wondered at the reasons. In truth, she had expected Christine to refuse such a cruel choice. *All for one and one for all.* But choose she had. And now Missy had a responsibility to execute that decision.

Neither child was aware who their mother had sentenced to death. And the irony was only the survivor would know. Christine did not want to live if either of her children were dead – yet her instinct had been to preserve life where she could.

Christine's hand did not waver. It did not tremble or falter. Once decided, her aim was true.

She chose Galen.

41

Ten months earlier

The Old Barn, Hawkstone, Essex: 4.17 p.m.

The letter was three weeks old.

The date was typed in the corner underneath the address of the hospital, and while the language was too formal for most thirteen-year-olds to fully understand, Galen Hardwicke was not most thirteen-year-olds. Her mother had told her they were still waiting for the results, but her mother was a liar.

ESSEX HEALTHCARE NHS TRUST
Hawkstone General Hospital,
Middlesex Way,
Hawkstone
HS7 4PQ

1 December 2021

The Old Barn,
Chalfont Avenue,
Hawkstone
HS9 5RW

ALL OF US ARE BROKEN

Department of Paediatric Neurology and Neurosurgery
PRIVATE AND CONFIDENTIAL
Galen Hardwicke

To the parent/guardian of Miss Galen Hardwicke,

The recent blood sample taken to determine the presence of defects in the huntingtin (HTT) gene confirms extra trinucleotide repeats of the specific chemical code in chromosome four. Therefore, as suspected, a diagnosis of Juvenile Huntington's Disease (JHD) is made.

This disease is inherited in an autosomal dominant pattern and most often, children inherit the genetic change repeat from their fathers. Given your family history, we would recommend genetic testing for Galen's younger sibling, if this has not already been undertaken. We would also recommend pre- and post-test counselling.

An appointment letter to the neurology clinic will follow in due course.

Yours sincerely,

Electronically signed by Dr Nigel Eustace
Consultant paediatric neurologist

I was hoping to write to you with better news. I know you'll both be devastated. Small mercies, then, that Tom's test was fast-tracked – and is clear. Official letter to follow. We'll see you in clinic next week or the week after. N.E.

With her father's body cooling in the bed behind her, Galen had read the letter three times before it sank in. She understood all about trinucleotide repeat disorders. When

269

Charlie had first been diagnosed, she'd read everything about them she could lay her hands on. And when she'd first started displaying symptoms of her own, she'd read everything else.

Here, though, was a new truth in black and white.

Except her mother hadn't got around to telling her yet. This made her furious and yet, in some ways, she didn't blame her. How could she begin a conversation about a progressive disease with her teenage daughter? Galen was supposed to be going to parties and sleepovers, experimenting with alcohol and falling in love for the first time. She was supposed to be arguing about her homework and curfews and the length of her shorts, not wondering when she might die. Life expectancy for JHD was approximately fifteen years from first diagnosis, although it could be much less, depending on the rapidity of the onset of symptoms. Much less. Nobody knew, least of all Galen.

In a detached way, she wondered if today would turn out to be the worst day of her life, or whether there would be other days of tragedy and heartbreak that would outdo even this. She didn't think so. It wasn't every day her father died and she witnessed an electronic signature on her own death warrant.

If her father had been alive, she would have talked it through with him. But the only person who could understand the undiluted horror of confronting her own mortality wasn't here anymore. He was lying in the bed behind her, and she hated and loved him in equal measure for passing on this illness and not sticking around to help her deal with it.

On the afternoon she went for her blood test, Galen

missed History, Mathematics and Religious Studies. Her school-friends had asked where she was going, and Galen, trusting, open-hearted and honest, and a girl who had not yet discovered the cloaking power of the white lie, told them the truth.

Her mother took her for a milkshake afterwards and they'd watched the rain roll down the windows and the sea crash into the bay. Talk had turned to her brother.

'If the result is positive, I'm not sure we should tell Tom. What do you think?' Her mother had stirred three sugars into her tea, even though she had given it up five years ago.

'I don't know.' Galen hadn't thought about it, but now she had, she said, 'Don't you think he deserves to know?'

'It just feels like another weight on his shoulders.'

Galen had wanted to shout, 'What about the weight on my shoulders?' But she had made the right noises in the right places, and she had parcelled it up and put it away.

Her mother had talked a bit more about taking Tom for genetic testing, and although Galen was a mature thirteen, she did not yet understand that her mother's coping mechanism was to deal in practicalities. She did not recognize that her mother, in her own understated way, was devastated by this tragic turn of events, and if she just kept talking and planning logistics, she could keep running from her own darkest imaginings, that her family of four would become one.

When Galen had finished her drink, and eaten the whipped cream and cherry with a long-handled spoon, and her mother had asked her how she was feeling about everything for the nine-hundredth time, all she could dredge up was, 'Fine.'

It had felt too far away, as if it was happening to somebody else in a parallel life.

Later, when they'd got home from the clinic, and Tom was playing Lego, and she could smell lasagne cooking in the oven for dinner, she'd slipped away for five minutes to spend time with her father.

'It's not your fault,' she'd said, resting her head on his chest as he lay prone in bed. 'It's one of those things.' But they both knew it was much more complicated than that. Or was it? When she thought about it, it was actually pretty simple.

Because sitting in this overheated room three weeks later, with the letter in her hand, breathing in the spores of her father's death, Galen's childhood fell into the Before and After, and she remembered that day by the sea, with the milkshake and the waves, and she was struck by a profound truth.

She and Tom were different now. They would always be different. Fate had thrown the dice and Tom had won this game with the highest of stakes without even knowing he was playing it.

That truth felt too amorphous, too vast to distil into platitudes that felt hollow or lacking, but there was a courage in simplicity, and a need to make herself understood.

Her mother would tell Tom that Galen had inherited the same genetic disease as her father, and that Tom had not. Lucky Tom with his curls and his football boots and his love of Minecraft. She would keep it factual and to the point, perhaps talk about medical treatment and progression. But no mention of death. No room for self-pity.

ALL OF US ARE BROKEN

But if Galen had been asked to explain it to her brother, she would have summed up the news in a much starker way. 'I've got the same disease that killed Daddy, and it's going to kill me too.'

42

The Lodge on the Loch: 9.01 p.m.

At the sound of another gunshot and the high-pitched cries of children, PC Alex Talbot sat up, unlaced one of his boots and hurled it at the closed door of the grand ballroom. He did not think about what he was doing, other than in the most superficial and instinctive of ways, and by the time Saul grabbed his arm to stop him, a scowl on his face, it was too late.

As acts of heroism went, there was something almost laughable about the stupidity of this one. Talbot gazed at his shoeless foot. Socks were a ridiculous construct, he decided. And then wondered how he could be thinking about socks at a time like this. It was odd how the mind disassociated itself during moments of fear. But then he felt Saul squeezing his bicep, nails digging into the flesh. Talbot turned to him, a questioning look on his face. With his other hand, Saul pressed a finger to his lips and pointed to the ballroom. Throwing his boot may have been stupid but it had served its purpose.

Less than five seconds later, the long nose of a rifle appeared in the crack of the door. Saul could see a flash of blue shirt, and caught the rush of sweat and blood. Dashiell Lloyd, no doubt about it.

'Who's there?' Lloyd sounded as if his mouth was full of

too much tongue. As he cleared his saliva, it made a sucking noise like a plughole.

Talbot paled and Saul, concerned he might fall to pieces under the pressure, murmured to him, 'Keep it together.' Both officers needed their wits about them. For all his bravado, Saul sensed a wariness in Lloyd, who'd been sharp enough to evade capture so far, and was likely on alert for trickery.

Lloyd opened the door a little wider and repeated his question. Saul and Talbot exchanged glances. The gunman was a loose cannon. If they handled this poorly, it would be over before it had begun. Talbot's breathing quickened, alarming Saul. A natural burst of adrenaline or the start of a panic attack? Saul wasn't sure but he understood it. His own hands were shaking and he forced them into stillness. His mouth dried. He was teetering on the edge of the precipice. Inch backwards to safety or let himself fall? He took a breath and stepped off.

'Hello, Dashiell. Where's Melissa?'

A silence from behind the door, as if the man had been expecting anything but that. Saul's chest felt tight, as if, on taking that breath, he'd forgotten how to expel it. Lying side by side with Talbot, his left shoulder glanced Alex's right. The young officer felt so rigid, so coiled with tension, that Saul was worried he might break cover like a greyhound out of the trap.

Lucky sixpence or bad penny? The coin was still spinning.

The crack in the door widened further still. Lloyd stood there, a gun in each hand, pointing in their direction. Five seconds to end a life, for this killer to depress the trigger and take from them what he'd taken from so many others that day. Talbot bent his head, but Saul met Lloyd's stare. If he was going to die, he would do it with his eyes open.

Lloyd took a couple of steps towards them, the barrel of the gun so close to Saul he could smell hot steel. But he was defiant, even in the face of death. He prayed that Talbot would not react, would do nothing that might tip this finely balanced moment of tension into tragedy.

Lloyd's gaze flicked between them and then he pressed his weapon into the cowering Talbot's shoulder. Time was suspended. Saul tried to swallow but he could not rid himself of the lump at the back of his throat. He could not breathe.

Lloyd spat on the floor. 'Get up.'

The anticlimax of it almost choked Saul. Talbot bounced to his feet, adrenaline making him unpredictable, frayed around the edges. His socked toe landed in Lloyd's saliva, but he was so keyed up, he didn't notice. Saul, knowing they had no choice but to do as Lloyd ordered, was a different beast, hyper-vigilant and exacting. He moved in a constrained manner, trying to think his way out, trying to buy them some time. But they were not dead yet. That was something.

Lloyd jerked his guns towards the half-open door, and the two officers entered the ballroom.

Three casualties, probably dead. Three hostages, two of them children. Two shooters. Six guns, two on the floor. Two exits. Eight windows.

Saul's unconscious brain had assessed the situation before he was even aware he was doing it. On seeing the victims and their broken bodies consumed by the creeping tide of a blood-slick, Talbot's face collapsed into misery.

Melissa Smith had one gun pointed in the direction of the children, and one at them. She relaxed her aim when Lloyd followed them in. When she raised her eyebrows, the resemblance to Detective Inspector Angus O'Neill was striking.

'*Polizei*,' said Lloyd, snuffling and grunting like a farmyard pig.

The change in Smith was abrupt. Her face hardened until she became someone else. 'My stepfather was a police officer. He's dead now.'

'We know,' said Saul. He gave her a level look. 'Was that you, Melissa?'

'He deserved it.' Her voice was clipped. 'Most police officers I've had the displeasure of knowing do.'

Saul glanced at Talbot. He was white-faced and trembling, but his shoulders were back and he appeared more composed than earlier. *Good lad.* The next part of their conversation would require delicate handling.

'He's not the only member of your family in the police force, is he?'

Smith, who had been picking at her nail polish with her teeth, stopped what she was doing, her thumb in her mouth, still holding her gun. 'What's that supposed to mean?'

He stared at her, determined to relay the message he'd travelled hundreds of miles to deliver. 'Your biological father. He's a detective inspector, I believe.' Smith narrowed her eyes. Saul was aware that Talbot had turned towards him and imagined his expression of surprise, but he would not look away from Smith. He held out his hands, so she could see them. 'I've got a letter for you. In my pocket. Your father asked me to give it you.' He waited a beat. 'Shall I get it?'

Melissa Smith turned from him without a word, walked over to the teenage girl and pressed the barrel of her stepfather's pistol into the base of her neck. Two words drifted across the ballroom, like the whisper of the music that had filled this vast space in happier times. 'Goodnight, Galen.' The older female hostage – Saul had been so intent on Smith he'd barely noticed her, but she was standing alone by a window – fell to her knees, a sob escaping from her.

Smith had a wild and uncontained air about her. He'd witnessed this once or twice before in those whose morality switch had been damaged or broken. Moments later, without fail, they'd committed some dark and terrible deed.

Saul didn't know what he'd expected but it wasn't this. He had set the rabbit running and would give his own life to turn back the clock. He'd shocked her, he could see that now. Unsettled and shaken her. His arrogance had led him to misjudge the situation and now a young girl would die because of what he'd done. For the first time in his life, a kind of panicked apathy seized him.

But before Saul had time to draw his next breath, he registered a blur of movement on his left. Talbot, modest and unassuming, was sprinting across the ballroom towards Smith and the girl, running harder and faster than he'd ever run before. In a twist of irony, Lloyd was bent over the holdall, searching for a length of rope to tie them up, and briefly distracted. He could have – *should* have – used their handcuffs against them, but he'd had other things on his mind. Two guns lay by the holdall on the floor. Finally, thought Saul, a chink in their armour.

But Lloyd was the type of man who had brutalized others since he was a boy. In his peripheral vision, he caught Talbot's sudden movement, and from the bag, he withdrew a six-inch survival knife made from carbon steel.

Everything slowed down.

Missy. Lloyd called out her name, and for the second time, Galen's life was spared by a beat in time as Smith turned to him, a questioning expression in her eyes, and then understanding dawned as Talbot ran at her, and Lloyd moved with the fluid precision of an athlete.

In his file, which Saul had read from cover to cover on the train earlier that day, it had said that Dashiell Lloyd had spent his formative years with his family in the countryside, hunting and fishing, firing arrows and throwing knives into the wounded bark of trees. He'd once impaled a neighbour's hand on a fence for six hours because she'd complained his football had broken her window. An accident, he'd said, on both counts, despite his uncannily accurate aim.

The blade – serrated, illegal – struck PC Alex Talbot in the gap between his body armour and his neck with such force and velocity, it ruptured the left carotid artery, inflicting cataclysmic damage.

Talbot spun, full of grace, before tilting backwards. His hands flew up, as if he was fighting to regain his balance, and all would be well if he could just stop himself from falling. In his haste to leave Midtown that morning, Talbot had not tried on his stab-proof vest until it was too late to swap it for a smaller size, and all that he'd feared – pain, bleeding out, his own death in the line of duty – had come to pass.

In some faraway corner of his brain, Talbot was aware of the sound of a woman screaming. The timbre of her voice reminded him of his mother. She played bridge on Monday evenings. He hoped his sister was home by the time the police knocked on their door.

But even as he confronted his own mortality, he reached

out a hand to Saul, as if to reassure him. And then his fingers were closing around the knife, trying to withdraw it, to rid himself of the taint of Dashiell Lloyd. But his strength was failing him, and the last sensation he was aware of was the glance of skin against metal, and no regrets.

Talbot's act of bravery had saved the life of Galen Hardwicke, and while he did not – could not – know it, perhaps, in some deeper way, he felt it. As his knees went from under him, he smiled at Saul for the last time, and that smile was a shining light, a talisman against the encroaching darkness. He was dead by the time he hit the floor.

The coin stopped spinning.

Saul shouted Talbot's name, the white heat of fury setting him alight – no space for cool-headed logic, but a need to burn. He flew at Lloyd, not thinking about his own vulnerabilities, but driven by instinct, by a need to inflict his own kind of vengeance and pain.

Lloyd laughed as their bodies collided, relishing it, and Smith fired at Saul, but missed him and shattered one of the windows. She would not make the mistake of missing him again.

Saul could feel the weight of gunmetal between them as they grappled on the floor. The children were screaming now too, but he tuned them out, his head filled with images of Lloyd's body in the mortuary drawer.

And Talbot, lying under a sheet while the pathologist tracked the trajectory of the blade.

Guilt, a new friend, slung an arm around Saul's shoulders, but he pushed it away for now. All he could think of was Lloyd, and how he wanted him dead, and he, Saul, with his anger and his pain, was heavier and stronger and fitter, and when his fingers closed around the trigger, he fired it, the bullet tearing into Lloyd's stomach.

But Saul had made a mistake he had sworn he never would, allowing emotion to cloud the rational, detached part of him. With Lloyd the focus of his fury, he had forgotten, just for a moment or so, about O'Neill's daughter.

But that was all it took. Saul felt a pressure at the base of his spine, and then a fire was raging inside him, taking hold. He felt wetness from the wound, and a weakening he had no control over, however much he resisted, and when he looked up, he could see only blue.

Noise. Everywhere. He rolled onto his back, Lloyd's pistol still in his hand, but no strength in him at all. Melissa Smith was standing above him, gun raised, and she was going to kill him.

'Your father loves you,' he said, because that was all he had left. 'He wants me to bring you home.'

Melissa Mary Smith – Missy to her husband – stopped to listen, just for a second. Ever since she was nine years old, she'd wanted her father to love her again. The police officer's eyes were closed and his skin was pale, and she wondered about the letter in his pocket, and whether he was telling the truth, or if it was a trick to reel her in, and then he would shoot her, like she'd shot him. With her gun trained on his head, she dug into his pocket, and there it was, just as he'd said. An envelope addressed to her, a letter and a photograph.

In fifteen years, her father's handwriting hadn't changed.

Fox said her name, soft as the rain that was falling outside, and there was blood on his lips, at both corners of his mouth. She retrieved the gun from the officer and placed it in Fox's hand. 'It's okay,' she said and sat on the floor next to him, lifting his head onto her lap.

Missy watched the blue lights catch the crystals on the chandeliers. In one hand, she held a photograph of a girl with a flower, and she stroked Fox's hair with the other, her own gun resting on his chest.

She thought, if it was still all right with him, that she would like to see her father again.

Six specialist firearms officers in full tactical dress entered the ballroom. She watched them move in formation towards her, weapons poised. Methodical. Determined. They were shouting at her to put down her weapon, and Fox said something too, although she couldn't hear him.

The noise, always too loud for Missy, became deafening.

She laid her gun on the floor next to Fox, and rose slowly, her hands flattened in a gesture of surrender. It was right they were here. She had done some awful things today, and even though she felt no remorse for the atrocities she'd committed, she could recognize, in an abstract way, that what she had done deserved punishment. The firearms officers surrounded them, but she wasn't afraid anymore. She was going to see her father, and that was enough for now.

Missy did not feel the bullet until it had entered the back of her skull, and even then, the starburst of pain that followed was as fleeting as the hope she'd allowed herself to nurture. Behind her, Fox, who had mustered the last of his strength to close his finger on the trigger and perform what he'd believed was a final act of love for his wife, had no time to put down the gun, before he, too, was shot in the head.

ALL OF US ARE BROKEN

In the last seconds of her life, Missy was transfixed by colours and flashes of light, and then she saw nothing but the glare of dead stars, winking out one by one until all that was left was ash.

At last, the katydids stopped singing.

43

The Lodge on the Loch: 10.37 p.m.

Blue was standing in the rain when they brought Saul out.

The paramedics had stabilized him, but he'd lost too much blood, and a doctor would later sit her down in one of the hospital's family rooms, and tell her they didn't know if he would walk again because the bullet had grazed his spinal cord, and she would tell them they didn't know Saul Anguish if they believed that.

As she'd sat in that room, with its benign decor that sharpened bad news, not softened it, the irony didn't escape her. A family room for a man with no family.

When she'd heard those gunshots, a part of her she couldn't explain had known Saul was hurt. It was an unthinking kind of knowing, the same kind that told her how to breathe or jump, and she'd stood outside the hotel, cold rain leaching the colour from her skin and her hair. From her life. A female paramedic had seen her distress and thrown her a safety rope.

'A minute,' she'd said with brisk compassion as they'd carried him from the ballroom and loaded him into the ambulance. 'No more.' *Thank you.* His eyes were closed – they'd sedated him – and he was so pale she couldn't make out the veins in his lids. His lips held a bluish tinge. With his mess of white-blond hair, he looked translucent, as if he'd been rubbed out from the world. Sometimes, with the shadows cast by his past and his obsession with collecting, she thought that might be true.

A minute to say godspeed. A minute to find his evidence bags filled with secrets, and to hide them away.

DC Eliot Williams went with him in the ambulance. For once, there had been no sarcasm or recriminations. There would be time for that later. He'd hugged Blue, an uncharacteristic gesture, and she'd surprised herself by hugging him back. 'You'll stay?' he'd said, standing under one of the forensics tents in that damp October night, and she didn't need to ask what he meant. 'Of course I'll stay.'

In the end, they'd all stayed. The officers from the Strategic Firearms Unit, and the detectives from Police Scotland's North division, Chief Inspector Shona McGill and the other commanders, and they'd formed a guard of honour as the sun rose on a new day, a ball of fire in the sky, and they brought PC Alex Talbot's body out of that hotel.

They stayed until they brought out all of the bodies, every last one.

Three hundred miles away, an older man, his shoulders bent now from grief and failure, made himself a cup of tea in the disloyal light of dawn.

In all his years as a police officer, Angus O'Neill had never stopped being surprised by the way the world continued to turn when one's own, or those of the victims' families, had stopped.

It had been a difficult twenty-four hours, and today would

be more difficult still. A young officer under his command was dead, another badly injured. He felt nothing about the murder of Baxter, the colleague who had stolen his first wife and daughter, but his feelings about Melissa were far more complicated.

Several newspapers were scattered across his kitchen table. He hadn't slept, and in the cold morning air, he had walked to the newsagents on the corner and bought a copy of every one.

His daughter's face stared up at him from the front pages.

The headlines were typical newspaper fodder, screaming their outrage at the events of the previous day. Rightly so. For now, they focused on 'Missy' and 'Fox' and their killing spree, their victims and the terrible ordeal of the Hardwicke family, but in the coming days, their attention would turn to him. It was no less than he deserved.

His finger traced the newsprint, the dark sheet of his daughter's hair.

When Melissa was six, she had appeared in her first ballet show. He still remembered her clumsy movements, the out-of-time dance steps, her extravagant wave to the audience which had sent a ripple of laughter across the theatre.

When he and her mother had collected her from the lobby at the end of the evening, she had run to them, her cheeks flushed with excitement, strands of hair escaping from her bun.

He had hoisted her onto his shoulders and carried her, triumphant, back to the car. As they had walked down the night-time streets, slick with rain, she had leaned down, her breath sweet against his ear.

'I'm going to be famous one day, Daddy. Just you wait and see.'

PART THREE

THREE MONTHS LATER

44

St Mary's Church, Midtown-on-Sea: 11.27 a.m.

Detective Constable Saul Anguish was dressed in a black suit and tie for the memorial service at the church stitched into cliffs that overlooked the bay.

It was the kind of morning that was sharpened by frost, the sky filled with flurries that eddied and whirled with such intent it was impossible to tell where the clouds ended and the snow began.

The congregation did not tarry outside St Mary's, a white clapboard structure with a tall grey spire that appeared to be reaching for a blessing from the heavens. April might be the cruellest month, but January held a bitterness all of her own, freezing the wellspring of hope and its tentative shoots. Men and women – snowdrops in their lapels or gathered into small bouquets for this special ceremony of thanksgiving – stamped their feet against the hard ground and rubbed their gloved hands together, the weather in sombre tribute to their fallen colleague.

Saul had left an hour ago, following the path from the coastguard's lookout, the salt marshes brittle with ice. It had taken him longer than he'd expected, even though he'd used his cane, and he cut a lonely figure as he limped through the graveyard enclosed by a white picket fence and long grasses that bowed when the wind rushed through them.

With his bare hand, he stopped to brush snow from Alex Talbot's headstone. Not for the first time, he wished he could remake the events of that day, to live it again but to choose differently. His skin burned with cold but he rested it on the granite until he could bear it no longer, and only then did he allow himself to go inside.

The church was full, standing room only, but murmuring his apologies, Saul slipped down a side aisle and into the seat that Blue had saved for him. He was healing, but it was painful to stand for long periods of time. Next week, he would return to work on light duties, although Detective Inspector Angus O'Neill would no longer be there. He had resigned in the immediate aftermath of the shootings, although he'd visited Saul in hospital, thanking him for passing on his letter and apologizing for risking Saul's life. For the loss of Talbot's. He had not asked Saul what Melissa had said to him in those last moments, and while Saul had wanted to offer him some words of comfort, he could not remember and would not lie.

'I thought you weren't coming.' Blue nudged him, the Order of Service held loosely in her hand. Saul glanced at the photograph on the front, an officer in his uniform, proud, smiling, neat and tidy.

'I wouldn't miss it.'

In a month's time, Saul would be wearing this suit again to collect, on behalf of Talbot, the Chief Constable's Commendation, posthumously awarded to the young police constable for the outstanding bravery he'd shown in saving the life of Galen Hardwicke. Saul, too, would collect his own medal for courage. Because of his fearlessness, and his fascination with bees, Callum Brown, the boy who'd been shot in the stomach, had survived the terrible events of that day. His father had written to Saul, a heartfelt letter of thanks. Callum's recovery would be slow, but he would recover, physically, at least. Smith's pupil – Katie Andrews – had not been so fortunate.

Music swelled in the church by the sea. Outside, the guillemots cut through the blizzard, their wings like blades of darkness, rending the sky. The vicar's voice rose and fell as he shared stories with the congregation about the officer's music-filled childhood, his school days and his career in the police force. He had recently been transferred, the vicar said, his future bright as the sun.

In the hollow hours of the night, Saul would wake, sweating and wild-eyed, reliving the last moments of Alex Talbot's life. He blamed himself for the young man's death, and the guilt ate into him, infecting the part of his soul that was morally sound and righteous, feeding the monster he'd struggled to contain since boyhood until it grew into something grotesque and savage, bloated with rage.

Blue tried to understand, but she was dealing with demons of her own. As Saul thrashed in his nightmares, her cool hands calmed him, but she had not been there with blade and blood. She was lost herself, haunted by the memories of that night, the bite of ties that bound her wrists, the weight of Lynch's body on her much slighter one, and the knowledge that even though she had resisted, even though she had fought against him with all she had, it hadn't been enough. His strength, his superior physicality had allowed him to overpower her, and she despised herself for her own weaknesses.

At first, she'd hated Lynch with a ferocity that stunned her, unable to shake the horror – the injustice – of the act of war he'd wreaked upon her, but now she felt nothing at all. Saul and Blue, lost to the dark. Him freighted with the guilt of Talbot's death, and her cursed by the memories of her assault. As each day passed, she watched in fear as he slipped further into purgatory, and she along with him.

Police officers from Essex, and the neighbouring forces of Kent and Suffolk, had crowded into the church to honour the life of one of their own. He saw DC Eliot Williams, and the bent head of O'Neill, their voices joined in a chorus of 'Amazing Grace'. Saul did not – could not – sing. He closed his eyes and listened, and thought about what he'd become, the broken parts of him.

One by one, mother, sister and best friend stood at the front of the church, their voices buckling under the burden of their sorrow. They, too, told stories from his life and wept at the cruelty of his death.

The vicar, solid and comforting, read from Psalm 51, Verse 17, 'The sacrifices of God are a broken spirit: a broken and a contrite heart, O God, thou wilt not despise,' and then it was over, and they were leaving the church, and Saul, who was not a man of faith, became inflamed with sudden anger at his words.

'What does God know about contrition? A broken spirit?' His voice rose, drawing glances from some of the departing congregation.

The vicar, who was standing by the church's heavy wooden doors, pressed his hand onto Saul's wrist to calm him. 'It's not about God, young man, but us. Repentance is remembering our salvation comes from His steadfast love and mercy, even when we have sinned. It is turning towards God without resistance or resentment, and asking for forgiveness. It is not a broken heart, but a renewed one.'

As they walked down the steps of St Mary's, Saul missed his footing and stumbled, and Blue slipped her hand into his, squeezing it as tightly as she dared.

'All of us are broken, Saul, but it's how we put ourselves back together again that matters most of all.'

The snow was falling harder and faster now, obscuring the headstones and the delicate lipped flowers of the winter honeysuckle the vicar's wife had planted the previous year. Keen to avoid the worsening weather, the mourners hurried to their waiting cars. Within minutes, the churchyard was empty.

By the bench that overlooked the bay, Saul said goodbye to Blue. Snowflakes shimmered in her fringe, a crown of tiny diamonds. He loved her then, with her sea-mist eyes, and hair the colour of summer skies. But when he tried to imagine their life beyond this moment, everything felt off-kilter and uncertain, subject to vagaries beyond his control. She was riding her motorbike and offered him a lift, but he told her he'd walk across the marshland, back to the coast-guard's lookout.

'It hurts though, doesn't it? Aren't you supposed to be resting?'

And his silence told her what she'd suspected. That he sought penance in his pain.

She looked into him then, and for a beat in time, they acknowledged what they had done, but she did not speak of it and neither did he. They would never speak of it. Not because they were remorseful or ashamed – both had glimpsed the darkness in each other's souls – but because Blue did not want to be reminded of her own fragilities, and Saul loved her too much to do that.

As he navigated the path through the cemetery, towards the salt marshes beyond, Saul leaned on his cane. The end was tipped with silver, and while not visible to the naked eye, forensic testing in a laboratory setting would reveal specks of blood in the grooves where metal met wood.

By the time he'd been discharged from hospital, Blue had cleared his cottage of the remnants of the chicks, scrubbing away the smell of decay until her hands were chapped and bleeding, but, on his first night home, Saul had asked her again what had happened, and this time, she had told him the truth.

A handful of weeks later, when winter had taken hold and the world was turned inwards, Blue borrowed her mother's car and drove Saul to a house they had been to once before. Again, it was during the secret hours of the night, and again, they had moved between the shadows, connected in perpetuity by the blackest of arts.

Blue chose the country lanes, away from cameras and traffic, the engine muffled by a storm they'd been waiting for days to arrive. Saul had carried a cardboard box on his lap and his cane by his side. Both wore gloves and overalls and both had covered their hair, those distinctive strands of white-blond and blue. They didn't talk much. The odd word here and there. And then, while the moon was low and hidden, and the rain played percussion on the rooftops and the roads, Saul held out his hand and Blue, his willing companion, followed him into darkness, leaning in to the power and pleasure of vengeance.

His cleaner found him the next day. His face was buried in his pillow and the back of his hair was matted with blood, although, according to the pathologist who carried out his post-mortem, that blow had been designed to subdue rather than kill him.

His hands and feet were bound, and when they rolled him over, there were multiple lacerations to his chest, cheeks, lips and eyelids, consistent with the beak of a large seabird.

Cause of death was takotsubo cardiomyopathy, a weakening of the heart muscle induced by fear.

Saul limped across the marshes, the bay filled with a swirling maelstrom of snowflakes that obscured the lighthouse and the estuary beyond, a thousand feathers tipped from the clouds. For a moment, a shaft of light appeared on the horizon, a pulse from the beacon that steered the ships home. *All of us are broken, Saul, but it's how we put ourselves back together again that matters most of all.*

Inside his suit pocket, he carried one of two bloodstained quills from the wing of an adult gull. It had seemed a fitting tribute today. He'd found them on the bedroom floor after their victim had tried and failed to fight off his attackers. Blue had the other one. For her own collection. Perhaps it was time for them to start one of their own. He would ask her. After all, they were bound together now, not by life but by death.

He leaned his cane against a fence that was falling down and flung out his arms, head thrown back to the sky, a stirring of . . . not joy, exactly, but a sense that reparation had been made, the scales of justice restored to their rightful balance.

His Order of Service drifted quietly into the grasses;

discarded, unimportant now. It would remain there, dampened by snow, until the photograph of the police officer had softened and blurred, and all that remained was a memory in printed ink and shadow.

A Memorial Service of Thanksgiving for the life of Detective Constable Douglas Lynch.

45

'Have you got a blanket?'

Galen rolled her eyes at her mother's question, but Tom pulled Charlie's favourite tartan rug over his sister's lap and tucked it around her legs. Then he beamed at her and shouldered her rucksack, which contained her camera, a bottle of water, her medication and special notebook. It was 398 days since she'd last seen her father.

In the immediate aftermath of the shootings, all three of them had given witness statements to the police – and there would be more interviews and more questions from the coroner and the procurator fiscal next month – but for now, the sun was rising, and so were the tides.

Christine pushed Galen's wheelchair across the wet sand of Chanonry Point, a slender spit of land between Fortrose and Rosemarkie. The seaweed stuck to its wheels, and every now and then, Tom stopped to pull it off, laughing as he chased his mother with ribbons of algae, squealing when she chased him back. It was out of season and they had the beach to themselves for now. Galen had been resistant to using a chair, but she was tired at the moment, and her worsening symptoms – a lack of co-ordination

297

and inability to judge distances – had made the decision for her.

The Moray Firth held the palette of a storm, slate grey and bruised. Christine fussed over her daughter, but she needn't have worried. Galen's cheeks were flushed with joy, not cold, and her eyes were fixed on the water.

She had not returned to school.

In the hours that followed their horrific ordeal, she had found the courage to confide in her mother about the loneliness of losing her father and being diagnosed with a life-limiting illness.

'I don't want to go back to St Agnes's,' she had said.

'Why not?'

'Because the girls there think death is catching.'

And then, relieving herself of the burden she'd carried on her own for too long, she'd told her mother about Gabrielle's messages, the social isolation, the clods of earth she had found in her locker. How when she'd confided in one friend about her genetic testing, Gabrielle had found out, and she'd screamed and run away from her.

Christine, white-lipped and reeling, had promised her she would never have to go back to that school again.

Galen had laughed then, and said if Gabrielle was stupid enough to believe that death was catching, imagine how freaked out she'd be when she heard about her part in the shootings. Christine had found an odd sort of comfort in that. In spite of everything, her daughter could still poke fun at herself.

And now – three months on – Galen was still laughing. Next week, she was going for afternoon tea and a manicure with Isla. Her friend had written a heartfelt note of apology to Galen. She, too, was leaving St Agnes's at the end of term.

As for Daphne and Frank, Christine would never forgive them for the way they'd treated Galen during that strained lunch when the family had stopped off to tell them about her diagnosis in the months after Charlie had died. If Tom wanted to spend time with his grandparents, she wouldn't stop him, but it felt freeing to know she would never have to see them again.

A small crowd had begun to gather at the water's edge. A man and his dog, who sat patiently and watched. An older married couple, who bickered about sandwiches, but never stopped talking to each other, smiling and affectionate, a love as comfortable as they were. Binoculars and flasks of tea and telescopic lenses.

Tom was collecting pebbles, smooth, flat ones. He waved to his mother and sister, and they waved back. Or tried to, in Galen's case. Sometimes her body refused to behave in the way that she wanted it to. She watched him, trying to skim his stones across the water, laughing as the spume licked his shoes. Galen loved Tom with a fierce, protective love. She did not begrudge him his good health, but revelled in it.

When she was gone, her mother and Tom could start again.

Christine hated it when Galen talked like that, but it was more than a year since her diagnosis and its progress had been swift and devastating. She did not want to die – she was scared of being alone in a coffin – but she was a pragmatist too. That's why they were here, on this desolate stretch of beach. Before the shootings, before the darkness that had come calling, this had always been a pilgrimage. Galen's last trip.

Her condition was aggressive. In a matter of months, it would rob her of her ability to speak and to swallow. Of all cognitive, physical and emotional function. No two cases were the same. If a disease had been crafted by the devil, this was it. She had wanted to come to Chanonry Point while she was still well enough to savour the memories. If the dolphins didn't come today, she wouldn't get a chance to see them again.

Galen scanned the horizon, but the waves were choppy, and it was difficult to tell the difference between the ink of shadows and a sleek dorsal fin.

Despite the brightening sky, the wind had bite to it. Christine was worried about Galen getting too cold, and Tom's hands were chapped from the sand and salt water. The beach was a bleak and windswept place, just a car park and a couple of picnic benches and the lighthouse keeping watch over the narrow inlet.

And then a woman cried out, pointing, and they followed the direction of her arm until a dark speck was visible in the distance – two, three, four of them – and they burst from the water, their grey flukes shining in the early-morning sun.

Galen felt a surge of great joy, of hope, at the sight of these majestic creatures. According to her book, bottlenose dolphins belonged to the genus *Tursiops*, which first appeared in the fossil record five million years ago. At the age of thirteen, that number felt too big for her to quantify, but they would still be here when she was worm food in the ground, and that was good enough for Galen.

Her mother chose her.

While some children might have struggled with this knowledge, or allowed it to destroy them, Galen held it close, embraced it. She loved her mother for it, more than she ever had. When Melissa Smith had put Christine in that impossible position, forcing her to decide between her children, there was only ever one choice, and Galen had mouthed it to her mother again and again: *Me.*

And her mother had listened.

Galen's illness. Her father's death. The incessant bullying at school. The barrel of a gun pressed against her head, as cold and hard as life itself. These things had happened to Galen. She had not happened to them.

By listening to her daughter's voice, by respecting her courage and grace and humanity, her mother had gifted Galen a sense of autonomy, a control over her life that had been lacking for so long. By accepting her sacrifice, by acknowledging her love for her family, she had handed the power back to her daughter. For once, Galen had made a choice of her own, the driver of her destiny. So much had been taken from her. But even in the face of death, there were stubborn signs of life.

Six or seven dolphins were swimming close to the water's edge, chasing the salmon in. One of them breached the waves and its aerial acrobatics made Galen laugh. Christine laughed too, and reached for her daughter's hand. Tom was tearing across the beach, giddy with the joy of being outside, made wild by the wind. She could smell the salt on the air, feel the breeze lifting her hair. Above her head, the kittiwakes and auks wheeled and danced. A seal bobbed in the distance, sleek and watchful. And there, on that windswept peninsula, a girl found she remembered what it was to be happy.

Later that night, when they'd returned to their cottage, Galen heard Christine talking on the phone.

Tom had been asleep for hours, exhausted by the fresh air and too many chips from a cafe they'd found along the coast, but Galen could not settle. Her strength, as well as her appetite, had left her, and she lay still, listening to the waves as they lapped beneath her window, and her mother's murmuring through the mouth of the open door.

With his permission, the police had passed on a number for Al's brother, and Christine had called him in the aftermath of the shootings. Despite her nervousness, she was determined to explain to him what his older sibling had sacrificed for her family, and how brave he had been.

Those calls, occasional at first, had become fortnightly – and then weekly – occurrences. Recently, her mother had been talking to him most days, and he had arranged for them to visit his home this week while they were in Scotland. He lived on a smallholding with hens, a goat and two bad-tempered cats, and he'd promised Galen and Tom could collect eggs.

Galen could not make out much of tonight's conversation, and part of her was glad. She knew it would be sad because of the way Al had died and the fact they were back here, near the place it had happened, and she could not face any more sadness, not at the moment. But an hour or so had passed, and her mother was still talking, and once or twice, in spite of everything, she heard her laugh. He was a widower too, her mother said. His name was Stuart, and he had a son, a boy of eleven.

Galen smiled to herself in the darkness.

Her eyes were heavy now, but she did not want to close them yet. The police had spoken to her mother about trauma counselling for their family, but she was not ready to relive the horrors she'd witnessed, let alone talk about them. It was too soon. Tom had started seeing someone a month ago and his nightmares had almost stopped, but Galen knew the darkness that had taken up residence inside her could not be vanquished by a therapist asking questions, however kindly meant. In any case, sometimes her mind wouldn't work in the way she wanted it to, and she groped for simple words that had once formed without thought or conscious effort. Today was a good day and she did not want to sully it with the blood-soaked memories of what had been. Instead she thought about the dolphins, somewhere out there in those watery depths, navigating their way through the shadows and the murk, always knowing how to find their way home.

She loved it here in this whitewashed cottage in a place called the Black Isle. Her mother had found it online last week, when the doctor had agreed that Galen could take her trip, and rented it for the night. Her bedroom had photographs of birds on the walls, and a square mullioned window that gazed across this austere body of water.

After her mother had helped her into bed and kissed her goodnight, Galen had asked her to leave the curtains open and sit with her for a few moments. The girl had hardly spoken about what they had endured during that October evening, but something compelled her to raise it now.

'That night,' she said, 'I thought she was going to kill me.'

Her mother had smoothed her daughter's hair from her face with loving fingers. Despite the coolness of the room, Galen's skin was glazed with sweat. Christine slid her hand beneath Galen's neck and held a glass of water to her lips. 'I thought I was going to lose you.' She shook her head, trying to dislodge the memory. 'No mother should have to make that choice. I did it because I trusted in you and what you were trying to tell me. You're braver than anyone I know, Galen Hardwicke. Daddy would have been so proud of you.'

'I'm not brave, Mum. I'm scared. Of the future. Of what I'll become.'

Christine had not replied immediately, the room silent apart from the distant scream of a seagull. 'We're all living on borrowed time, sweetheart. The only difference is we know your clock is running a little faster than we'd like. But that means nothing is left unsaid between us. Like the fact I love you more than anything else in the world.'

'Even Tom?'

Christine pretended to think, a grin softening her face. 'Well, I *suppose* I love him too. If I have to. But it's neck and neck, okay?' Her eyes had darkened then, her voice low. 'I'm scared too. But we can help each other to be brave.'

Galen had half smiled at her mother, basking in the warmth of her love, secure in it. Her eyes had closed and opened again. Her mother, recognizing her daughter was tired, kissed her, savouring the familiar smell of her skin, and stepped out of the room. 'I'll leave the door open. Call if you need me.'

And now, an hour or so later, Galen was still not asleep. She thought about those dolphin mothers, half sleeping while on the move, always looking after their calves, loving and protecting them, even at great cost to themselves, and her own mother, doing the same while navigating a pathway through grief, trying to make things better for her, trying to make things right.

From her bed, Galen could see the moon, high and bright, and its light fell across the waves like handfuls of stardust. She would never forget this day. She wished she could stay here forever.

You can, her daddy said.

A thunderclap of pain in her head consumed everything. The part of her that loved facts would have been interested to know she was experiencing a sudden bleed in her basal ganglia, known as an intracerebral haemorrhage, a rare but catastrophic side effect of her condition. It interrupted the blood flow to her brain, depriving her of oxygen. A numbness settled across the left side of her face and her arm. She tried to call out – and then to swallow – but could not.

Two or three minutes passed. But even if someone had come to her then, the sands of Galen Hardwicke's hourglass were almost exhausted. An excess of blood in her brain had caused the pressure to build up too rapidly. Her breathing slackened. Another minute went by. The cells in Galen's brain began to die. Her vision blurred at the edges, and through its ragged hem, she tried to look upwards at the moon again, but it was lost to her. She closed her eyes and let herself fall.

Six years old. Swimming in the sea with her father, the light dappling his face. Dolphins surrounded them both, nudging the backs of their legs, and Galen cried out, a sweet and joyful sound. The sun was so bright she could not see her father's features, but she knew it was him because he was laughing, holding out his arms, and she watched him until the light was brighter than them both, and she swam towards him, and she did not look back.

ACKNOWLEDGEMENTS

The first time I saw dolphins leap from the water at Chanonry Point, I couldn't believe what I had witnessed. As a nature lover like Galen Hardwicke, there was something unimaginably beautiful about watching these majestic creatures in their native environment and I knew I had to find a way to put them into a book.

But the genesis of *All Of Us Are Broken* began many years earlier during a trip to the Scottish Highlands. I fell in love with the landscape, which still holds my heart in a way few things do.

At the time of writing, it's a beautiful August evening in Pitlochry and I've just travelled the road from Newcastle to Loch Tummel, Saul and Blue riding beside me, chasing down Missy and Fox. And let's not forget the Hardwicke family on a journey of their own. I hope you've enjoyed reading about these characters as much as I have loved writing them.

When an author is writing about real locations, mistakes can and do slip in. Some of these are deliberate – there's no pub or pharmacy in Oxton and the police station at Lauder isn't manned – but if there are others, the fault is all mine.

Please remember that while most of the places in this novel exist, the characters are a work of fiction.

Heartfelt thanks to Ethan and Rob at Rules Of Engagement Firearms for their expert knowledge, patience and generosity in showing me how to handle different types of guns; to ST for his insight into hostage situations; and to former senior detective Stuart Gibbon for answering my emergency questions with such good grace. I've tried to present an authentic picture of this kind of traumatic and fast-moving situation, but sometimes facts are blurred for artistic purposes, so please forgive my transgressions. Thanks to Keely Buckle for answering my questions about teaching, and to her children for inspiring me with their love of hand-knitted blankets. A special shout-out must also go to Ed James for reading an early version and correcting my 'Scottish' errors, and for letting me cadge a (very helpful but slightly stressful) lift to Berwick-upon-Tweed for research purposes.

I've long been fascinated by the outlaws Bonnie Parker and Clyde Barrow, who provided inspiration for the characters of Missy and Fox. *Go Down Together: The True, Untold Story of Bonnie & Clyde* by Jeff Guinn was invaluable in my research.

Thanks to my agent Sophie Lambert, who is calm and unflappable and always has my back, the team at C+W, and publicist extraordinaire Laura Sherlock, who is a force to be reckoned with in the best kind of way.

But no book makes it onto the shelves without the support of a publisher. Thank you to my fantastic editor Trish Jackson, who has believed in me since the beginning, and the rest of the team at Pan Macmillan for their continued support and hard work, including Jeremy Trevathan, Lucy Hale, Neil

ALL OF US ARE BROKEN

Lang (isn't the cover design amazing?), Stuart Dwyer, Rory O'Brien, Rebecca Lloyd, Leanne Williams, Claire Evans, Jamie Forrest, Kinza Azira, Samantha Fletcher, Amber Burlinson, Kate Berens, Gillian Mackay, Andy Belshaw, David Adamson, Kate Bullows, Keren Western, Tom Clancy and Richard Baker.

Thank you to the brilliant booksellers, bloggers, reviewers, librarians and readers – authors like me wouldn't be here without you – and to all my writing friends, with a special hat tip to the Ladykillers and Colin Scott. Love, too, to my family, who never complain about all the time I spend in the Writing Shed.

This is a violent and brutal book, and for that reason, it was important to me to include the back-stories of Missy and Fox's victims, and their determination to fight for their lives, even in the face of death. All real-life victims of shootings deserve to be remembered. Life is precious. As Christine Hardwicke shows us, our instinct for survival is what makes us human.

Pitlochry, August 2022

ABOUT THE AUTHOR

Fiona Cummins is an award-winning former journalist and a graduate of the Faber Academy Writing a Novel course. *Rattle*, her debut novel, was the subject of a huge international auction and has been translated into several languages. It received widespread critical acclaim from authors and reviewers. She has since written bestsellers *The Collector, The Neighbour, When I Was Ten* and *Into the Dark*, in which she introduces DC Saul Anguish, a brilliant young detective with a dark past. Fiona lives with her family in Essex.